HOME FOR JUNE

JULIET MADISON

To my favourite chef, Zeynel.
With you, I am home.

CHAPTER ONE

It was time for Hannah Delaney to do what she'd promised herself exactly one year ago. No, she was not getting a new hair colour, joining the gym, taking up embroidery, or getting a tattoo. She was leaving Tarrin's Bay—for good.

She'd tried. She'd persisted. She'd waited. But things were exactly the same one year on, though the pain of the breakup was less now. When her friends (and boyfriend) had moved on to greater, grander places, with bright lights and hustle and bustle, she had stayed put, like she always did. Kept busy, like she always did. And looked after everyone else's needs before her own, like she always did. But if things were to change, and she was to experience her full potential, *she* had to change. Starting now. June the first.

Hannah called her friend in Sydney to confirm acceptance of her offer, then made a quick call to the real-estate agent to book an appointment, before stepping out onto the wide, north-west facing verandah. She breathed in the rich, lush air, both salty and sweet from the combination of ocean and farmland. It awakened her airways, nourished her lungs, and comforted her soul. The only bright lights she really craved were those of the morning sun reaching through the trees towards the land, and the moon lighting up a clear night sky. And the only hustle and bustle she loved was the hurried but seemingly aimless wanderings of the chickens around her feet when she tended to them. She loved the coastal farm she'd grown up on that was now her own. But as much as home held a place in her heart, it also held her back from moving forward… to discovering life for herself, not one that was expected of her, or that she felt obligated to continue living.

'Eight years,' Hannah said with a sigh. She stepped off the verandah and onto the slightly overgrown grass she hadn't gotten around to mowing. Despite the natural slowdown of winter, the soil was rich, and the grass had always been healthy and full of life. She crouched and threaded her fingers between the crisp, cool strands. 'Eight years of doing this on my own… mostly.' She glanced backwards at Scarlett, her border collie who was comfortably flopped in her favourite spot on the weathered verandah, beside the white wicker armchair, eyes squinting in the low afternoon sun. Hannah stepped onto the verandah and crouched again, this time in front of Scarlett, threading her fingers between the orangey-red and white strands of hair. 'Having a nice rest, Scar?' She stroked the top of her dog's head, a slight waxiness gliding onto her palm. 'How about a pampering bath tomorrow, huh?' She tickled behind the animal's ears. 'Maybe even with extra bubbles.'

Hannah's parents had adopted the dog from the animal shelter fifteen years ago, partly to give her a home, and partly to tempt a young Hannah to stay on at the farm instead of moving closer to the city like her friends. It had worked, but the truth was she hadn't felt truly confident to forge an independent life for herself back then… not at twenty, but now, at thirty-five, it was definitely time for a long-overdue change.

She stood and placed her hands on her hips, surveying the

property with scanning eyes like a lighthouse on guard beside the ocean. The willow tree in the distance swayed gently in the breeze, the chickens hustled and bustled in the right-side paddock, and the red ride-on mower inside the open shed glared at her with the arched panels above its front lights, reminding her of her neglect. She'd had her parents help for a while after they moved into a low-maintenance but independent retirement village, or 'Senior Land', as her comedian father called it. But after his heart attack and her mother's increasing anxiety, *easy living* was the doctor's prescription. And there was Nathan, the general all-rounder who helped out when needed, for a price, but things had become awkward over the past year after she'd developed a minor rebound-crush on him, and he'd rejected her. Too much baggage to recognise something good in front of him, her parents had agreed. They had seemed more distraught than she was, originally considering him as the perfect partner option to share her life with on the farm.

And Samuel had helped out before that, with a few things here and there whenever he stayed with her, as any good boyfriend would do, until he figured out that he'd rather keep his eye on the stock market than the stock, returning to the city to focus on his finance career.

The glare of the ride-on mower intensified. 'Okay, okay.' She hopped on and when the engine growled to life, she took off, and the fresh scent of coumarins releasing from the grass trailed behind her. She did a one-eighty and the breeze picked up, pushing her hair onto her face and masking her view. 'Damn it.' She slowed to a stop and pulled off the elastic from around her wrist, sliding it over her hair and making a short ponytail at the nape of her neck. 'Knew I should have kept it short.' She puffed a few rogue, blonde strands from her face as she continued riding.

The property should sell for a decent price, she hoped. It

had a distant sliver of an ocean view, and was in a prime location not too far from town but isolated enough to be private and serene. She would want a high-enough offer to make it worthwhile selling. If not for her, then her parents, who had lovingly restored the old farmhouse over the years into the elegant, subtle beauty that 'Iona' was today. The real-estate agent would probably advise on an auction, but she would discuss the options with her tomorrow. A place like this required a commitment, and she hoped someone willing and worthy would take over the reins.

When she had finished weaving back and forth across the yard, she returned the mower to the shed and went back inside to check her phone.

Did you make a decision?

A text from her mother said on the screen.

A twinge of guilt twisted inside, but was soon replaced with a sense of purpose.

Yes, I did. Estate agent is squeezing me in early tomorrow to discuss. Time for a fresh start, Mum.

Her heart beat a little faster as bouncy dots appeared on the screen, disappeared, then reappeared, eventually transforming into words:

It's ok, darling. I understand. What time do you want me to come over and help get the place spick and span?

Hannah smiled. Of course her mother would want to help prepare the house for inspection, but it was also her way of avoiding difficult emotions. Cleaning, organising, being useful...

Hmm, a bit like what Hannah tended to do herself, while her father responded to everything with humour.

> Let me make a list and a plan of attack first, then I'll be better equipped to give you your instructions ;) So how about midday, discuss over lunch and then get to work?

> Perfect.

Every task came with a written plan for Hannah. Farm work was automatic and second nature, but everything else benefited from her expertise in organising. It was why she was also a trusted part-time events manager in and around town, planning and running important occasions including weddings, corporate retreats, product launches, and the like.

When the familiar surge of ideas and options rose up in her mind, she became energised. Not only would she enjoy giving the place a bit of oomph to get the best price, she would enjoy the anticipation of her potential exciting new job at the large events company her friend worked as a PA for. Karen had also offered her a room for rent in her Sydney house for as long as was required. The bonus was it had a small backyard that would suit Scarlett. Not that she needed much space these days, preferring to sit quietly in the sun in her old age. But her dog had grown up in the outdoors, so keeping her inside wasn't an option.

Hannah brewed a cup of lemon myrtle tea with leaves freshly picked from her own tree and sat on a chair at the kitchen table. She opened Facebook and posted:

> The time has come for this bird to leave the nest. Sydney here I come!

Within minutes comments appeared, one friend saying 'Finally, yay!' and another saying 'What??' Everyone would find out the details soon enough, but until she had a confirmed job she would only reveal she was simply moving out to start anew.

She scrolled through Facebook without really reading anything, until a photo caught her eye. One of her Tarrin's Bay friends, who ran a market stall of handmade baby clothing near to where Hannah sold her eggs, had posted a selfie in her running gear, saying:

It's been a while but I'm back in the game! My legs are killing me

She was always posting selfies, but it was the background that had attracted Hannah's attention. She clicked on the photo and zoomed in, zeroing in on a person standing by the harbour, hand sheltering his eyes from the sun, but the familiarity of his face unmistakable, even twenty years later.

Luca Antonescu.

'Oh my God,' Hannah said. 'What's he doing here?'

He could be on holiday, or visiting someone. Or he could be back, as in *really* back.

She looked at his face a little longer than was probably appropriate, but she hadn't seen him in so long. Not since the night of the Year Ten school formal when he'd left early, and she'd later found out his father had died.

She'd only known him two years. But those memories stuck like glue in every cell in her body. They'd been friends, worked on some school projects together, and hung out sometimes with mutual friends. But he never knew just how much she had yearned for him.

And when her long-awaited intent to ask him to the school formal had failed when another girl had beaten her to it, she'd vowed never to let feelings like that take hold of her that strongly again. Especially after he'd left town and all opportunities had left with him.

She'd moved on, and so had he.

Or so she thought.

CHAPTER TWO

'Mum, why are you late?' Hannah stepped aside. Her mother entered the house and glanced at her watch.

'Eleven fifty-nine, darling,' she said, plonking her handbag on the kitchen island bench with a chuckle. 'One minute to go. Not too bad.' Kathleen Delaney was always ten minutes early for everything.

'Ooh, I don't know, Mum, this might really throw out my plans for today.' She winked.

Her mother pecked her on the cheek then glanced around the kitchen and living area, placing her hands on her hips, a trait Hannah had inherited whenever strategic planning was required... there must be some special connection between the planning part of the brain and the hips, her mum used to say.

'Don't worry, Mum, I've done the hip thing and the results are right here.' She tapped a sheet of paper that lay on the island bench.

'So everything we need to do is on that one piece of paper? Your skills have become even *more* efficient. I remember when you used to carry around spiral-bound planners with different-coloured sections and all sorts of fancy stuff.'

Hannah smiled. 'I still do that for some events, and this paper is only a summary of what I typed up into my spreadsheet.'

'Ah, okay,' she said. 'So give me the rundown.'

Hannah held up the sheet of paper and pointed. 'Number one on the list...'

Kathleen took it from her daughter and smiled. 'Large print, don't even need my glasses. You know me too well.'

'All part of the service.'

'Lunch first? Shouldn't we get stuck in and then take a break for a late lunch?'

Hannah shook her head. 'We can discuss things while we eat. Save time.' She opened the fridge and withdrew last night's vegetable soup, still in the saucepan.

'You should freeze that, make some handy quick meals when you've had a long day.'

'Already did, but there's just enough left in here for two.' She smiled and placed it on the stove, then ignited the gas hotplate. She then popped two pieces of organic sourdough bread in the toaster.

'You could always try running a cafe or restaurant.' Kathleen slid open a drawer and took out two placemats, placing them on the nearby dining table. 'Put your good home cooking and friendly service to use.'

Hannah laughed. 'Meal preparation for two or three people is a lot less work than for a whole room full of hungry, fussy patrons,' she said. 'Anyway, it's nothing special, just the basics. I haven't strayed from my usual choice of recipes in... forever. Whatever is easy; tried and tested works for me.'

'Well, maybe it's time to try and test something new. Just for a change.'

Hannah shrugged, and the enormity of what she was preparing for shook the sheet of paper slightly as she picked it up and looked at it, even though she had practically memorised it. The sensation surprised her.

'I know, darling,' Kathleen sidled up next to her. 'Moving away will be enough of a change for you. You're absolutely sure it feels right for you?'

Hannah nodded. 'Had a year to think on it.'

'Of course.' Kathleen collected two spoons from the cutlery drawer, turning her back for a moment.

Hannah tipped a small amount of locally made extra virgin olive oil into a dipping bowl, adding a splash of balsamic vinegar. A few drops stained the benchtop and she wiped them away with a tissue. Oh, how many spills and meals this timber island bench had seen over the years...

Iona was part of the family, but it wasn't like it had been in the family for generations or anything. That's what Hannah had told herself. It could have led to that, decades down the track, if she had decided to stay and eventually have a family of her own. But there was only her, and her life was stagnant and needed some forward movement, some spice. Some *newness*.

'Mum,' Hannah said, as her mother placed the spoons on the table. 'I know you were only nine minutes late, but even so, there was a reason, wasn't there. I can tell.'

Kathleen sighed and lowered her gaze. 'As I was leaving, your father asked me if you thought you might reconsider selling.'

Hannah's insides clenched a little.

'Don't worry.' Her mother approached and placed her hand on her daughter's forearm. 'I reassured him it was for the best, and he agreed. It'll just take a bit of getting used to. You do what you need to do, it's your life and we support you in whatever you choose.'

Hannah glanced up at the pendant lights overhanging the island bench. 'We could still keep it. The agent is just sorting out the details and market comparisons over the next few days before listing it. We could rent it out, or make it holiday accommodation, something like that. Even for a year or two while I try out new opportunities in Sydney, then if I don't like it I could still come back, maybe?'

Kathleen shook her head. 'Too much uncertainty and hesitation. And it would still be a lot to manage behind the scenes, and you won't find many people interested in renting a place like this, it requires a—'

'Commitment, yes I know. You're right. It's all or nothing.'

'And you've given it your all. We're proud of you.' She held Hannah's arms in a gentle show of support.

'Thanks, Mum. It might be a while before anyone sees it anyway, give us some time to get used to the change. Not everyone wants to run a small farm with five hundred chickens!' She laughed and ladled the soup into bowls. 'Let's eat.'

Hannah's phone rang, and as she answered and spoke, her mother asked with her eyes what the other person on the line was saying.

'Well,' Hannah said after ending the call, 'the agent already has potential interest.'

'Already?'

Hannah nodded. 'They're coming on Monday to have a "preview", as she calls it. Before it's officially on the market. And the agent is popping by after work today to have a quick look, though she's already seen the photos I had prepared and sent earlier.'

'That's only two days away.' Kathleen stood. 'No chance of changing it to Tuesday, or Wednesday at least?'

Hannah shook her head. 'The buyer is seeing other properties. And, oh! I forgot to tell you, on Tuesday I'll be in the city for a job interview with Karen's boss.' Karen had emailed her the details last night and Hannah had confirmed the time that she could come in.

'That's quick. I mean, that's great! Okay. Right. Well...' She did the hands-on-hips thing again. 'We'd better get cracking.'

'We'd better.'

Kathleen picked up the sheet of paper and pointed. '*After* we complete item number one on the agenda.' She placed a smile on her face and ushered Hannah to a chair at the table.

This was it. It was all happening. And a lot faster than she imagined.

CHAPTER THREE

Scarlett smiled her doggie smile as Hannah stroked her pet's smooth, silky, freshly washed hair. The promised bath with extra bubbles had been delayed a day and a half as Hannah and her mother had been busy cleaning and tidying the house. Her father had come over the day before also to help with the yard, pretending to move in ultra-slow motion whenever Kathleen watched him to check he wasn't overdoing it. Hannah had giggled, just like she always did whenever he did things like that.

'A couple of visitors coming today, Scar. Just so you know.' She always talked to her dog like she was a person. She'd become not only part of the family, but a best friend to Hannah from day one, as her other friends gradually moved away. She would come home and sit on the armchair on the verandah, Scarlett at her feet, and tell her all about what was going on in her life... from her studies in business management and event planning, to how many eggs the chickens were laying, to the injustice about the lack of nightlife in town for twenty-somethings, and to romance and sometimes the lack thereof. Scarlett knew everything. At least, that's what it felt like to

Hannah. She wasn't yet sure how to tell her they would be moving. Not that she would really understand, but still. She wasn't quite there yet.

Hannah left Scarlett on the verandah and went inside to double check everything. She washed her hands and put on some naturally scented hand cream. She checked her reflection in the mirror and bared her teeth. Then she laughed. It was like she was going on a date, but she wasn't, and she couldn't really care less about how she looked but she did want to give a good overall impression, in every possible way. She would greet the real estate agent and potential buyer, then make herself scarce on the verandah to let them look around in peace, but still be available for any questions about the running of the property. She hoped it would be a family with a couple of kids. There were four bedrooms and plenty of living space, not to mention the ample space outdoors for playing, climbing trees, kicking a ball around, and making mud cakes... all things Hannah had done herself as a child.

Pebbles crunched and crackled outside and she went to the front door, opening it and placing the stuffed fabric-hen doorstopper her grandmother had made in front of it. Hannah waited there casually, or trying to be casual; one hand in her pocket, the other resting against the doorframe. The trousered legs of Lily Symons stepped out of the white Lexus sedan, which would probably need a minor wash after the trip down the initial dirt driveway to the property, before it reached the pebbled circular area in front of the house. She smiled and waved as she walked across, expertly handling the inconsistent surface of the pebbles in her high heels. Hannah would probably have fallen over by now. She only ever wore work boots, rubber thongs, bare feet, or thick, sturdy, low heels when she had to attend a professional event or important social gathering.

'Hi, Lily.' Hannah held an outstretched hand.

'Hannah, good to see you again.' She clasped Hannah's hand and gave it a single shake. 'I trust you got a lot of preparation done since Saturday's visit?'

Hannah nodded. 'All the essentials at least. Though I didn't have time to bake any bread or cookies.'

Lily chuckled and flicked her hand in the air. 'Not to worry, it's always a nice, welcoming scent but I think this place will sell itself. It's unique.'

'It is.' Hannah's eyes fell on one of the white timber posts framing the entry up to the front steps, the etchings of her name still visible under the new coat of paint. She couldn't remember how old she'd been, but it was about waist height, and she had been learning to write and spell. *'What are you doing?'* her mother had asked. *'I can spell my name proppaly now, Mummy,'* she'd replied. Her mum had shaken her head and smiled, bending down and then adding a heart shape around her name. *'Shh,'* she'd said. *'Don't tell your father.'* Hannah had giggled and covered her mouth.

Lost in her memory, she didn't take notice of the approaching car until it parked next to Lily's.

'Ah, here he is,' said Lily, stepping off the front verandah steps.

The man stepped out of the old Toyota Corolla, and turned to walk towards the house. Hannah's heart doubled over. The man stopped, his eyes widening. She gripped the doorframe where her name had been carved, and tried to dampen down her automatic bodily responses by taking a quick, deep, breath. 'Luca?'

'Hannah?'

He walked closer, and with each step she took in more detail of his face, older but even more handsome, his eyes still embodying an intense depth that looked right into her.

'Oh, you two know each other?' Lily said. But their eyes remained on each other.

'You're still living here?' he asked.

Hannah held her arms out wide. 'Home sweet home,' she said. 'Well, not for much longer.'

He stopped at the base of the steps while Hannah stood at the top. His presence, all these years later, was like opening an old box of memories, the smell of history taking her breath away.

'Your parents?' he said. 'Are they...'

'Alive and kicking, but in a low-maintenance place.'

'Glad to hear it,' he replied.

She didn't want to ask about his, already knowing about his father, but hoped all was well with his mother and brother. She stepped aside and held out her arm to usher him up the steps. He stepped up, his height and proximity overpowering her senses. 'It's good to see you again.' He held out his hand.

She took it, he shook it, and she thought for a moment he was going to lean in and give her a kiss on the cheek, but he hesitated. How were you supposed to greet someone you hadn't seen for twenty years, when you'd only known them a short two, but enough to establish some kind of bond? She released his hand and stepped back a little, hoping to avoid any awkwardness in front of Lily. Perhaps if it had only been them alone he may have kissed her, or hugged her, or gently patted her on the arm or back, like old friends.

'Looks like you two will need some catching-up time later,' said Lily. 'Have you been here before, Luca?'

He nodded. 'Long time ago, as a teenager.' He chuckled, then turned back to face Hannah. 'Remember when Ben tripped on the step back there,' he pointed to where he'd just walked, 'and Karen tried to help him up but then *she* fell?'

Hannah let out a laugh, probably with a bit too much

volume. 'Oh yes, that was a classic. As clumsy as each other, those two.'

'You still in touch with Karen, she still in town as well?'

'Nope. Sydney. But yes, I mean, I'm still in touch.' She closed her mouth before she continued explaining how she would also be moving in with her soon and hopefully working at the same company. There were years to catch up on, if they even really wanted to, but now was not the time. 'Anyway, I'll let Lily do her thing and show you around, and I'll be on the back verandah if you need me... need anything,' she added quickly. 'Like, questions and stuff.' Oh God, she was starting to talk like a teenager all over again.

He smiled and nodded, and a thick strand of black hair fell over his left eye. He ran a hand through his hair and stepped through the door with Lily, into the house that had been her home, her life, for *all* of her life. And now could become his.

Luca breathed in the homely atmosphere as he entered the house that seemed smaller than he remembered, even though it appeared to have had renovations and a wall removed between the kitchen and living area. When the real estate agent had told him of the opportunity to preview a four-acre property on the edge of town, he'd jumped at the chance. And when he'd found out the address, he'd remembered it was the Delaney's, where he'd visited a few times to work on school projects with Hannah, Ben, and Karen.

He hadn't even thought to ask Lily if Hannah was still there, though he thought there might have been a chance that her parents would be here today, and had planned to ask them about her and see where life had taken her. But clearly, it hadn't taken her away from her home. He wondered what had prompted her to sell up, considering her parents were still alive.

'As you can see, the home has still retained its country charm but has been modernised in certain ways for functionality and to create more light and open space.' Lily gestured to the kitchen and living areas.

Luca nodded, but his mind was still processing Hannah's presence. She was right outside. He wanted to ask her a million questions. But for now, he had to focus on what he was here for: finding a new home, a new start to build the life he had promised his mother. At that thought, resolve strengthened his posture and his mind switched back to the task at hand.

'It's been well looked after, I can tell.' He walked to the kitchen, always the first place of interest for him. 'Solid benchtop.' He knocked his knuckles on the island bench. 'I think this was here before.'

'Yes, Hannah mentioned the kitchen has been completely renovated a few years ago, but the island bench has been kept as is, which adds a rustic charm.'

Luca opened the oven door, the pantry, then stood near the stove to get a feeling for it. He'd be spending most of his time at the restaurant, but his home kitchen was just as important when it came to decision-making.

'Like cooking?' Lily asked.

He laughed. 'I'd better. It's how I pay the bills.'

'Oh, you're a chef?'

He nodded. Though it was more than a way to pay the bills. It was his love, it was his passion, and it was his father's legacy, living on in him. And it was thanks to his mother and her finances that he was even here right now, being able to consider buying a place like this and starting a new business. Even though he'd give it all up in a heartbeat to have her back. To have them both back. But he would make them proud, do what he'd said he'd do, and make this work. Somehow.

'Got work in town?'

'Yep. Well, I will have. Once I open the place. Not far from Lookout Point.'

Lily's eyes widened. 'You're setting up there? Oh, wow.'

The premises had been leased to him by a different agency who specialised mostly in commercial premises. 'That's the plan!' He smiled, but his heart also beat a bit faster at the thought of the huge task that lay ahead of him.

'Well, you'll definitely need to find a place to move into asap then, I take it.'

'For sure. I'm at the caravan park at the moment, but found a temporary share house I'm moving into this afternoon until I can get my own place.' He didn't know why he was telling her all of this, but the people of Tarrin's Bay tended to be a bit more open and friendly than many in the city, generally speaking. In places like this it was hard to keep secrets for long.

He wandered through the living room, forcing himself not to look at the family photos on the mantelpiece and surrounding walls. He leaned closer to the fireplace, and a faint warm scent drew into his nose... *still works*, he thought. There was nothing like sitting by a warm fire, which is why he wanted to put one in at the restaurant, but it would probably have to be a gas one that looked like a real one. He would also put a fire pit on the open-air deck where people could sit and relax in the cooler months. It was these little thoughts and ideas that kept his spirits up, motivated him to keep going, to avoid running away and starting over elsewhere in a busy place where he didn't have to be the boss and could just do his job and then go home. Wherever home was, or would be. But he would stick to his plans this time. He had to.

The hallway led Luca to three bedrooms, a bathroom (also

renovated), a laundry, and a master bedroom with en suite and French doors that opened out onto a small patio overlooking a willow tree in the distance, not far from a small creek that was part of the neighbouring property.

Mum and Dad would have loved this.

It was a beautiful home. Hannah was probably just moving somewhere with less maintenance, like her parents had. Maybe right in town within walking distance to everything. He'd have to ask her. He wouldn't mind catching up and even getting to know her now as an adult, now that he was staying in town.

He asked Lily a few questions about the sale of the property, then stepped out onto the back verandah. Hannah was sitting in a wicker armchair, looking at her phone, an old dog at her feet.

'Hey there, beautiful,' Luca said.

Hannah's head shot up, her eyes wide, until he bent down and patted the dog. 'I don't remember you as a puppy. It really has been a long time, eh?' He glanced up at Hannah whose cheeks held a slight hint of rose.

'She's fifteen.' Hannah patted the animal too. 'Tough as nails, she is.'

'Runs in the family, I think.'

Hannah shrugged.

'You've been doing all this on your own since your parents left?'

'Yep.'

'How many eggs do you get a day?'

'About one-hundred and fifty to two-fifty, more in summer.'

Luca gave an impressed whistle. 'Wow.' His mind tried to calculate how many he would need per week in his restaurant. *Number of meals requiring eggs, yolks, or whites, and house-made mayonnaise, times the number of eggs per menu item, times the number of patrons likely to choose those menu items per day, times number of opening days...* It was hard to know, until he had sorted out a menu. He was used to simply preparing the meals on a menu, not designing a menu, though he had always made up his own recipes for personal use. But having his own eggs would save money and he could be sure they were free ranged and healthy and fed the right diet. Though he would probably need some help, in the early stages of his business at least, to collect them and care for the animals.

'I supply them to some local places. I have a courier who comes to pick them up and deliver them for me, and the rest I sell myself at the weekly produce markets.'

'So you don't end up with any overflow?'

'Hardly ever.' Hannah stood. 'Feel free to walk around and look at anything. And if you decide you're interested, I can show you my operations manual, which details everything you need to know about running the place.'

He smiled, and was reminded of how good she'd been organising their school projects and breaking them down into easy-to-manage tasks. 'So I don't need any prior training or qualifications?'

'Nah, just a few basics which I'm happy to teach to the lucky person who buys the property, and the rest you'll learn as you go along and get used to it.' She slid her hands in her pockets and smiled.

Though he was here to inspect the property, he couldn't help also inspecting her. Various shades of sun-kissed blonde in her hair, pulled back into a short ponytail, golden skin and a few enchanting lines around her blue eyes as she smiled. What a beautiful, natural woman she'd grown into, from the skinny teenage tomboy she used to call herself. He'd never thought of her like that; she was always a real girl who never put on a fake face or tried to be someone else. What you saw was what you got.

'Lucky I'm a fast learner,' he said, unable to hold back his usual self-confident charm when speaking to the opposite sex. Even though he wasn't trying to impress her. Didn't need to. Just years of habit.

'I know. I remember,' she replied. Then turned her attention to the shed. 'All the equipment, the ride-on, for example, will be staying. So the house will come equipped with everything you, or anyone else, may need.'

'I'll have to hire you at the agency, Hannah,' said Lily. 'Doing too good a job here.' Lily stepped onto the verandah, and pointed out some of the property's other features to Luca.

They all walked around the yard, to the shed, the paddocks, the large chicken coop. 'It's all mobile,' Hannah said. 'So they can be moved to the other paddock every now and again to give the land a rest and time to regenerate, and give them a healthier supply of food and bugs to graze on.'

'That's such a great idea. This wasn't here back then, was it? I think I remember a barn of some kind.'

'That's right, Dad brought in the chicken tractor around ten years ago.'

Luca nodded with interest. And he *was* interested. Though it would be a big change, as he'd told her, he was a fast learner, always had been. And being busy was exactly what he needed right now. But the right kind of busy. Busy with a purpose, an aim, a promise. Busy to achieve results instead of working aimlessly without any long-lasting reward. And this place could be a perfect complement to his business.

After forty-five minutes, he had seen all he needed to see of the place for the time being, but he was nowhere near finished with seeing Hannah. The past echoed every time he looked at her, and knowing he never got to say goodbye, not to her or anyone else from town, left a feeling of unfinished business somewhere inside him. He didn't know what, if anything, needed to be *finished*, only that his departure back then had felt premature... then again, so had his father's.

He thanked the agent (who not so casually mentioned she had a couple of other people looking for this type of property who she was going to get in contact with today), and stepped off the front verandah.

'I'll be in touch soon, Hannah,' said Lily before getting into her car, and Hannah thanked her and waved.

'I'm seeing a couple of other places soon, but I always liked your place. I'll have a think about things,' he said.

'No problem, Luca. It was, ah, nice to see you again.'

'You too. Been so long, and we never really got to...'

'Say goodbye,' she completed the sentence for him.

Luca nodded, but what he'd been going to say was that they never really got to get to know each other more, outside of school. At least not without a group of people. She'd always intrigued him, and conversation was never difficult, but she'd never seemed interested in him in any other way. They say that boys, or men, liked women who played hard to get, but he'd always liked the ones who were clearly interested in him. And many had been. It took away the guessing games. But she was different and never put on a show for anyone. Not even Matthew, who he'd seen kiss her suddenly next to the school canteen, right on the *one* day, at the *exact* time that he'd *finally* decided to break from habit and an assured outcome, and ask her to the school formal. But seeing her with Matthew made him step back, and the next day he asked Tracy instead, who he'd known was interested in him, and she'd said yes. Funnily enough, right after he'd asked her and she'd put an arm casually around his waist to say 'I can't wait', he'd noticed Hannah glancing towards him. But as quick as their eyes had caught each other's in that moment, they had diverted, and when he glanced back in her direction after answering Tracy's question about what colour dress to wear, she was gone.

He didn't want the same thing to happen now.

'We should meet up sometime,' he said. 'Catch up on the latest gossip, you know, just the last two decades or so.'

'Oh,' she said, sheltering her face from the sun with her hand. 'Yeah. I'd, ah, make you a cup of coffee, but today is full-on and I actually have to collect all the eggs and do a few extra duties because I'll be in Sydney all tomorrow, and then Wednesday I have the markets on, and...'

'It's okay, no rush,' he said. 'And don't worry about things getting awkward with the house, if I'm interested I'll put in a decent offer, I won't go back and forth forever and ever. If it's meant to be it's meant to be. And either way, I'd love to catch up. If you'd like to.'

He watched her facial expression soften slightly and wondered if she was going to explain her next fortnight's to-do list to him, kindly telling him that he didn't factor into any of her tightly scheduled plans. But she simply said, 'Sure.'

'I'll give you my number, and you can get in contact whenever it suits you, no rush, and you can let me know a day and time that suits you. No rush. Did I already say that?' He scratched his temple.

The corner of her mouth lifted into a half-smile. 'You did.'

'Sorry. Anyway I'll leave it with you, see how you go.' He took out his phone, but she was already halfway inside. He stepped onto the verandah and peered inside.

'Here, write it down.' She handed him a pen and a Post-it note.

'Oh, okay. I was going to text it to you, but paper works too.' He jotted it down and added a smiley face.

She stuck it on the fridge. 'Thanks.'

He gave a nod, and shook her hand again, which seemed

strange, yet he thought it would also seem strange to give her a hug at this point, so a handshake it was for now. She stayed on the verandah as he stepped off and got into his car. She gave a quick wave, then the engine rumbled and the car reversed, before turning towards the road. When he glanced in the rear-view mirror, about to offer another wave, the verandah was empty.

She would have had to give him her number to receive his via text. Why had she not wanted to? Though Hannah had been a calm and practical 'what you see is what you get' girl, he wondered if over the years a few sneaky defences had worked their way into her persona. She'd seemed genuinely surprised and pleased to see him again, but also restrained.

Now he wanted to find out her story even more. But he would have to either keep communicating to her through the real estate agent, or wait for her to get in contact in a more personal way. Whether she actually would or not, he did not have a clue.

CHAPTER FOUR

Hannah sat at the dining table and exhaled. Long-buried emotions and desires swirled within, looking for an outlet but not knowing where to go.

So that's what he was doing here, looking for a place to buy. She stood, twisted side to side, then sat again. She had things to do, but her mind was scattered, which was unlike her. And she just realised that she still didn't know what he was doing back in town, apart from house hunting. It obviously wasn't for an investment, since he'd asked about looking after the chickens. Maybe he had a wife and kids and was checking out a few places first before showing them. Surely he wouldn't want to take over this place on his own? And what did he do for work? She'd heard muffled conversation between Luca and Lily while they were in the kitchen and she was on the verandah armchair but couldn't hear details.

Maybe she *should* meet up with him, if only to settle her curiosity. If they were going to catch up, she wanted it to be her decision, she didn't want to get caught up in past emotions and unresolved desire, which was why she didn't give him her number. Though he knew where she lived, so it wouldn't take much to get in touch anyway, but that would look desperate, and Luca was never desperate. Never needed to be. He'd had no shortage of admirers at school. But right now, she was preparing to move away and start fresh, not get to know someone she'd always liked and been truly comfortable with all over again and risk rejection. She'd been so proud of herself, mustering up the courage that day at school to ask him to the formal, and also because she wanted to have an excuse to say no to Matthew before *he* asked her... he was okay but she hadn't been ready for that kiss the day before, which is why a few seconds into it she'd pushed him away and told him to slow down. But just when she'd been about to approach Luca, there he was with Tracy's arm around him. And a few weeks later, there they were at the formal together, while she'd accepted Matthew's invitation. And that was that.

She had to keep moving. She got up and went outside, giving Scarlett a quick pat, then went to the shed to get the egg trolley. She opened the gate and wheeled it into the paddock towards the chicken coop. Luke the courier would be coming this afternoon, as he did every Monday and Thursday, to pick up the cartons for local deliveries. The pungent scent of feathers, hay, and chook feed that was as familiar to her as Scarlett's doggy smell comforted her as she worked on autopilot, collecting the eggs and checking for any cracks or imperfections. She placed them into the custom-made egg trolley her father had built, which had layers of trays for cartons to sit securely, allowing the eggs to be transported back to the house easily without breakages. She worked quickly, some of the chickens coming in from outside and weaving around her legs and between each other. Their food was half gone, she'd noticed on the way in, and as usual, she would refill the trough before sundown this evening.

The cartons filled up bit by bit, and as she worked she

wondered more about Luca. Remembered more about Luca. He had always left that 'what if?' feeling inside her, like an unopened letter waiting to be read.

'Gah!' she said as she dropped an egg onto her foot. She cleaned it up then finished working, the trolley three-quarters full. In summer she'd usually fill it twice, or at least one and a half times. As a child she had happily collected the eggs dozen by dozen, bringing them back to the house, a carton at a time, until her dad had built the trolley when their chicken numbers had grown.

She closed the gate behind her and wheeled it to the front verandah, placing the required number of cartons in the wooden chest by the front door, then running inside to get the order and delivery list for Luke, placing that inside the chest too. Then if she wasn't home, he was able to pick up the contents and deliver them to the buyers.

There was always something to do here on the farm, it was hard to take time off but at times she had, paying for help to come and do all the daily tasks. Tomorrow would be an early start and a late night, and then the next day was market day, so despite her curiosity, she would have to see how the next couple of days panned out before deciding whether to contact Luca.

'Gah!' she said the next day, as the train started moving before she'd had a chance to get onto the platform at the station. Luckily she had planned for such a contingency and allowed extra time before her interview. With trains only running every hour from Tarrin's Bay, she would have to wait another forty-five minutes or so in town. 'Coffee time,' she said to herself, walking down the road towards the end of the main street near the harbour.

She stopped at a cafe, not her usual one, and ordered a takeaway mocha. The warm cardboard cup welcomed by her hands, she walked back down the street and looked up towards Lookout Point. Cold, and a bit windy, but the walk and ocean air would do her good.

She walked up the slight incline of the main street, past the bank, and then where the old beauty salon used to be, which was now empty with windows taped up with newspaper, and... she did a double take, as someone exited the premises. Luca?

Okay, so maybe he was taking over the beauty salon. Nothing wrong with that. She stayed put and watched as he locked the door, then turned and walked down the street in her direction.

'Hannah.' His eyes brightened, connecting with hers. Then they scanned the length of her body. She had put on a flattering grey trouser suit that hid her knobbly knees. 'You look nice.'

'Hello again,' she said. 'And thanks.' She was about to mention where she was going when he spoke again.

'You could have just called, no need to come all the way in here to meet up with me.' He winked.

She smiled. 'I had no idea, I mean, wow, so you're opening up this place?'

'Sure am. Tarrin's Bay will never be the same again once I've made my mark here.'

'For sure. A male beauty therapist, in a small town, that's really cool. Well done.'

He laughed. 'Beauty?' He tipped his head back in another laugh. 'The only pampering I'll be doing for people is for their tastebuds. I'm a chef. I'm opening a restaurant.'

'Ahh.' It all fell into place. His parents had been preparing to open a family restaurant in town twenty years ago, but just when they had begun to get it ready, well, that's when his father had died the night of the formal. 'How exciting,' she replied. 'I hope it all goes well!'

'You'll have to come to the opening night. Once it's all set up. I have a lot to organise.'

'Hmm. I could. But it depends when it is. I'm moving to Sydney.'

His eyes blinked and his mouth opened. 'Oh, right. Thought you might be downsizing or something.'

She shook her head. 'I'm going for an interview today. And Karen, actually, is letting me rent a room at her place.'

He nodded. 'Sounds like you and I are doing a swap... I come here and you go there. Either that or you heard I was coming and decided to get out of town while the going was good.' He grinned.

She chuckled. 'Of course not, just time for a change.' She took a sip of her coffee.

If only he'd come a year ago...

She pushed away thoughts of 'what if?'. She'd made her decision. And it had been a long time ago. People change, so who was to say they would even get along now? But sometimes people didn't change, and if that was the case then things wouldn't be any different, he would always have a girl, or now, a woman, available to him, and it was never ever Hannah.

'I was going to get a coffee myself actually, do you have to rush off to the train?' He gestured in the direction of the station.

'Just missed it actually, but I can get the next one, I have time.'

'Fancy a walk and a talk? And you can tell me all about this job you're going for.'

She couldn't really back out now. She didn't have an excuse. She couldn't say *sorry, I just can't handle the idea of dredging up old memories and feelings and risk feeling them again and being disappointed once more.* 'Um, sure.'

They went to the same cafe Hannah had just come from.

'Need another so soon?' asked the barista, eyeing Hannah.

She shook her head and gestured to Luca.

'Large mocha please.' He turned to Hannah. 'Do you want anything extra, a muffin, a cupcake?'

'No thanks. I'm good with my mocha.'

'Oh, you too? Great minds.' He smiled and so did she. He used to say that to her at school whenever they would come up with the same idea or way of doing something. 'Coffee and chocolate together, it's genius really,' he added as he turned back to the counter.

'I agree,' she said softly, but the coffee machine got noisy and she wasn't sure if he heard her.

And by the time they were at the lookout, she could barely make sense of her own thoughts as they jumped around her head all at once like bouncy balls... *Forty minutes till the train... Interview answers all prepped... House on the market... Luca's back in town...*

She was so used to consistency and routine, being in control, and knowing what was going to happen next. But like the turbulent water lapping below the rocks where they stood near the railing, things had suddenly become more free-flowing. As they sipped their coffees walking up the hill to the lookout, Hannah had updated him on how the town had changed since he'd been here before.

'Mrs May's Bookstore is still open, that's so cool,' he said. 'My mum used to buy books from there when we lived here, she loved Mrs May.' Luca's eyes lowered.

'Yes, it was sad to see her go, such a special soul. It's great that her daughter and granddaughter were able to continue the family business.' *Unlike me*, a hint of guilt said from somewhere deep inside.

Luca nodded slowly, his eyes still low and gloomy.

Somehow it came to her, and she realised. 'Luca, is your mother still...'

He shook his head. 'It's been just over a month now.' He took a gulp of his coffee and looked far out to the ocean, drawing a long breath. 'Complications from a heart condition she'd developed.'

'Oh my God, I'm so sorry.' She placed her hand gently on his forearm where his left hand rested on the railing.

'We had a bit of warning at least. Gave us time to sort out legal matters and finances, and also...'

Say goodbye.

'I'm sorry.' She pressed her hand more firmly against his arm, like it was the most natural thing in the world to be touching him and comforting him.

He twisted slightly to look at her, and had it not been for the coffee cup in his hand she thought he may put his hand on top of hers, but he looked at her with genuine appreciation instead. 'Thanks, Hannah.' He drank the rest of his coffee and chucked it in a nearby garbage bin. 'So, your interview,' he said, and Hannah checked her watch.

'Oh yes. It's for an events company in the city where Karen works as a personal assistant. I do event planning and management, both business and personal.'

Luca's solemn expression dissolved and his face lit up. 'You've been doing that in Tarrin's Bay?'

'Yep. And surrounding areas. Weddings, business functions, product launches, corporate retreats, you name it.'

'So you help people organise things and make a detailed plan?'

'Yep.'

'And make everything run smoothly and successfully?'

'Yep.'

'And you're leaving town?'

'Yep.'

He shook his head and grabbed the railing. 'Oh man, bad timing. You sound like the exact person I need right now.'

How she'd longed to hear those words before, in a different context.

'You need some help with your restaurant?'

He nodded. 'I guess so. I've been figuring things out myself, but the sooner I get things happening the better, so I might need professional input to help me with the branding and launch of the restaurant.'

Part of her wanted to reach out and say 'I'll do it! Pick me!' Hannah hated having to say no, to anything. She'd declined any requests for work after May until she knew what she was doing, and said she'd keep her repeat clients informed. 'I would if I could, but until I confirm my situation in Sydney I can't commit to anything. Even so, I'd need to focus on packing up the house before moving.'

'I know, it's okay. I'll manage. But if you're anything like the Hannah I remember, I know you would have been great at it.'

She shrugged. 'Timing, huh?'

He nodded. 'Timing.'

It seemed it was never on her side.

'Speaking of timing, I better start heading over to the station. I want to make sure time is on my side today.'

'Oh yes, let's go.'

Let's?

'I'll personally take you there and make sure you make it, and if not, I'll drive you to the next station, and the next, until you catch one, and if not, I'll keep driving until we're in Sydney, so nothing to worry about, you'll get to your interview.'

'Ha, no need, I've still got plenty of time. And anyway, I thought you were bummed that I was leaving.' She sipped the rest of her coffee as they walked down the hill, then put it in a bin.

'I am. But who am I to stand in the way of your dreams, Sydney will be lucky to have you.'

'Well thanks.' They walked briskly, and as they passed the restaurant premises she said, 'Don't you have a lot of work to get back to?'

He shrugged. 'Sure. Soon. When I get home, my temporary home at least, I'll try to channel Miss Hannah Delaney and create a plan and timetable for the launch. But for now, I'll see her off at the train and hope that some of her skills will rub off on me on the way.' He grinned, and his smile arched into his cheeks, the winter sunlight accentuating his angular jaw.

He was still the chatty, friendly guy he'd always been. And she loved how he had grown into and filled out his tall, broad frame, and how the dots of stubble on his jaw were like tiny sprinkles of pepper spicing up his face.

'If you have some basic questions, I don't mind answering them,' she found herself saying, as they turned and began walking up the street to the station.

Hannah, you have enough to do.

'I can recommend some local tradespeople, some suppliers, resources, etcetera.'

Don't make things complicated for yourself. Stop now.

'Feel free to run any of your plans by me for a quick check.'

What on earth are you doing?

'Wow, thank you,' he replied. 'That's very kind. But I would want to pay you, I don't expect you to help me out for free.'

'Oh no, I couldn't accept payment for giving you a bit of general guidance.'

'Then I will manage perfectly fine on my own. You have enough to do without giving away your valuable time and advice for free.'

'True, but—'

He held up his hand. 'No buts.'

'Okay, I hope it all goes well anyway, keep me posted.'

'I will. I mean, I would, but I don't have your number.' He nudged her gently, like he used to do sometimes in class when pointing out something amusing like a twig in another student's hair, or the teacher with a mark on his forehead from the whiteboard marker.

'Then you'll have to wait for me to contact *you* for updates.' She nudged him back.

'Hannah Delannah,' he said with a shake of his head. 'You still have a touch of that cheekiness in you.'

She turned to look at him and laughed. 'No one's called me that in years.' She too shook her head. 'Luca Antonuca,' she added.

Oh my God, what's happening? It was like they'd stepped into a time machine and landed in the past.

'Ha!' His laugh was like a glorious burst of flavour inside a chocolate truffle. 'Same for me. And anyway, no one else, as far as I know, used to call you your rhyming name, only me.'

'I know. Like I said, no one's called me that in years. Twenty years to be exact.'

'Well I'm going to. Unless you'd prefer to be called something with a more modern feeling to it, like... HD.'

'They're my initials, nothing exciting about them.'

'Nothing exciting about High Definition? Technology is a lot better now than it was when we were at school, HD are pretty cool initials to have if you ask me.'

She chuckled. It was as though they were walking home from school, backpacks bouncing against their backs, bubblegum popping between their words. 'If only your initials were LR instead of LA.'

'Why's that?'

'Then I could call you Low Resolution. And I'd be much more advanced than you, being all HD and stuff.'

Another of his delicious laughs burst from his mouth, and she wanted another, and another, and another. Like chocolate truffles, one was not enough.

How could she even try to avoid him now that he was back? She missed this. The talking, laughing, and just hanging out together. It was like barely any time had passed at all. But it had, a lot of it had. And things were different now. And she couldn't let herself fall under his spell again, no matter how tempting. It wouldn't lead to what she had wanted years before; if it were to happen, it would have happened a long time ago. He had clearly never thought of her in that way, only as a friend, and although that was still nice, she knew it would lead to her wanting more. And she couldn't let that happen. Not now, not when she was starting to take control of her life. It was time to move on, starting with the eleven o'clock train to Sydney.

CHAPTER FIVE

After grabbing some lunch, Luca went back home. Although it wasn't home, it also wasn't *not* home. It was just a place to stay until he found a house of his own, a small but modern two-bedroom townhouse only a couple of minutes' walk from the main street. But choosing his own house wasn't a decision he could make lightly. Hannah's place would be wonderful, just what he'd love, but he'd have to think carefully about the maintenance involved.

'Hey, mate,' he said to his housemate, Nathan, who was grabbing his keys from the hall table and about to head out by the looks of it.

'Hey. Just on my way to a job.'

'Same place as yesterday?' he asked.

'Nah, that was a one-off. Today is some garden maintenance at South Haven, a B&B not far from Serendipity, that health retreat at the entrance to town.'

'Ah yeah, I've heard about Serendipity. I think their restaurant might be a bit of competition, not many other fine dining options in town.'

'Unless you count Bayside.' He shrugged. 'But it's more of a casual set-up.'

Luca nodded, and a slight rush of cold made him shiver inside. He'd already checked out all the eateries in and around town before confirming his lease. Bayside was in the next block down from his premises. They specialised in buffet dinners, with an à la carte option. But they were also in the premises that his parents had secured in the past. So, had his father not died, Bayside might not even exist or may have been set up elsewhere, and *Viata* might have been there instead. The thought sent more shivers up his spine. He could have trained with his father and ended up working side by side with him at the lively and homely family restaurant. But, ironically, given the Romanian meaning of the restaurant's name, *life* had not turned out the way they'd expected.

'Anyway, dude, enjoy your afternoon,' Nathan said. 'Back around sunset.'

'Leave dinner to me,' Luca said. 'A thank you for letting me shack up here while I look for a place.'

'How can I say no to that? My last roomie was a baked beans on toast kinda guy.' He chuckled.

'Ew. I bet you had to keep the windows open a lot.'

'Ha-ha, yep. Anyway, thanks, mate.' He went for the door then turned around. 'How many places have you looked at so far, by the way?'

'Seeing a couple tomorrow, but I've only seen one so far. A chicken farm up on Jasmine Road, you know it?'

His eyes went wide. 'Hannah's place? It's for sale?'

He nodded. 'Yep, you know Hannah too?'

'Helped out with the garden for a few years when she needed an extra hand. Haven't been there for several months though. Figured she was handling it well enough on her own.'

'She's done well by the looks of it, but she's planning to move to the city.'

'No way, Hannah? She's as much a local as Tarrin himself,' he said. 'I only moved here in my twenties but I know she's been here her whole life. Wait, you know her already?'

'I lived in town for a couple of years in my teens. We were schoolmates.'

'Ah.' He tilted his head back. 'Blast from the past for you then, huh.'

'Indeed.' Luca had even woken up with a twenty-year-old song in his head... he couldn't remember the name of it but knew the tune. By the time he'd awoken it had slipped away from his consciousness. 'Anyway, see you after work.'

'Sure thing.' Nathan left and Luca sat at the kitchen table, opening his laptop.

'Where to start, where to start?' he mumbled to himself, opening a Word document. He then opened a spreadsheet, but it only confused him, so he went back to the plain white virtual sheet of paper.

Restaurant To-Do List, he typed.

Get kitchen built—process already started.

That was the main thing, everything else revolved around getting that done right. He'd organised a commercial kitchen company to come down and work on it for a week or two, based on how long they said it would take.

Create menu & organise suppliers.

That was the fun part, he could have anything he wanted, as long as it made good use of local produce as he'd heard that was important to those who lived in Tarrin's Bay, and it was also a drawcard for visitors who wanted to experience all that the town of new beginnings had to offer.

Hire staff.

Well, he couldn't do it all on his own. He hoped he could

find some decent permanent staff and a few casuals to help during times of demand.

Create website.

His brother was good with anything tetchy, but had signed him up to a free website provider so he could start writing his content before publishing it to the internet. So far all it said was: *New Tarrin's Bay restaurant—coming soon!* At least it was a start.

Order furniture and décor. Decide on furniture and décor first. Work out table arrangements.

The more he added to his list, the more it grew, along with a sense of overwhelm.

Decide on a NAME.

He wrote it in capital letters because it was a crucial step and needed to be decided upon asap so he could register the name, get the website domain, plan the colour scheme and design around the theme, and get a sign made to put up out the front of the premises to start attracting attention.

He opened a new document...

Name Ideas:

Ocean View

Seascape

Bay Vista

Luca's

They all sounded either too clichéd, not specific enough, or were already overused names in the hospitality industry. He didn't want to use the same name his parents had chosen, *Viata,* because although it was tempting, he wanted it to be his own creation, and also an English word so that the majority of people could tell immediately on hearing the name what sort of restaurant it was.

And also, he didn't want to jinx it.

He drummed his fingers on the table, random words

running through his mind. None of them caught his attention enough. *Hmmm.* He wondered if he could at least ask Hannah if she had any name ideas, that wasn't a big ask. Oh, but he didn't have her number.

He opened Facebook, searched her name, and on recognising her photo he clicked her profile. He smiled. It was a picture of her with her arm draped around Scarlett, the dog with a wide smile as natural as hers. He hardly used Facebook, he could never sit still long enough to look through all the posts, and preferred talking face to face, but he may have to start if he wanted to take advantage of social media marketing.

He scrolled a little, though nothing was public except her profile pictures. He'd also never looked her up until now. He'd thought of her over the years, yes, but never searched for her. Up until now he had always wanted to keep his Tarrin's Bay time in the past, as even though it held some fantastic memories, the ones that lingered were the ones that hurt. And it was easier to leave them behind than associate with anything that reminded him of that time.

But here he was now, facing his past. Starting anew right where it all began, and ended, for his parents' life dreams. He owed it to them to give it a shot. Owed it to himself too. He'd always liked the idea of owning his own restaurant, but the commitment had scared him. Not because he didn't think he could stick to it, he knew he could, even though many other people who knew him probably thought otherwise. It was because he didn't want to get it wrong. Didn't want to make any mistakes. Didn't want to fail.

It had been the same with women. He'd never stayed long enough with anyone to fail at a relationship. If he didn't stay, he didn't have to fail. And he didn't have to risk losing yet another person he loved.

But now, at thirty-five, he was feeling the pressure of time getting away from him lately. Faster than it ever seemed to. Not that anyone was pressuring him with anything, but something just seemed missing from his life. Some kind of stability, certainty, and... companionship. Not just casual companionship, but deep, connected, meaningful companionship. Love, some might call it.

He closed down her profile without sending a message or friend request.

He put his to-do list back on the screen. He needed to get to work. He could do this. And he would come up with a great name by himself.

Despite those longings that had been starting to simmer in his mind, or his heart, for a while now, in the foreseeable near future he wouldn't have any time or mental energy for companionship, for distractions, or even the possibility of the L word with someone.

There was only time for one thing.

His promise.

He didn't make promises often. But when he did, he kept them.

CHAPTER SIX

'How did it go?' Karen asked, when Hannah met her at the entrance to the office building just after four o'clock.

'Great,' she replied. 'Let's discuss over a cup of tea, where is a good place?' Hannah glanced around. While waiting for Karen to finish work, she had wandered around the city streets looking at various stores... brand-name clothing and handbags, shiny sparkly things, and luxury items everywhere; so different to the coastal-themed homewares, quirky ornaments, handmade candles, and local artists' creations in Tarrin's Bay stores.

'Right here.' Karen pointed across the road. 'I think you need their *Restore* tea blend, after your interrogation by my boss.' She winked.

Hannah chuckled. 'She wasn't that bad. But extremely... direct. And... well, does she ever smile?'

'Ha-ha, yep, she does sometimes, maybe an average of three-point-three-three times per month.' They waited for the pedestrian crossing to light up green then walked across. Tarrin's Bay didn't even have crossings like these, just a couple of zebra crossings. 'Usually coincides with when I bring her a surprise slice of cake or something.'

'That would make me smile too.' Hannah eyed the menu when they got to the cafe. 'Restore tea, huh?'

'Definitely. My shout. And something to eat?'

'Hmm.' Hannah tapped her chin. 'Slice of cake, now that you mention it. Vanilla cream.'

'Oh yes. Make that two.'

Karen ordered and they took their seats with a smile that widened when their tea and cakes were set down on their table by the window; people rushing past in suits, others wearing fancy backpacks, earphone cords trailing down from their ears like extra appendages.

'So by the end of the week you should know?'

'Yep. There are a couple of other applicants with similar experience to me, although I bet most are not from a chook farm down south.'

'But your varied experience should set you apart. You've handled many different types of events and in different locations, so you'd have some fresh ideas.'

Hannah nodded. 'We'll see, I guess. So if it's a yes, should I move in as soon as possible or do things bit by bit?' Hannah took a bite of the cake and the heavenly texture melted in her mouth. 'I've never moved house before.' She mumbled.

'I know,' Karen said. 'It's like you're fresh out of high school, starting life as an adult.'

'Tell me about it. I feel so strange, but it'll be good.' She took another spoonful. 'Speaking of high school...' She leaned in closer across the table, as though speaking too loudly would cause everyone in the cafe to turn towards her and point. 'Guess who showed up in town the other day, *and* might be interested in my property?'

'Benedict Cumberbatch?'

Hannah chuckled and shook her head.

'Idris Elba?'

'Guess again.'

'The Prime Minister?'

Hannah curved her hand beside her mouth and whispered, 'Luca Antonescu.'

It took a while for Karen's face to register recognition. Then her mouth opened a bit. 'Oh! As in, high school Luca? Your two-year-long crush you never got to follow through with?'

'Yes, that one.' Hannah's cheeks flushed.

'Wow, long time no see. Where's he been all these years, why didn't he come to our ten-year reunion? Has age treated him well? What's he doing back? Wait, he wants to buy your place?'

'Hang on, hang on.' Hannah poked her fork towards Karen. She took a sip of the fruity herbal tea. 'All I know is that he's been working as a chef in Sydney, and is opening up a new restaurant in Tarrin's Bay, so he's looking for a place to live. Likes the idea of supplying his own eggs, and growing some produce I guess. And his mum recently passed away.'

'Oh no, how sad. Poor guy, both his parents now.'

'Yeah, not fair is it. Makes me feel so lucky to still have mine, especially after Dad's health scare.'

'Same here.'

They were silent for a moment while sipping their tea.

'And?' she asked.

'And?'

'Does he still have that dark, thick hair falling all over his face?'

Hannah nodded. 'No greys yet either. Though they would suit him.'

'So, ah, I guess seeing him again brought back all the feels?'

'What? No, of course not.' She flicked her hand in the air. 'That was ages ago.'

'Hannah, you absolutely adored him. Though you never

showed it. You two acted like best friends. Surely it must bring back some memories.'

Hannah fidgeted with the napkin. 'Well, yeah... but still, time has passed, and we all grew up, and now I'm moving anyway, so once again life has shown me that nothing was ever meant to happen, or will ever happen. Just one of those things.' She shrugged and ate more cake. 'Besides, I'm sure he's good at what he does, but for all I know he might give it a shot in town for a year or two and then leave. It's not like Tarrin's Bay doesn't have enough places to eat. And maintaining my place, if he wants to buy it, would be hard work on top of that. To be honest, I wouldn't be surprised if he can't stick with it.'

'You mean like all the girlfriends he used to go through? Hannah, he was a popular teenage boy. He's now a grown man. I'm sure he's matured a bit over the years.'

'We'll see. But I'm focusing on a new life now, no distractions.'

'You haven't been wondering... what if?'

'What if what?'

'What if you stayed?' Karen moved the salt shaker to the middle of the table. 'What if him arriving in town was meant to happen,' she moved the pepper shaker close to the salt, 'so you can finally tell him how you felt all those years ago, and see what happens?' She clinked the two shakers together.

'He's one year too late. I'm over it now, don't want any unnecessary drama in my life.'

Karen sat back in her seat. 'Fair enough. And I *am* looking forward to hopefully working with you, and having you at my place so we can binge-watch TV shows and have more tea and cake.'

Hannah smiled. 'Me too, my friend, me too.' She held up her teacup towards Karen, who gently touched it with hers.

They sipped and refilled the cups from the pot. 'He actually wanted my help setting up his restaurant, even offered to pay me.'

'Really? Well, why not do it for some extra cash? It wouldn't take you long to whip up a launch plan, you've done it before. Then you can leave him to it and get on over here.'

'Still, I have a lot to organise with the house, I don't want to overdo things. It'd be fun, yeah, and okay, part of me wouldn't mind catching up a bit more on the last two decades, but what if your boss wants me to start real soon?'

'Evie is still working in the role and yet to finalise when she's going to take her maternity leave. It could still be several weeks. Anyway, see what the verdict is at the end of the week.'

'Yep, will wait and see. It'd be nice to have some spare time, though, before moving. And get Scarlett accustomed to the new place gradually.'

'Oh, I'm so looking forward to having her around! I've set up a nice dog bed on the back patio, and an extra one in the laundry. Hopefully she'll be comfortable there.'

'Thanks, Karen.' Hannah touched her friend's hand. 'I wouldn't be able to make such a big change without your support.'

'That's what friends are for.'

A slow smile oozed onto Hannah's lips, and then onto Karen's, as she remembered the karaoke they once did at a high school disco, where they sang that old song together. She also remembered Luca watching her from the crowd, and she'll never forget the relaxed smile on his face at the end of the song when he gave her a simple thumbs up.

Yep, friends. Friends supported each other, hung out, and had fun. Friends didn't complicate things by pushing the boundaries of their friendship into the 'what if' zone.

It was nice, in a way, to remember those intense young teenage feelings. But it was bittersweet to remember them disintegrating after he left. From necessity, not choice. But she was an adult now, life was moving forward fast, and she had things to do. Delving into the past wasn't one of them.

CHAPTER SEVEN

Before dinner on Wednesday, Luca flipped through the pages of the two property brochures; both viable options, though one a little pricier than he would like to offer. They each ticked most of the boxes. But he'd have to start from scratch if he wanted chickens, whereas Hannah's house was good to go. But one of the other properties also had plentiful mature fruit trees which would come in handy for his menu ingredients. But he couldn't base a decision on plants, or chickens. First and foremost, it had to be a home. With future potential. Not just a place to sleep. Somewhere he could imagine building a life. Maybe even with a family, when the time was right. If it would ever be right for him.

He looked at his phone photos of the Jasmine Road property; as it was only a preview at the moment it didn't have a brochure, apart from Hannah's instruction manual she'd mentioned. It had a better feeling than the others, but he didn't know if that was from his memories clouding his judgement. It ticked *all* the boxes though.

He needed to see it again.

He made a call to the real estate agent and requested another inspection.

Over dinner he ran through more restaurant name ideas in his mind, and thought more about the house. With both topics of thought, Hannah kept popping into his head.

I just need her opinion on the names.

Maybe he could casually ask her at the next inspection. He looked through more photos, especially of the kitchen. The large rustic island bench reminded him of the one they used to have at home before moving to Tarrin's Bay as a young family. His father on one side, expertly chopping ingredients, his mother next to him, swiftly taking the chopped ingredients to the stove. They had worked well as a team. He imagined doing the same one day, not at work, but at home. It was funny how a simple piece of furniture or equipment could trigger memories. And how one thing could potentially be the deciding factor for the house he wanted to start fresh in.

Yep. He was definitely interested. He wanted it, but... at the same time, he didn't want Hannah to leave.

***

Hannah switched the lights on inside as soon as she entered from the back verandah, having fed the animals and cleaned the water troughs before refilling them. The island bench burst to life under the glow of the pendant lights. Her phone was lit up. She glanced at the screen. A missed call from the real estate agent, and an 'important' email notification, from the events company.

She resisted the urge to check the email first and listened to her voicemail. Lily had brought another prospective buyer through to see the property today while she'd been at the produce markets. They had seemed mildly interested, Lily had said, but not as keen as Luca. And speaking of Luca, he had requested another inspection. Hannah called Lily back and said Thursday or Friday would be fine, and an appointment for Thursday at ten o'clock was confirmed.

Hannah glanced at the phone number stuck to the fridge. She glanced at her phone.

Might as well...

She added him as a contact. But that did *not* mean she was going to contact him. But if anything happened to the piece of paper, it would be backup. If she needed it. Which she didn't. But if she did.

'Oh!' She remembered the email.

She opened her inbox and prepared herself for the 'thanks for coming in, but we're afraid we'll have to decline' message, with a thoughtful and sincere 'All the best for the future!' added on to it.

Dear Hannah,

Thanks so much for coming in for an interview. Our team has reviewed the shortlisted applicants and are pleased to say that your variety of experience and unique ideas will be a wonderful asset to our company. We would be delighted to offer you the position, subject to a one-month trial period, for a confirmed duration of fourteen months, and with a view to continuing either part-time or full-time after the contract period.

We will require you to start on Monday 6 August.

    I will give you a call tomorrow to
discuss.
    Regards,
    Janelle.

Hannah's mouth dropped open. *They've decided already? August 6? That's eight weeks. Oh my God. I got it. First go, and I got it!*

She wiggled a little and grinned. Then texted Karen. And then her mother. And then:

> Hi Luca, if you wanted to talk further about how much more advanced High Definition is, you didn't have to go to the trouble of booking another inspection ;) But I'll see you tomorrow. And just wanted to let you know I got the job and will be starting in 8 wks, if that has any bearing on your decision with the house. I'll be needing it sold asap. ~ Hannah.

She pressed send before she changed her mind. And then second-guessed herself...

I could have just told him that tomorrow.

I should leave all the house business to Lily to talk to him about.

But he's not just anyone, he's... he's Luca.

She sent off a quick reply to the email and then took some vegetables from the fridge for dinner.

Her phone buzzed.

> Well well well, look who's decided to give me her number! Too bad she's leaving town, but a BIG congratulations on your new job. Great stuff HD. You deserve it.

She smiled and tucked a loose strand of hair that had fallen from her ponytail behind her ear.

Her finger hovered near the screen. She typed a longish reply then deleted it, changing it simply to:

> Thanks!

No need to go into detail. She'd see him tomorrow. And then she'd know how serious he was, if at all, about her place.

CHAPTER EIGHT

'So once a day isn't enough?' Luca asked.

'Twice a day is great if you can,' Hannah replied, as they stood near the chicken coop. 'One wheelbarrow full of feed morning and evening. If you're working nights you can hire a local teen to do the job at the end of the day. I know a few who can sometimes help out.'

He nodded.

'You open this hatch on the silo here.' She opened it. 'And let the feed drain into the wheelbarrow.' She let a small amount fall in as an example, as she had already filled up the feeding troughs this morning. 'When full, carry it over to the troughs and tip it in.'

'Got it.'

'I use only organic feed, makes for healthier chooks and better eggs. There's a good market here for organics, as not everyone does it. Health-conscious people are willing to pay a bit extra for it, as the feed costs more than others.'

'Where do I get it from?'

He sounded even more interested than she had expected.

'A delivery truck comes regularly and fills the silo, so I

would have to change all the accounts to your name, and they'll invoice you via email.'

'Uh-huh.'

'So food, fresh water, fresh air, open space to roam and forage, and shelter overnight to roost and that's the basics.' She gave a nod and blew a wisp of hair from her forehead.

He looked at her a moment, as though he was absorbing and memorising what she was saying. She raised her eyebrows. 'Any questions?'

He took a moment to respond. 'Ah, nope. Not yet anyway.' He turned away and ran a hand through his hair. 'But if I do, I'll...'

'Get in touch with Lily,' she suggested.

'Yes. That's what I was going to say.'

They took the wheelbarrow to the troughs and filled them up. 'Luca.' Hannah softened, as they began walking back to the house. 'It's okay, contact me directly with any queries about the running of the place, if it makes your decision easier. And anything else, go through Lily. Sound good?'

'Sounds good.' He smiled and gave a nod. 'Also, can I just—'

'Hannah!' Lily called out from across the yard where she stood near the house. 'Ah, I think she's... I'm not sure if...' she moved towards Scarlett. 'She might have eaten something, I think it's stuck.'

The dog was semi-standing, hunched forward, her chest heaving, and she clawed at her mouth.

Hannah ran. 'Scarlett!' She was there in a flash. Scarlett's mouth was open, drool dripping out, and she seemed to be both trying to inhale but also exhale or expel something. Hannah tried to pry open her jaw further to see inside but it was too strong. Luca appeared beside and placed his hand firmly on the dog's back. He gave it two firm slaps. A slight cough sound emerged, but still Scarlett struggled.

'Oh my goodness,' Lily said. 'Should I call a vet?'

'Hang on. Try a bit harder,' she instructed Luca. Though it pained her to watch Scarlett like this. He gave her two more sharp slaps.

'Oh, no. C'mon, Scar!' She shuffled around behind her pet and lifted the top part of her body off the ground, nestling her fist in the hollow underneath her rib cage. She was old and Hannah wasn't sure if this would damage her chest but there was no time to think. She pushed her fist quickly upwards and the dog lurched forward. A choking sound emerged and Hannah did it again. This time, something popped out and landed in a puddle of drool at her feet. Scarlett sucked in breath after breath, and slunk onto the ground in recovery mode. Luca stroked the dog's back calmly and reassuringly.

'Oh, hallelujah,' said Lily. 'Phew!'

'There we go,' said Hannah, 'Everything's okay, Scar. You just rest now.' She snuggled close to her for a moment. Then picked up the object. A gumnut. She'd put a few in a bowl on the small round table on the verandah to add a decorative touch before the first house inspection. Somehow one had found its way to Scar and she'd decided to see if it was tasty or not. The dog breathed heavily. 'I might give the vet a call and see if I can bring her in for a quick check-up.' Hannah got to her feet and called. 'He'll see her shortly,' she said a moment later. 'Sorry to cut this short today.'

'It's no problem, I got to see how the chooks work. The basics anyway.'

'I can always meet you again later, Luca, if that's okay with Hannah,' Lily offered.

Hannah nodded.

'That's okay, I think I've seen enough to have a good think about this,' he said.

'Right. Well I'll be looking at putting it officially on the market tomorrow, so if you're keen, if you could let me know by the end of today or first thing in the morning, that'd be ideal.'

'Will do,' he replied. 'Thanks, Lily. And Hannah, I'll come with you to the vet.'

'Oh no, it's okay.'

'I can help you lift her, she might be too weak to walk right now.'

He was right, it would be handy to have an extra set of hands. 'Okay, thanks, that'd be great.'

They took Scarlett to Hannah's car, Lily left with her dust-coated high heels, and Hannah locked up house.

An hour later she brought Scarlett back to the car, along with a nutritional supplement for ageing dogs, and the vet said it should stop her from wanting to eat random things like gumnuts, which can sometimes be from a mineral deficiency such as iron. Her ribs were a bit sore to the touch but otherwise intact, as was her diaphragm, and throat. She was suffering the expected effects of old age, but there was no need for any immediate treatment apart from the supplement. He'd advised to bring her back for another more comprehensive check-up in a couple of months. Which would be right when she was moving, so she made a note to do it in her last week in town.

'Thanks for helping out.' Hannah turned the key in the ignition.

'I didn't do much. You got the thing out, lucky you knew what you were doing. I just tried the human version I learned at my occupational first-aid course.'

'I'm so glad it worked.' Hannah glanced at Scarlett in the back seat. 'She's my best friend, this old girl.'

'I can tell.' He smiled. 'I miss having pets. Haven't had one for a while. Might have to change that.'

'Well, if you buy my place you'll have five hundred pets,' she laughed.

'A dog would be nice as well.'

'They are great company.'

'I bet. You are too. Always were, Hannah.'

Hannah caught his eye. She was about to put the gearstick in reverse but wanted to look at him a moment longer, so that if only one last time, she would be satisfied. One last look, like she didn't get before. Even though she knew she'd see him again before she moved. But still...

'I'm glad we bumped into each other again,' he added.

She put the gearstick in reverse, but kept her foot on the brake. 'It's been nice to catch up again.' She smiled and nodded. 'Oh, what were you going to say before? Before the thing with Scarlett, something about, can you...' She raised her eyebrows.

Luca flicked his hand in the air. 'Ah, nothing really. Doesn't matter.' He looked into the back seat. 'Let's get this girl back to her favourite spot beside the armchair on the verandah, hey?'

'How did you know it's her favourite spot? You've only been there twice.'

'Yes, and both times Scarlett has been sitting there. So a wild guess. Besides, the chair has that old blanket thingy on it that you knitted when you were at school, remember? You brought it out to the lookout that night we all got pizza to watch the comet in the sky?'

'Space station.'

'Was it the space station? I forget.'

'Yeah, a quick bit of light arcing through the sky. I think you blinked when it passed by.'

'Ha-ha. Probably. Anyway, I was stupidly wearing only a T-shirt so was pretty cold and I'll never forget that you gave up your blanket for me. I remember it smelled like vanilla or something, like you.'

'Vanilla is my favourite scent. My mum used to make her

own vanilla-scented hand creams and body lotions. Still does actually.'

'So I figure Scarlett likes that spot because it smells like you.' He smiled.

Hannah tilted her head. 'Huh. I never thought of that before. You notice the little things, don't you.'

'Attention to detail is an asset in my job. I've learned to notice it.'

'I like that. So many people don't see those little things, don't notice what's right in front of them.'

Just like he hadn't noticed her in *that way* when they were younger. But he wasn't a chef then so perhaps his attention to detail came with his training.

'That's where the beauty of life lies. In the little details. It's also what my,' he rubbed at his jaw, 'what my mum used to say.'

Hannah put the gearstick back in park. 'Did she get work in another restaurant, after you left town?' she asked, hoping it wouldn't be upsetting for him to discuss it.

He shook his head. 'She went back to dressmaking, which is what she had done on the side while Dad was planning the restaurant. She actually designed and made wedding dresses. Ended up with her own brand and shop, *Teadora*. Her name.'

'Oh, wow. Actually, I think I may have heard of her brand, through some of the wedding planning I've done. What a beautiful occupation to have. She must have been very clever.'

'She was. She said her dresses were different because of the extra details she would put in, each dress had something unique added to it. Like a swirl of beads somewhere unexpected, or the bride's initial sewn into the ribbon trailing from the back, or diamantés attached in a heart shape to the front hem. She said, "The beauty is in the little details, not in the perfection".'

'I'd love to see some.'

'Google "Teadora wedding dresses". We sold the business after she died, but many of her designs are still for sale.'

'I'll do that,' Hannah replied. Not because she needed a wedding dress, but to see what his mother had made. To show her respects by admiring what she had created.

Luca smiled. 'Still knitting these days?' he asked.

'Nope,' she chuckled. 'That was a one-off, that and the few scarves I made. It was a fad for a while, kind of trendy and daggy at the same time.'

'A bit like my choice of clothing?' He made a scanning movement with his hands down his body; dark jeans, tan shoes, a knit top and a tan leather jacket. 'Leather jackets are old school, but this one is a bit more...'

'On the trendy side,' she added.

'My thoughts exactly.' He grinned.

'Anyway,' Hannah put the gearstick back in reverse, and her mind back on track, 'time to go home.' She reversed. 'My home, I mean. So you can get your car and go home too. Your temporary home. Until, unless, you buy mine, and then it *will* be your home. Then it won't be mine anymore. But for now.'

'Hannah,' he laughed. 'Don't stress. It'll always be your home.'

She looked out at the shops as she passed through the main street, then turned the corner to head up towards her part of town. It would. This town, and the family property, would always be home for her, no matter where she ended up. If only she could figure out how to take some part of home with her. To keep the feeling alive.

She arrived back and Luca helped bring Scarlett inside to the laundry, where Hannah set her up in her indoors dog bed.

'Tea, coffee?' she asked. 'Mocha?' She chuckled.

'No, but thanks. I need to go and work out some options, go through the finances, and weigh up some pros and cons.'

'Of course.' Hannah accompanied him to the door. 'Well, let me know if you have any questions.'

'I will,' he said, stepping outside. She stayed at the door, holding on to the frame. Luca turned around. 'Hannah,' he said, stepping forward.

Her eyes widened.

His arms lifted and he slid them around her, and hers naturally followed his lead. 'It's really good to see you again.' He softened into her, and despite initial restraint, she allowed herself to soften into his embrace.

'Ditto,' she whispered.

And as he pulled away, she tried to figure out how to take some part of him with her.

CHAPTER NINE

'Thanks, Lily, I'll await the verdict,' Luca ended the call that evening and sat on his bed with a sigh.

I did it. I made an offer.

He blew out another sigh and lay back on his bed. He could have taken longer to deliberate, look at more properties, wait for the house to go on the market and see what happened, but the idea of someone else offering higher made him anxious. He didn't want some stranger to take over Hannah's pride and joy. He wanted to give it a damn good shot. And live somewhere that had meaning, to honour its history while creating its future.

His dad would have loved the chickens, and the herb and vegetable garden. There were even blueberries and lemon trees. All the basics for a good, healthy kitchen. Fresh produce was key to a meal's flavour, and nutrition. He hoped that if the sale went through, his dad, somewhere, somehow, could see him there in that garden, and then in that kitchen, making him proud. He hoped that his mum could see too, and know that keeping his promise to finally build something of his own would be fulfilled.

To distract himself, he scrolled through Facebook and

watched a few random funny videos that showed up, until he got hungry enough to grab a bite to eat. Nathan had already eaten, and gestured to a container in the fridge.

'You sure?' he asked, and Nathan nodded. 'Thanks, man,' Luca said. 'No need to save them for me, but it's nice to have the odd night off from cooking.'

'I figured as much. Though if it's too overcooked let me know and I'll pass on the criticism to the chef and tell him to do better next time.' He smiled.

Luca chuckled. 'I'm sure it's fine. No need to worry.'

He ate the spaghetti bolognaise and gave Nathan a thumbs up. Though it was a meal that was hard to get wrong. If he ever did happen to come across a not-so-great spag bol, he probably *would* be passing on the criticism to the chef.

His phone rang. 'Hi, Lily?'

'Hannah is going to think about your offer overnight and let me know in the morning. Just so you know, it *is* a little under what we believe it's worth, and what she's prepared to accept, so if you'd like to increase your offer, now is the time.'

Luca's heart beat a little faster. 'Hmm. I'm not so sure I can offer any higher, but leave it with me. I'll have to think about it.'

When he ended the call, he tapped his fingers on the table. He'd made a decent offer. And at this stage there were no counteroffers, so the agent would no doubt want to encourage Hannah to decline the offer and hopefully achieve a higher one, or allow other inspections by prospective buyers. But she was in a rush to sell. There's no way he would short-change Hannah, but he had to think of his needs first when it came to using his mother's inheritance, and his brother's investment as a silent partner in the restaurant, which he also had to budget for. But if all went well with his business, he should expect to be making a decent profit within about six months or so. He could increase his offer by a bit more, if necessary, but not too much or he would have to go back to the bank for an increased lending limit.

Should he do it now in order to increase the chance of a quick sale, or wait and see what Hannah said about the first offer?

What do you think, Mum? He wished he could ask. She'd become a savvy businesswoman over the years and he trusted her opinion.

He cleaned up the kitchen then took his laptop to his room and opened his to-do list.

He knew what he had to do, but there was no order to his plans. It was a bit of this and a bit of that, and doing what appeared to be the next best step each day.

But he needed someone to take his list and his ideas and formulate them into something more workable and efficient. Hannah was leaving in eight weeks, and he'd probably need at least eight to ten weeks to do what he had in mind, so he thought. He would have to find someone else who could help.

He googled for a while but didn't find much, not around this region of the country anyway. He could always call Hannah and ask for a recommendation at least.

He picked up his phone, but hovered his finger over her number. He didn't want to disturb her while she was considering his offer. But in case things got weird between them if she declined his offer and the house was put on the market and sold to someone else, perhaps now was a better time.

He pressed the call button.

'Luca, hi. Um, I haven't decided yet, I need to—'

'It's okay, I'm not calling about the house,' he interjected. 'It's about my restaurant.'

'Oh, okay then.'

He was about to ask if she could recommend someone who

did a similar thing to what she did, but his mind had other ideas...

'I know you're leaving. That's cool, but here's the thing. I *really* need some professional input on my launch. I could find someone else, but... I know you're the best. And I want the best.' He took a quick breath. 'I can't fail at this.'

'Luca, I...'

He continued before she could object. 'So I'm prepared to pay you whatever you need to charge to make it worth your while. I know you're going to be busy packing up to move. But I just need someone to create a plan for me, and then I can do most of the work. You can contribute as little or as much as you can, but I need expert management skills... to give me something to work with.'

There, done.

'Luca, I understand. But there's no halfway. I'm all or nothing when it comes to this sort of stuff.'

'Then do it all. I'll pay extra.'

'I don't want... I need to...' She sighed, and he was filled with a sudden sense of guilt.

I'm being selfish, he thought. *I can do this myself, I should do this myself.*

His pride wanted to take it all on and make it work, but it was more important that it was a success than being able to say 'Hey, look what I created ALL BY MYSELF!'

Pride needed to take a back seat, to allow what was needed to get the job done properly to be a priority. But she had enough on her plate.

'It's okay, sorry, I got a bit overexcited. I'll find someone else. Can you recommend anyone?' he asked.

Silence.

'Hannah?'

'Six weeks,' she said softly, but firmly. 'It'll have to be all complete within six weeks.'

His chest rose in anticipation and he held his breath in his throat. 'Does that mean you'll do it?'

'On one condition.'

'Anything.'

'You increase your offer on the property.'

His chest sunk. When did she get so assertive and ruthless? 'By just how much?'

'Luca, I'm not interested in having our own little auction and draining all your well-deserved funds, I just want an easy sale. No stress. But I promised my parents a minimum sale amount, and yours is a bit under. So unless it rises, I'll have to put it on the market tomorrow.'

He nodded, even though she couldn't see his response.

'I understand,' he said. So now he would not only have to increase his offer, but pay her a good amount for her services too. He hoped he wasn't getting in too deep. But *something* felt right about the Delaney house, and *everything* felt right about Hannah helping him out with the restaurant. He exhaled loudly. 'Okay. I'll revise my offer and get back in touch with Lily. But I'll only make the one higher offer. If you need any more than what I offer, I'll have to pass. But if it's acceptable, then great, and we can work together for the next six weeks on my launch.'

'Okay.'

'Okay.'

Silence.

'I guess we'll find out in the morning,' he said. 'I'll leave a message with Lily now, and go from there.'

'Sure.'

He was about to thank her and say goodnight, when a

question reappeared in his mind that he'd forgotten to ask when Scarlett had that incident. 'Oh, Hannah?'

'Yep?'

'What is the significance of your house name, Iona?'

'My ancestors were from the Isle of Iona, in Scotland,' she said. 'I've never been, but my parents have when they were younger. Dad said it's the most peaceful place, like a second home. So when they bought the Tarrin's Bay property, he wanted to include a little piece of our heritage in it.'

Luca pondered this. He didn't know much, if anything about the Isle of Iona, but made a mental note to google it. 'I'll keep it,' he said. 'The name. If you accept my offer. I'll keep that part alive for your family.'

'Thanks, Luca. It's okay, though, I understand if you would want to make it something for yourself, with your own significance.'

'No. I can do that with my restaurant. Iona will stay Iona.' He gave a firm nod to confirm his decision.

'That's lovely of you,' she said softly, then yawned. 'So what is the name of your restaurant going to be?'

'Umm.'

'That's unique.'

'No, I mean, umm, that's another reason I need your help. I haven't come up with anything yet that feels... right.'

'Oh. Well once you have clarified the type of restaurant, the cuisine you'll be offering, and the market you want to attract, names should come at you from everywhere. You'll probably come up with several and then have to choose between them.'

He chuckled. 'You must find this stuff really easy. I've thought as much as I can, but still... *nada.*'

'Well,' her voice brightened up, 'let's hope this offer is what I'm looking for, and then you'll have yourself a restaurant name in no time once I get my mind onto it.'

He could easily picture her chin held high, a satisfied grin on her face. She was still laid-back, go-with-the-flow Hannah from school, but she was also... confident, don't-mess-with-me grown-up Hannah. And he had to admit, he kinda liked it.

After ending the call he thought about his new offer, and before chickening out, and despite the butterflies in his belly, he pressed the real estate agent's number.

CHAPTER TEN

This was it. No turning back. Hannah didn't get butterflies in her belly often, but she did now. She pressed Lily's number, and a minute later she had accepted Luca's offer. It was actually a tiny bit higher than she expected, which made her think that he really wanted her house, and that gave her confidence. He really was serious about this.

She sat on the couch and exhaled. *Done.*

But the butterflies remained. She opened Luca's number in her contacts, then closed it. She'd have to wait a while so he could speak to Lily, and no doubt probably sit on his couch too and exhale in relief, or maybe he would jump on it with excitement like he did once at Ben's house when they'd gathered there for another session of their school project. It took her a moment to remember why he'd been excited, but then the visuals formed in her mind. Something about a new flavour of potato chips Karen had brought along, and back then, that was a big deal, because unlike today's abundance of fancy flavours, twenty years ago it was mostly plain, salt and vinegar, or cheese and onion. Now there was everything from chilli and pepper, to paprika and thyme... Life was better in many ways now, but she still longed for the more simplistic ways of life back then.

And yet, the city was beckoning her now. But strangely, she felt it would be even simpler. Go to work, come home, finished. Not the endlessness of running the property here, and running a business, with no delineation between them and between her work and personal life. Life could be more easily segmented. And if she wanted to go on dates, there would be an abundance of men. New options. New flavours. But no pressure, someone who could just fit around her life and she didn't have to bombard with farm life. *If* she wanted someone, that was. She would want to just settle in first and get her own life on track.

Hannah allowed herself a while to flip through one of the coffee-table books she'd collected over the years. Mostly style and design books, coastal living, farm living, and home organising ideas. They inspired her for the events she created and managed.

She looked at some pages dedicated to kitchens and thought of Luca. A combination of stainless steel and rustic timbers, a mixed yet matched array of textures and styles that somehow worked well together.

I wonder what kind of feel he's after...

She knew she'd have to make that call soon. Accept his other offer. They'd made a deal and it was time to confirm it.

I bet he wants coastal chic, relaxed and airy, with whites and blues; a welcoming feel rather than a dimly lit, atmospheric restaurant with rich hues and accents of red. Then again, he'd come from the city so maybe he wanted to inject his own brand of city-ness into the coastal, country lifestyle.

Ideas formed in her mind even without having a clue what he was looking at doing with the place. She'd been hesitant before, but now... that familiar excitement of new ideas built up inside, the feeling of endless possibilities, and her in control of all of it. She actually wanted to do it now. Yes, she'd be busy preparing for the move, but the immediate cash flow would be handy, until she received the profits from the sale.

Okay. Time.

'Luca, hi,' she spoke into the phone.

'Hello, city girl, I am now a chicken farmer, you know.' He sounded quite pleased with himself. 'Did you know that chickens apparently originated from dinosaurs?'

'Is that so?' she replied. 'But does the chicken come first or the egg?'

'I am on a mission to find out. I will have to get back to you on that.' He chuckled. 'Well, I guess a thank you is in order. So, thanks, Hannah, I'm really excited to get moving and make the most of your place. Our place. My place. You know what I mean.'

'I'm glad it's going to someone I know. And keep me posted on the chickens. I'll miss them.'

'I'll send you updates and a few chook selfies, don't you worry.'

'Ha, thanks.' She paced slowly up and down the living room. 'So, in the meantime, you've got a restaurant to launch?'

'I do indeed. Are we... still on?'

Six weeks. She could do it. Well, she kinda had to now. And it would be a good way to give closure to the 'thing' with Luca after all these years... maybe he was meant to turn up in her life now, not for a second chance at romance, but for him to be the one to take over her house. It sounded like he needed to start something new after his mother's death, and maybe being back here was a way for him to honour his parents' memories and the life they tried to start here back then. It made sense. And helping him out with his business would also help him indirectly with the house, by making sure he gave the restaurant the best chance of success. And maybe, just maybe, after six weeks she'd finally be able to move on properly and lay her old feelings for him to rest.

Yep, this was perfect.

'Absolutely. When should we start?' she asked.

'Now?'

'Now? You don't want to waste any time do you.'

'Uh-uh. I'm getting old you know, we're not teenagers anymore. Time to get cookin', good lookin'.'

'Um, I think I'll leave the cookin' to you and I'll do the plannin'.'

'Of course. But I reckon I can get you into the kitchen. Help me work out the best menu to use.'

'For sure, if you want to cook me expertly prepared meals, I'm happy to oblige.'

'Well, yes, but I may just have to rope you into helping out. I'm sure you're a bit of a good cook yourself. You might be able to add some input on what these locals like to eat.'

'Hmm, we'll see,' she replied. 'Anyway, I can meet with you in about an hour if that suits?'

'Fabulous, my dear. Meet me at the premises so I can show you around. And let me know what to pay you and when.'

'Sounds good. Once I've assessed the situation and discussed your requirements, I'll write up a plan on Monday, then meet with you again soon after to go over it, then if you're happy we'll begin, or if you want changes I'll rework the plan and we'll go from there.'

Luca was silent for a moment, and Hannah could practically see him smile through the phone.

'I can hear your brain ticking away. This is going to be good. Thanks, Hannah Delannah.'

'No problem, Luca Antonuca.'

She arrived first, and squinted through the gaps of the mostly covered windows. Too dark to see much. She remembered the beauty salon had stairs to the top level, where they used to do their more luxurious pampering treatments, and had some kind of outdoor relaxation zone. She'd only been once, for a friend's hens' afternoon.

Hannah tightened the collar on her jacket around her neck as a gusty wind rushed past in an icy flash. Winter was definitely here. Though it was never so cold in Tarrin's Bay as to snow or need thermal underwear, unlike a visit to the Blue Mountains once for a wedding, when she had come underprepared and found herself sleeping with a few extra blanket layers weighing her down so much she could hardly roll over in bed.

Another gust of wind approached her, Luca approaching along with it.

'Hey there.' He grinned.

'Hey. Hi.' She held out her hand, instinctively, as she always did when beginning a business meeting. Then she instinctively pulled it back, remembering it wasn't needed. This was Luca she was dealing with. But he took her hand away from its hiding spot by her side, his skin warm despite the cold wind. Before she could give it a fifty per cent professional shake and a fifty per cent personal shake, he tapped her hand with his palm twice, then curved his hand around her thumb and tugged it down, his eyes catching hers.

'What are you doing... oh my God, the handshake? *The* handshake?'

He nodded, tapping her hand again with his palm, and her hand (instinctively) following his lead, forming a fist and lightly tapping his knuckles before opening her palm and holding it up for a high-five. Her head tipped back in a laugh as she remembered when they had made it up in high school, and how many attempts it had taken to get *just right*. 'Just one fist tap, Hannah,' he'd said, 'any more and it's overkill'. And she'd tried to add more and more movements, but it had gotten too complicated so they'd agreed on a quick and simple but unique handshake that they could do without thinking.

'Twenty years later and still as fresh in my memory,' he said. 'The body doesn't forget.'

Neither does the heart, she thought.

In truth she'd tried to take longer working out the handshake back then because she simply loved touching his hands. And also, it had just been plain fun.

But now they had business to get down to, and fun would have to wait. She needed to focus so she could do the best job possible in the time she had available.

'Well, before I forget why I'm here, let's have a look at this future award-winning restaurant, shall we?' She straightened her shoulders with a swift smile and gestured to the door.

Luca unlocked it and held the door open for her.

'Thanks.' She walked inside. Stark white light brightened the bare walls as Luca flicked on the switch.

'I want more atmospheric lighting than these bare globes,' he said. 'I was thinking some glass fittings with those old-fashioned Edison bulbs?'

'Oh yes, they are quite popular. But we'll get to that. There are bigger priorities first.'

'Of course.' His cheeks rounded with a smile. 'Such as the kitchen, the reception, tables and seating arrangements, menu, staff, marketing.' His hands made circles as he paced the room. 'I could go on.'

'You could, but I'll work it all out bit by bit. No need to feel overwhelmed.'

'Overwhelmed? Me?'

She smiled. 'You can't keep still when you have a lot on your mind.' She stated. He stopped moving at her observation, then resumed moving.

'You're right, my mind does have a few too many browser tabs open. Do you know how many browser tabs you can have open on a computer at any one time?'

'No, how many?'

'Don't know.' He shrugged. 'Thought you might. I must find out, will google that later. And now I have another browser tab open.'

She chuckled. 'Let me put those browser tabs from your brain into my spreadsheet and let your operating system reboot.'

He smiled. 'Sounds good. I'm a good multitasker, in the kitchen at least, but all this planning has been doing my head in.'

'Leave it to me, I love this stuff.' She grinned and gave his arm a light punch. 'And I get to tell you what to do. Ha-ha-ha-ha.' She gave a fake evil laugh and rubbed her hands together.

Luca responded with a real and non-evil laugh. 'Enjoy it while you can, Han. It won't last forever.' He gave her a light punch back.

Her light mood deepened on realising...

Neither will this time with him.

'Okay, well,' she cleared her throat. 'Show me around and then we'll have a chat about your grand vision for this place.' She withdrew her clipboard, and pressed the top of the pen with a perky pop. She wrote the date at the top of the paper and then held it poised in her hand.

Luca led her into the rectangular kitchen, a combination of white walls and stainless steel. 'As you can see, the kitchen basics are nearly complete. Just waiting on delivery of some extra equipment on Monday, then the kitchen people will continue the set-up and all should be complete by later that week.'

'That's been fast,' she said.

'It was the first thing I organised. Once the kitchen is done, I'll feel like everything else is easier to organise.'

She nodded, then stepped out of the kitchen and glanced at the staircase towards the back of the room. 'Now, you have two levels, so will the top be reserved for functions only, or also dining?'

'Dining when it's not being used by a private function.'

'And have you considered non-slip steps to help protect wait staff carrying food?'

His eyebrows raised. 'Nope, but good thinking, Ninety-Nine.'

She gave a brief nod. 'Just things popping into my mind.' She gestured to the stairs. 'Can we?'

'Of course, after you.' He held his arm out and she stepped onto the steps, vaguely conscious of him stepping behind her and hoping he wasn't too close to her backside.

When she reached the top of the L-shaped staircase, she blinked at the natural light flooding the room. Floor-to-ceiling glass doors were on the far wall, and as though drawn to a light at the end of a tunnel, she walked towards it. 'Wow,' she said.

Luca unlocked and opened one of the doors, and they stepped out onto the large square balcony that overlooked the ocean, Lookout Point visible on the left. 'This is my favourite part.' His smile was contagious, hers grew and she could feel his excitement and gratitude at securing this place.

Hannah loved her rural views, but there was nothing quite like the sight of the ever-flowing ocean.

'You are one lucky chef.'

'Sure am. Though I won't get this view when I'm in the kitchen.'

Filled with a sudden urge, Hannah got out her phone camera. She put down her clipboard and snapped a photo of the view. 'There you go,' she said, and a moment later his phone chimed. 'Print it, frame it, put it in your kitchen.'

'I like that idea.' He looked at his phone. 'Thanks.'

She smiled, picking up her clipboard and turning around. 'Okay, so tell me... what do you envisage as the end result here?'

She pushed away the thoughts that asked the same question, but of her upcoming six weeks with him.

'End result? You mean, how I want it to look, etcetera?'

'Yes. And feel.'

How would *she* feel after all this?

How would *he* feel?

'And how will this place be different from other restaurants? Give me a few sentences to describe your vision.'

'Oh man, this is like a job interview.' He shifted his stance and ran a hand through his hair. 'Umm... Well, there's nowhere in Tarrin's Bay that's got really classy fine dining, so I want the food to be world class, but not posh and too fancy, know what I mean?'

She nodded.

'I want the meals to be satisfying. Artistic and creative, but not skimpy on portion size. If my dad was here, I'd want to know that he could order an entrée and a main and be happy with that, whether or not he had dessert.' He paced again. 'But I don't like wastage. So many places I've worked at throw out so much food, I can't help but think of people in poorer countries with nothing, it makes me feel guilty. My parents worked hard to provide for us. So, sufficient, but not too much wastage.'

'Uh-huh,' she nibbled the tip of the pen. 'I understand, and I agree. What type of cuisine did you have in mind?'

'I don't want to be limited by a specific type. Everything is so defined these days... Chinese, Italian, Vietnamese, French... I mean, I *could* do traditional Romanian, or a mixture of modern Australian and European, but to be honest, I want a bit of everything. Multicultural.' He shrugged. 'I want there to be something for everyone, both culture-wise, and food preference-wise, and also with health considerations for those who like to be conscious of their choices or have allergies.'

She gave a thumbs up, while still holding her pen, which looked plain weird, so she lowered it and looked at her paper. 'And what about the overall feel, not just the food, but the atmosphere?' She joined him in the pacing, but more slowly, walking from corner to corner, taking in the environment and wondering what it may look like six weeks from now. A few ideas formed shape in her mind already, but she wanted to let him express what he wanted first.

'I want people to feel like it's a really special place to go to, but also feel comfortable and relaxed.' He stopped pacing and his eyes went a little distant. He took a seat on one of four plastic chairs that were in the corner, near a few cardboard boxes. He exhaled. 'I want everyone to feel welcome, people from all walks of life. For every customer to feel as important as any other, like my parents made people feel.' He clasped his hands together and rested his elbows on his knees.

Hannah's heart warmed. She sat on the chair next to him, placing the clipboard on another, and leaned slightly forward, eager to hear more.

'I want people's eating experiences here to be memorable. And for them to want to come back again, and again. I want the place to feel new, but familiar. Clean and tidy but relaxed. Stylish but quirky. I want people to know they can come here after a long, hard week and relax with a delicious meal, or be here with friends and family for a fun and lively dinner to celebrate a special occasion. I want it to feel like...'

'... Home,' they both said softly at the same time.

Luca's gaze rose up from his hands to her eyes. Unblinkingly, his eyes widened, connecting with hers, as a clear and definite knowing emerged that he had perfectly encompassed what this restaurant was about.

'Home,' he repeated, his voice a bit louder, stronger, certain. 'Home.' A smile transformed his face into an expression of joy, and he stood suddenly. 'Yes!'

Hannah's smile grew, as his hands flew up in the air.

'That's it! Oh my God, Hannah, you're a genius.' He moved towards her and his lips met her cheek in a fast but firm kiss. 'That's it. The name of the restaurant. *Home.*'

She stood with a delighted laugh, and not just from the name being decided. 'It's perfect! But you said it too, it was pretty much your idea.'

'Oh, then I'm a genius!' He kissed the palm of his hand then patted his cheek with a chuckle. 'It's really hard to kiss oneself, you know.'

'Then I'll do it,' she said, before her professional side kicked in and tried to resist. She stood on tiptoes and planted a quick kiss on his cheek, now rosy from excitement and maybe her light hint of dusty-rose lipstick she only ever wore when on the job.

His hand brushed accidentally against hers, and his little finger entwined itself with hers for just a second before he grasped her hand and kissed it too. 'Thanks, Hannah. Ten minutes here and already things are starting to get better. You're my good luck charm. Just like back in high school.'

She lowered her gaze a bit and stepped back, but collided with the chair and lost her balance, her arms circling rapidly to try to regain it. 'Oh!'

He stepped forward and his hands gripped her upper arms, holding her steady before she could fall backwards. 'Whoa! I don't have insurance yet, no accidents on the premises yet, please.' He kept hold of her arms until she was still, then moved the chair to the side.

'Yet?' She chuckled. 'Do you mean once you do have

insurance you'll be like, "Hey, Hannah, come on over and trip up the stairs! And while you're here, there's a spill in the kitchen you might slip on! And watch out for those loose nails on the floor!"?'

He laughed. 'I *will* have to pay for insurance, might as well make it worth my while.' He winked, and she smiled warmly.

To distract herself from the unexpected feelings simmering up in her chest, she picked up the clipboard and wrote 'HOME' at the top, with a swirly underline.

'So it gets your tick of approval?' he asked.

She drew a large tick next to it. 'Yep. It does.'

'Name decided then. Phew! What a relief. Do you know how many names I've been going through in my head? I feel like one of my browser tabs has closed now.'

'And with each one of yours closing, one of mine opens. But that's good. Now we have something to work with.' She needed to have a sense of the purpose of a place, or a product, or an event, before she could really work out the nitty-gritty details of what she had to do to make it successful. Home. A word she knew all too well, as she had only ever had one in her entire life. Unlike many other people who moved from home to home, never really knowing what it's like to have that one special place where everything feels normal, balanced, comforting. She imagined Luca had probably lived in quite a few different 'homes', and that no matter where he lived now, it would never be the same again without his parents' presence. No wonder he felt the need to create a new home symbolically through his work.

Hannah jotted down notes.

'What are you writing?'

'Uh-uh.' She moved the clipboard away from his sight. 'No peeking,' she joked. 'I will let you know in good time. But I will say that the ideas are flowing to me now.' She wandered around the premises, as though walking through another realm, seeing things that weren't really there but could be. 'You could have a cosy couch over here,' she said, pointing to the corner near the glass doors. 'For people to have an intimate drink or dessert with a special someone.' She walked closer to the balcony with the view. 'And out here, a fire pit or chimenea, with cosy seating and cushions and small tables for groups to gather and bask in the starry night sky.' She walked over to the top of the stairs... 'And portraits hanging on the wall at different heights, like family portraits, as you go up or down the stairs.'

She momentarily returned her awareness to the room and to Luca's gaze, which was bright and curious and hungry for more. 'Go on,' he said, gesturing with his hand.

'Menus with faded and torn edges, like old family photographs,' she said. 'And a photo wall, different from the portraits above the stairs... just one feature wall for photos of customers who've dined here. Those who want to have their photo taken and included can do so, like they are part of one big family. Like this is their second home.'

'I love it, Hannah.' He moved closer to her, his eyes scanning the surroundings as hers were doing, as though her vision was imprinting itself into the air and he could see it too. 'It's like you can read my mind. Or see it.'

'The vision is everything,' she said. 'Start with the big picture and everything else will fall into place. With a few tweaks and strategic decisions along the way.'

'I'm *so* excited. This is great.' He held a hand to her lower back. '*You're* great. And that company in Sydney is lucky to have you.' He removed his hand, and despite the cold weather outside, and the lack of heating in the future restaurant as yet, she was as warm as though she was snuggled up in front of a cosy fireplace. She already felt at home here, even though it was cold and sparse and mostly empty. She was at home with the possibilities, the potential that would be realised, with knowing that things would evolve and develop as she helped him plan everything and get it set up.

'I'm looking forward to helping you out over the next six weeks,' she said. 'It *is* going to be great. This place is going to be great, I can feel it.' She smiled and took a deep breath, absorbing the moment and the vision she had just described. Imprinting it all into her memory.

She was moving away from home, to find a new one. And he was creating his own, right here. Not only here, but in the place that had been hers, and would one day be only a memory.

CHAPTER ELEVEN

By the end of the day Luca had sorted out the initial details with the real estate agency, registered his business name and website domain name, and sighed with relief when he arrived 'not home' at Nathan's house.

'Long day?' asked Nathan, his bare feet propped up on the coffee table and the newspaper in his hands.

Luca sat on the couch opposite. 'Not long, but full-on. Started plans to launch the restaurant. Oh, and bought a house.' He shrugged with a small smile.

Nathan's feet dropped from the table to the floor. 'Already? Really?'

Luca gave a nod. 'Yup. Should all be settled and ready to move in in about eight weeks.'

'Awesome, man.' He held up his hand. 'We should go out for a drink later to celebrate.'

Luca laughed when he high-fived it. 'That's the second high-five I've had today.'

'Did the estate agent give you one when you made the offer?'

'Nope, Hannah did. As part of our old special handshake. But it was kinda to do with something else as well.'

'Oh yeah?'

'I've hired her to manage my restaurant launch.'

'Great idea. She'll do a good job.'

'I know she will. Already has and we've barely begun. Name all decided and registered thanks to our first meeting today. *Home*, it's going to be called. Fits what I want for the place perfectly.'

Nathan's gaze went upwards. 'Home... Hmm, I like it. Different. And not lame or predictable.'

'Thanks. Might get confusing though... "I'll see you at home!" "Wait, which home? Home, or *home*?"' He chuckled, as did Nathan.

'You should get the paper to do a story on it.' Nathan jabbed his finger at the newspaper.

'Yeah. I guess Miss Delaney will advise me on that in her six-week plan she's presenting to me on Monday.'

'Ha, she likes her plans, that one.'

Luca tilted his head a little to the side. 'Do you know her well?'

Nathan shrugged. 'Guess so. Sorta. Not much to do with her anymore.' He flipped the page over, then glanced at Luca over the page. 'What about you, were you two an item back in school?'

Luca shook his head. 'Us? Nah, never. We were just good friends.'

'And now?'

'Now? It's been two decades, bro. Hopefully we'll keep in touch after she moves.'

Nathan put the paper down and rubbed at his jaw. 'I hope I didn't have anything to do with her wanting to leave town.'

Luca leaned forward, his elbows on the coffee table. 'What do you mean?'

He sat back and relaxed into the couch. 'Ah. Nothin'. I'm sure she's forgotten all about it.'

Luca narrowed his eyes, and his hands tightened with the sudden feeling of wanting to defend or protect Hannah. 'Did you two have some sort of falling out?'

'Not really. No hard feelings. She's awesome and we always enjoyed a good chat. I just wasn't interested in her in that way.'

How could he not be? Luca found himself wondering. Especially being an outdoorsy, practical guy. Nathan and Hannah would be a good match.

'Wasn't interested in anything really, back then, even if Jessica Alba had made a move on me.'

'Whoa, mate, someone must have hurt you bad.'

'You could say that. Anyway, all in the past now.' He flicked a hand in the air and picked up the paper again.

'But Hannah... she felt otherwise?' Luca didn't normally probe anyone for personal information like this, but he couldn't restrain his curiosity, and he cared about Hannah. If someone had hurt her, even unintentionally, he wanted to know about it.

He scratched his cheek. 'Seemed so. No big deal, just a misunderstanding. But in hindsight I think I overreacted when she tried to kiss me.'

Luca couldn't imagine Hannah making the first move. She was too patient, too proud, too... Hannah. But maybe she had changed.

'I didn't mean to reject her so... directly. I just wasn't into it at the time. I apologised later but she shrugged it off as if nothing happened, although things became different between us after that and she stopped asking me over to help out with work.'

'Probably didn't want you to feel awkward.'

'Yeah. Anyway, all in the past.'

'As you said.'

'Yep. So,' Nathan got up, 'let's get that drink, dude.'

'Sounds good to me.'

In truth, Luca wanted to collapse into bed early, as he had a big weekend ahead of him in the city to pack up some more things and see his brother for his birthday. But he hadn't realised how much he'd missed this... having a good ol' chat with a friend over a relaxing drink. Nathan was a new one, but they'd hit it off pretty well and he seemed genuine. And he didn't appear to have done anything bad by Hannah, except for not feeling the same. Nothing one could do about things like that. But still... he couldn't completely understand why he wouldn't have been at least a little bit interested. Especially if she'd clearly indicated she liked him.

If Hannah had made a move on *him* back then, he probably wouldn't have objected. But as for now, he wasn't so sure. Life was more complicated the older you became. And he wouldn't do anything to risk his friendship, or reunited friendship, with Hannah HD.

CHAPTER TWELVE

The chooks scooted around Hannah's feet as though sensing that changes were afoot, and an earthy warmth settled in her skin after the physical labour of cleaning up the coop. 'It's okay, girls. You'll like Luca. And I'll be back to visit.'

I will?

Or would she make a clean break from the town, and Luca, and only come back to Tarrin's Bay periodically to see her parents?

Time would tell, but if she was going to make a big change in her life she may as well do it properly. No half-hearted attempts. All or nothing, like her work.

'And your eggs will be going to a brand-new restaurant, how exciting! People will love them!' She crouched down to chook level and watched them moving about, making noises as though talking to each other.

Yep, this was what her social life had become. Having conversations with chooks. They had always been good company, and she would miss them. She might even be able to convince Karen to get a few chooks for her small backyard. It could be done. But... one step at a time. And at least she would be bringing Scarlett with her to Sydney and would have her loyal animal friend by her side to ease the transition.

Her verbal reassurances seemed to work, as many wandered out into the open air and scattered themselves around the paddock. She stepped outside the coop and inhaled the refreshing winter air, the light film of sweat on her skin cooling down.

Now that the chicken duties were done for the morning, she could get to work on sorting through the belongings in the house, donating unwanted items, throwing out anything that wasn't needed, or even selling anything that was valuable and no longer needed. But with her temporary job with Luca, she would now have some immediate cash flow, so her original plan to do some eBaying before the move probably wasn't as essential.

Hannah left the paddock and returned to the house, stopping on the verandah where Scarlett sat, nibbling on an old ball. She gave her a pat and looked back out at the landscape, as though she needed to continually check it was still there... as though by her decision to move it would suddenly rebel and disappear. But it was the same wide-open space she'd known her whole life. The hills to her right in the distance, the grassy paddocks in the middle, and the willow tree in the far-left corner of the property that her first dog, before Scarlett, had been named after, and buried under. Willow had been a great companion, growing up alongside Hannah. She hadn't wanted a new pet after Willow died, and when adolescence came with intensity, she focused on other things until Scarlett came into the picture. She was glad her parents had surprised her; Scar had become another life companion, growing with her into adulthood. They'd suggested calling her Rosie, but Hannah took one look at the scarlet-coloured sunset that graced the sky on the day she was presented with the gift, and knew her name had to be Scarlett.

So many sunsets she'd watched right here on this verandah. The spring and summer ones were the best, but she'd be out of this place before then and would see them no more.

She had many photos of such sunsets, and even one with Scarlett in the foreground, which was framed in a padded fabric frame her mother made, and positioned on her bedside table.

Compelled with the urge to get out her photo albums, Hannah went inside. She would have to go through the boxes anyway and figure out what to take and what to leave with her parents. And many of the older photos should really be scanned and stored digitally to preserve the memories. Maybe she could take a bulk load into the local printing place and get them to do it.

She stood on a chair and pulled down an old shoebox from the linen cupboard in the hallway. There were several more, but she grabbed the nearest. She took it to the rug in the living room and sat cross-legged on the floor, the box in front of her. She rifled through old dusty envelopes containing printed photos and negatives and chuckled at how much technology had changed. It was easy now to take photos, but she preferred this old way, when you knew you had a limited number of photos to take in a roll and had to pay for each one, you made them count. No 'hang on, the lighting's not great' or 'let's take it again, I have a double chin in that one!' With the old way, you took it and had to accept it. And you didn't even know what they would look like until you got the film developed. There was an excitement in that, not knowing what the pictures would look like until that moment. It was like life, you never really knew what would develop on a particular day, and what photo opportunities would present themselves. She wanted more of that. Consistency and predictability were nice and comfortable, but she wanted more of a chance for life to develop in an exciting way.

She lifted out an envelope containing slides. Actual slides that her dad used to put in a slide projector for family slideshow nights. She thought he had taken them all with him when they moved out, but this one had been mixed in with the regular photos.

Her mind wandered back many years to her early teenagehood and one of their slideshow nights, when her dad had included photos from her parents' wedding and honeymoon. She'd been all 'Dad, c'mon!', covering her eyes at the pictures of them cuddling and kissing on the ski slopes at Thredbo and seated near a fireplace in a candlelit restaurant. 'That's gross!' she'd said.

But now, she realised what a gift it was. How lucky they'd been to find each other and stay together all those years, when divorce was so common nowadays and relationships ended via text messages, an old-fashioned love and loyalty like her parents had, and still had, was a fading treasure.

She took out a random slide and held it up to the light. It was of the willow tree. The next one was of her dad building part of the old chicken coop. The next was a laughing young Hannah trying to put a knitted hat on a chicken as it scurried away. The third one was of a young Hannah also, probably around seven years old, wearing denim overalls and sitting next to Willow on the front step of the house. Of home. Her smile so wide and free, so natural, exuding joy and the certainty of being loved and cared for.

Hannah's chin trembled a little and her vision became glossy. She was so lucky. She'd had a safe, loving, and fortunate upbringing with hardworking parents who'd taught her everything they knew. She wiped at a tear falling from her eye and sniffed. How she'd love to have the chance to do that herself, to live a life like they'd had... to raise a child like they had.

But at thirty-five, the chances of that were less likely by the minute.

Life didn't always turn out as planned, as hoped. But she had a great one, and planned to make the most of it.

She shoved the slides back into the box and wiped away the remaining tear, then stood and took the box back to the cupboard.

Better focus on the practical things first, she thought. *Not the sentimental.*

If she didn't, she could get carried away with emotions and cancel everything. And she couldn't do that. Wouldn't. She'd made her decision and she would make it the right one, even if it wasn't.

While the linen cupboard door was still open, she withdrew a pile of sheets and blankets that she wouldn't need in the next eight weeks and put them into a large, plastic, zip-up clothing bag she'd got from the discount store, which would be perfect for packing and moving lightweight items.

She also removed the spare quilt and quilt cover, and a couple of spare pillows.

No sleepovers or guests coming up in the near future.

She shoved them into the bag.

Soon, only the near-future essentials remained. Apart from the photo boxes. She would get back onto them later.

She was about to close the door when the slide images flashed into her mind, and then the memory of the family slideshows again.

A smile tickled the corner of her lips. She dashed to her notebook from yesterday and jotted down an idea:

> *Old-fashioned slideshow for the launch event.*
> *Photos encompassing 'home'. Possibly an ongoing*
> *feature.*

And then another idea:

> *Different slide shows for different events. Theme*
> *nights. Classic movie nights. Family movie nights.*
> *Photos of customers from the feature wall...*

She imagined the restaurant having slides clicking over on a screen or wall while patrons dined, a much nicer and atmospheric option than just music or a TV screen with sports like the bars and bistros had.

And he could have special pre-booked themed nights to break up the usual night-by-night dining, such as... 1920s fancy-dress night with vintage table decorations and meal ideas... Nights for different cultures and their associated traditional food... Seafood nights with an underwater theme... Even trivia nights and fundraisers...

The ideas flowed and she couldn't wait to share them with Luca, and considered calling him now to run them by him. If he was here now they would probably get excited and jump on the couch and high-five each other. But this wasn't a school project, this was her job, and she would do it properly and professionally. Just like any other client, Luca would receive a detailed plan and schedule on Monday or Tuesday once she had written it up. But this was the weekend, and she would focus on her house-related tasks. By the end of the weekend, her goal was to have removed as many things as possible from the house that she no longer needed. But she knew that getting rid of a lifetime of memories could be a little challenging. As would getting through the weekend without thinking about what lay ahead for the next six weeks, and what would also have to be let go of after her time with Luca.

CHAPTER THIRTEEN

'Happy birthday, bro!' Luca gave Stefan a man-hug (AKA: back slap) as he entered the inner-city apartment, then an over-the-top squelchy cheek kiss that he always used to give him, despite his reluctance, since they were kids.

'Oh man, c'mon! I'm thirty-two now, I thought that kissing business would end at least on my thirtieth.'

'Never.' He gave him another one. It had started when Stefan was about six months old, and their mother would go crazy over Stefan's chubby cheeks, gently pinching and squeezing and kissing them with such affection. Three-year-old Luca latched onto the act, and Stefan would giggle in delight whenever he received one from either of them. He eventually resigned to kissing his brother only on birthdays and special occasions. But thirty-odd years later, the giggles were no more.

'At least we're not in public.' Stefan gave a sigh of relief. 'Until tonight anyway. No cheek kissing at the bar, please.'

'Wouldn't dream of it. I'll leave that to all the ladies. How's the online dating going?' He placed his overnight bag, mobile phone, and keys on the coffee table and sat on the couch.

Stefan sat next to him and got out his phone. 'One week in, and twelve matches already. At this rate, I'll have a wife by Christmas.'

'Wife? Who said you wanted a wife?'

'Just joking around. But I have a date tomorrow. Hopefully I'm not too hungover. I'll be happy just to get some action and take my mind off everything that's happened in the last few months.'

Luca shuffled on the couch. 'Why not take it easy, man. Don't jump into things. Try getting to know some women as friends first.'

'Since when did you get all fatherly?'

Since Dad died, actually, when you were only twelve.

Although, in truth, the only way he'd acted like his father back then was to train as a chef. He wanted to carry on some part of his dad's life, while Stefan was the opposite, doing something completely different by working in finance and the safety of numbers, and drowning his grief in an oversupply of pastries and cakes.

'We're not getting any younger. When you get to my age you start to realise that instant gratification isn't so gratifying after all.'

'It is from what I remember.' Stefan chuckled, and held his phone in front of Luca, a pretty woman on the screen. 'This is her. Can't believe she wants to meet up, actually. She must get loads of dates.'

'Not everyone is who they say they are online, you know. Don't get your hopes up.'

'Nah, she's legit. We're already Facebook friends. I've checked her out.'

'Ah, well if Facebook says so, then it must be,' he said with a tone of sarcasm.

'You should try Tinder as well. Go on, download the app. Might help you meet some new women down south, it's not as populated as in the city, you know. You might not be able to rely on your usual good looks, charm, and kitchen skills.' He gave his brother a light punch on the arm.

He'd never considered doing that before. Had never needed to, to be honest. His social life had always been as full as his stomach after a three-course meal.

Stefan took Luca's phone and went to the app store. 'Here. I'll do it for you.'

Luca grabbed it. 'No.'

'C'mon, man.'

'No.' He sighed. Maybe he'd look into it later, once the restaurant was set up and he was in a routine. 'Not right now.'

Not while he had a business to launch, a house to move into, and... *a friend from the past he wanted to get to know all over again.*

Stefan sighed too. 'Okay, but you're missing out. It's so much fun. Except when you get the crazy weirdos who match and unmatch you, then the ones who start chatting and get all clingy, then the ones who ask you a billion questions like you're going for some job interview, and then the ones who—'

'Sounds delightful.'

Stefan laughed. 'You're even speaking like an old man.' He put down his phone and looked at his brother. 'You're really doing this, aren't you? The house and business. Settling down.'

He shrugged. 'Don't know if I'd call it settling down. But planting some roots, yes.'

'Well, good for you then. I look forward to seeing the place. You're absolutely sure about it, this... chicken-farm place?'

'Yep.'

'And the premises, sounds like you've got the most sought-after location in the town.'

Luca nodded. 'Thanks for investing, I do appreciate it.'

Stefan shrugged. 'It was a no-brainer. Good location, gap in the market, experienced chef... I know you can do it.'

The slight irritation at his brother's irresponsible ways (that reminded him of how he used to be before his mother's death) dissolved, and a sense of gratitude washed over him. His parents may be gone, but his brother was still here. And Stefan believed in him, unlike many others who didn't think he could stick to anything. 'Thanks.' He patted him on the back. Then, leaned in closer...

'No more kisses!' Stefan held out his hands like a barrier and leaned back.

Luca laughed. 'Ha-ha, scared you there for a minute, didn't I?'

Stefan stood. 'Next birthday I'll be wearing a mask and full-body armour.' He went to the kitchen. 'Coffee?'

Luca stood too. 'Let me shout you one somewhere. It is your birthday.'

Stefan smiled. 'Let's go.'

'But no cake. Save your appetite for tonight, I have it on good authority there'll be a cake to remember.' He winked.

Stefan's smile widened.

So did Luca's. He had organised a cake to be made that looked like a stack of hundred-dollar notes. 'Afterwards, do you mind if I drive over to Mum's house?' Luca said quietly, not wanting to dampen his brother's joyful mood, but needing to ask. 'You can come if you want, or stay here. Up to you.'

Luca had been wanting to clear the house and get it rented out, but Stefan kept putting things off, citing the excuse of not enough time yet to sort through everything. Even though they'd had plenty of time to prepare before her death, they hadn't wanted to waste any of it, choosing to spend that time with their mother and deal with the consequences afterwards.

'Today?'

'I have to get back by dinner tomorrow, got a lot to organise for Monday. I'll probably go round tomorrow too, but would like to get a good look at things while I'm here and see what needs to be done and what I can take with me to my new place. Once my restaurant opens in six weeks, I won't have as many opportunities.' Truth was, he also wanted to feel close to his mother again. Look at the mementos lying around, the photos on the wall, and inhale the scent that he could never quite decipher but that smelled like his mother and made him feel at peace. He hoped for some kind of sign from her that he was doing the right thing and that everything would work out well. He didn't know how, or if that was even possible, though he believed in the afterlife... he just felt he needed to be there. Be in the family home, before he created his new home.

'I'll see how I feel after my coffee,' Stefan said, and the brothers went off in search of the world's best birthday mocha.

Just over ninety minutes later, Luca arrived at his mother's house, on his own. He checked the letter box and removed some junk mail, despite there being a no junk mail sign, then walked up the old concrete pathway to the front door. The warm, floaty, floral scent hit him as soon as he entered, and he had to steady himself with a hand against the doorframe. At first it was confronting, then comforting. He turned on lights, opened windows, and wandered from room to room.

'Hi, Mum,' he whispered. 'Just checking up on things.'

He entered the home workroom, or *joyroom* as his mother had called it, where she drew her designs and sewed and created. 'It's not work,' she would say. 'It's my joy.'

A dressmakers' mannequin stood proudly in the corner,

wearing one of her dresses, a simple and elegant ivory satin dress with an embellished V-shaped bodice and droplets of sparkling gems hanging from the A-line hem. Luca had grown used to dressmakers' terminology almost as much as culinary terminology, his mother often discussing her dresses and asking for opinions. He slowly reached out his hand, touching the soft material to his fingers, knowing his mother's hands had done the same thing at some point.

He could use one of the rooms at Iona to store his mother's important belongings. He had the space. Maybe a memory room. But... as much as it would be nice, it would be heartbreaking too. It might be easier to keep a few small things around to honour her memory, as he'd done with his father, and keep the rest in storage somewhere. But his mother's memories weren't small things. Dresses took up a lot of room, and she had four one-off designs in this room that the new owners of Teadora were not allowed to take, the three others hanging from a rack near the mannequin. He was happy for others to buy and reuse her main designs, but not the special one-of-a-kind dresses she'd kept to herself for her own satisfaction. Luca knew deep inside that she'd hoped her sons would find partners and she could give the dresses to them and have them tailor-made to fit, when they finally tied the knot. A wave of sadness overwhelmed him as he realised she would never get to see that day, if it ever came, for him and for Stefan.

His hand trembled as he touched the other dresses, one by one, the fabric swaying gently after he removed his hand, as though a light breeze had entered the room. His legs weakened, and he let them soften and sat on the floor, his arms around his knees. He looked up at the photos on the wall of models wearing the dresses, the framed drawings of her trademark designs, and a photo of his mother accepting an award.

He covered his eyes with his hand as they warmed and

stung with fresh tears. He let them fall softy, freely, quietly, down his cheeks.

After a few moments he stood and wiped his eyes with the sleeve of his jacket, and grabbed a protective clothing bag from the rack. He placed a dress inside it, and did the same for the other two. When they were put away, he eyed the mannequin. He didn't want to remove the display, but needed to protect the dress. Carefully, he unzipped the dress and helped it fall to the ground. He lifted the mannequin out and put it aside, then slid the dress inside the protective bag.

He took the dresses to his car and placed them in the boot, then came back inside for the mannequin which he had to disassemble to fit in his car. He closed the boot with a muffled clunk. There. Done. Progress made.

It was something, at least. Something important. He would bring them to Tarrin's Bay and keep them safely in his care. He went back inside to close windows and lock up. The rest would have to wait, he couldn't handle anything more today. And he had a brother to spend time with, right here, now in the present.

Driving back to the city, Luca slowed when he rounded the corner into a street containing various shops and cafes. He pulled over quickly for a moment so he could get a look. He glanced to the left. His mother's old bridal store. 'Under New Management' a sign near the door said. He chuckled, thinking that such a sign would probably reduce their business, as his mother and her designs had been the drawcard for many. Now that she wasn't there, they would have to rely on her existing dresses and designs, and when fashion trends demanded new designs, someone else would have to create them, or they would have to order in dresses from other suppliers and designers. His mother's business would go on in her memory, and he was glad for that, but it would never be the same without her.

A car horn beeped, and he returned abruptly to the present moment, turning his head to see a delivery van driver gesturing to where he was stopped. 'Can't you read the sign? No parking, delivery vehicles only. Move!' the driver called out.

He waved an apology and drove forward. It was only when he was parked again near his brother's apartment block when he chuckled again. He had hoped for a sign, and had found two. 'Under new management', and 'no parking'. Maybe that was his mother's sense of humour coming through, telling him everything would work out.

Either way, it was nice to think it were true.

***

Luca strained to open his eyes the next morning. He rolled over, reached for his phone then realised he'd left it charging in Stefan's kitchen. He checked his watch, then sat bolt upright. 'Damn.' He hadn't expected to sleep in so late, but had lain awake for who knows how long the night before, after getting back from the party and ushering Stefan to his bed to sleep off the alcohol.

He got up and went to enter the bathroom, but the scent of toast and coffee caught his attention. 'Up already?' he called, eyeing Stefan in the kitchen at the end of the hallway. 'I thought I'd have to tip a bucket of water over you, you were practically asleep before you hit the pillow. Feel okay?'

'I feel great. And it's a delightful day for food, fun, and an afternoon date.' He grinned widely. 'And that rhymed.'

'Ah yes, something to look forward to, eh?' Luca rubbed at his eyes. 'And now who's speaking like an old man.'

'Me, my brother, me indeed.'

He chuckled as he went to the bathroom and when he

arrived in the kitchen, sat at the counter in front of a plate of vegemite toast. 'You didn't have to go to so much trouble. Especially as it's your birthday,' he joked, taking a bite of crispy toast.

'It's the least I could do, after the show you put on last night, and that cake, wow, how will you outdo that next year?' He laughed.

He shrugged. 'Good thing I have a year to think about it.'

'Speaking of thinking... you got me thinking,' Stefan said, taking a seat on the one other bar stool. 'You're right. We are getting older. I'm going to take life a bit more seriously now. Or try to.'

'Yeah?' Luca raised his eyebrows.

'I figured I put so much effort into my career, what could happen if I paid as much attention to my personal life.'

'Agreed.'

'So tonight, I won't even sleep with her. Even if she wants to. I'll say "No, not on the first date, I'm not that kind of guy".'

'Good for you, bro. And what if there's a second date?'

'Second date is fine. One bit of progress at a time, man, sheesh.' He sipped his coffee and gave a shake of his head.

A strange chime sounded. 'Is that your phone?' Luca glanced at Stefan, but then looked at his phone next to the kettle, plugged into the power point, where the sound had strangely come from.

'Nope. Must be yours.' Stefan seemed to be hiding behind his coffee mug.

Luca picked up his phone to find a stream of notifications displayed on the lock screen. All from Tinder. 'What the?' He glared at Stefan. 'You didn't.'

He nodded. 'I did.'

'Argh.' Luca scrolled down through the messages, most saying 'you have a new match!' or 'so-and-so sent you a message'.

'You made a profile for me?' he asked.

Stefan nodded. 'It's easy, it just links to your Facebook.'

'But how...'

'C'mon man, I know your password is *Viațamergeînainte7777*.' He shrugged. 'What Dad used to always say, plus his favourite number, and one for each member of the family.'

Luca's eyes widened; he wasn't sure if he was more taken aback by his brother setting up his dating profile or by him guessing his password.

'I laughed when it worked. Because mine is similar, same phrase but different numbers at the end.' He covered his mouth. 'Oops. Now I'll probably have to change it so you don't guess mine and log in to my profile in revenge.'

All Luca was concerned with right now was seeing what damage his brother had done. He swiped one of the notifications and the Tinder app opened. 'Is this going to show on my Facebook?'

'Nope, no one will know.'

'Can the Tinder people see my Facebook stuff?'

'Nope, only if you friend them.'

A screen appeared showing that he had three matches, and two messages.

Stefan laughed as he peered at Luca's phone. 'Looks like Sunday mornings are the perfect time for connecting with some new people online, I only did this an hour ago!'

'I don't want to chat with anyone I haven't met.' He pushed his phone away.

'Luckily I took the liberty of doing it for you. Getting you started, at least.' He hid behind his mug again.

'Stefan!' Luca reclaimed his phone and opened one of the messages.

Hi, nice profile. You're a chef?
    Sure am.
    Cool. What's your favourite food?

'My favourite food?' Luca furrowed his brow. 'I don't have time for this right now.'

'Reply. It could be fun.'

'Now if I don't, she's going to think I'm one of those arseholes who lead women on and then ignore them.'

'Then reply.'

He sighed. 'One reply, then I'm going to forget about it and get on with what I have to do today.'

He typed in:

Meat pies.

Which wasn't a complete lie, he really liked a good meat pie, but they were by no means his favourite food.

A reply came in pretty quickly:

Hmm. I thought it would be something more fancy.

He replied again:

Meat pies with gravy.

He added a wink emoji.

She replied with a 'meh' emoji, followed by:

I'm a vegetarian.

Stefan burst out laughing. 'This is awesome!'

'No it's not.' Luca exited the message and went to the other one, a woman with dark brown glossy hair whose face was decorated digitally with one of those bizarre animal noses and whiskers. 'What the hell?'

Hi. Are you looking for a serious relationship or just a hook-up?

'Wow, straight into it.' Luca shook his head. 'I'm not going to answer that, and I'm not going to date someone who thinks they look cute with fake animal noses.' He briefly glanced at the other match who had not yet sent a message. Her picture was without fake animal noses, but she was sporting an unattractive pout. He put his phone to the side. 'So, moving on... would you like to come with me to the house today? I'm going to pick up a few more things of Mum's to take back with me. I can store them at the new place.'

Stefan shrugged, took a deep breath. 'Why not.'

'Yeah? You'll come?'

He nodded. 'I'd like to keep something of hers here too. Don't know what yet, but something.'

'Of course. Whatever you want.' Luca stood and went to the fridge, withdrawing some eggs, which made him think of Hannah and the chooks. 'And how about an omelette to accompany this *delightful* toast?' he asked.

'Thought you'd never ask.' Stefan smiled.

Luca grinned, placing the eggs on the counter then grabbing some mushrooms and an onion. They were a bit on the way out, but still edible enough.

As the vegetables sautéed, he patted his brother's back. 'It's going to be a good day. We can do this.'

Stefan nodded, his lips clamping together.

'I'm glad you're coming.'

Stefan downed the rest of his coffee then said, '*Viaţa merge înainte.*'

Luca nodded in agreement. He held out a fist and Stefan pushed against it with his own. 'Indeed it does, my brother. Life goes on. Starting today.'

CHAPTER FOURTEEN

B y Sunday afternoon, Hannah had completed about half of what she intended to do, and spent the other half distracted by more photos and sentimental items. She'd already gone through one box of tissues.

It was time to let some things go.

She packed up some old toys from her childhood, but kept a doll her grandma had made, and a toy tractor that she had loved filling up with dirt and tipping all over things. She hoped that one day she'd have a child who would love it just as much... but would hopefully refrain from tipping dirt all over things.

She sighed, taking the bags to the car.

She also packed up old clothes she no longer wore, including some farm-esque clothing that she wouldn't need in Sydney. Hannah drove to the nearest donation bin and pushed the bags inside the overflowing container. When that was done, she picked up a takeaway mocha and an almond friand just before the cafe closed. She'd only just finished the friand, realising she hadn't eaten for hours, when the sound of a helicopter buzzed overhead. It flew in the direction of the lookout.

Her eyebrows drawing close together, she wandered up the street and towards Lookout Point. Maybe there was a shark sighting, although they weren't common around this time of year, but anything was possible. When she realised several people were gathered around the side of the lookout, not taking photos of the view but peering and pointing, she knew something was up.

She scurried up and recognised a local man who sometimes bought her eggs from the markets. 'What's happened?' she asked him.

'Rock fisherman. Got swept away, the helicopter has just located him.' He pointed to an area to the far left of the lookout. Squinting, she could faintly see someone's arm raised, and then it disappeared, then it surfaced again.

'Oh no.' She leaned over the railing. 'Are they going to get to him in time, he's clearly struggling.' Her muscles buzzed with nervous energy and she wished she could jump in and save him somehow.

A rope extended down from the helicopter, a rescue person attached to it. 'Oh thank God.' After a few moments, the rope began to rise, two people now attached to it. She held her free hand to her heart, and took a sip of her mocha, which seemed trivial now.

'Lucky bugger,' said the man, as a few people clapped. 'He was wearing a life vest, someone said. If he hadn't, as many rock fishermen don't bother to...' The man shook his head. 'We might be watching something completely different right now.' His expression was sombre.

'Lucky he did then,' Hannah said. She breathed in relief.

The man turned with a shuffle to walk away, then stopped. 'See you on Wednesday, for more of your lovely eggs,' he said.

'Oh, yes. Of course.' She smiled.

'Your yolks are much creamier than the store-bought eggs.'

'Great to hear. Thank you.'

'I'll be buying them till the day I die,' he said with a chuckle. 'Which at this rate, could be any day now!'

Hannah flicked her hand in front of her. 'Oh, don't be silly. Looks like you have many years left in you... I'm sorry, what was your name again?'

'Reg.'

'Reg,' she said, holding out her hand. 'Hannah.'

He shook it. 'Ah, now it sounds familiar.'

How had she not known this man's name all this time? And here she was about to leave town, and finding out for the first time. 'Oh, by the way, so you know, in another couple of months I won't be doing the markets anymore. Iona Eggs will still be produced, but I'm not sure if the new owner will be doing markets or not. He might.'

Reg's coarse eyebrows rose. 'Well he'd bloody better,' he said. 'Or I'll be having words with him, don't you worry about that.' He tapped the side of his nose.

Hannah chuckled. There were quite a few interesting characters among the older people of Tarrin's Bay. 'I'll be sure to let him know there are people counting on him.' She sipped her coffee and waved the man away as he shuffled down the hill.

Hannah checked her watch, and got out her phone, typing a text to her mum:

> I have some things to drop over, do you need anything while I'm out?

After witnessing the rescue, she felt a need to see her parents.

Life was so fragile and she was a lucky bugger.

'Welcome to Senior Land!' Douglas Delaney greeted his daughter with open arms, then faked back pain when he leant forward to embrace her.

'Oh, you poor senior you.' She patted his back and he straightened up.

'Stay for dinner,' her mother said when Hannah entered the modern, compact, yet airy open-plan living area and kitchen. 'Unless you need to get back to the packing. But a couple of hours break will do you good.'

Hannah nodded in agreement, the scent of something cooking enticing her, and then told them about the fisherman.

'Those guys,' her dad said. 'Always putting their lives at risk.'

'This one was wearing a life jacket, actually. Luckily.'

'Oh, well that's good then,' he said. 'Too many have died over the years.'

Hannah placed the large garbage bag next to the dining table. 'This isn't garbage, by the way, just some things I thought you might want to keep. Or look through before deciding what to do with them.'

'Let me at 'em,' her dad said, bending to the bag and this time wincing in real back pain.

'Doug, your knees. Bend your knees first, remember?'

'Apparently I forgot to remember.' He straightened up with a hand to his lower back. 'Pilates, I have to do, can you believe it?' he said to Hannah. 'Next thing you know I'll be prancing around town in tights.'

'You might give a few people a fright. Me included.' Kathleen giggled.

'Dad, no need to be scared of Pilates, it's just a form of exercise. Will be good for you.'

Hannah moved the bag to a chair. 'A few old things, and some photos. And slides.' She untied the bag.

'Coffee, tea?' asked her mum.

Hannah shook her head. 'Thanks, but I've just had one.'

'Okay. Dinner is in the slow cooker and will be ready in an hour.'

That would be five minutes to six on the dot, Hannah noticed, as she checked her watch. Making it six pm serving time once it was plated up. 'Great. I'm starving.'

'Did you say slides?' Douglas asked.

'Uh-huh.' Hannah sat at a chair. 'Remember those slideshow nights we used to have?'

'I was just going to say the same thing!' Doug rubbed his hands together. 'Let's have one, for old times' sake. Tonight!'

'Tonight?' Kathleen leant her hands on the back of a dining chair. 'Do we even know where the old slides are, apart from the ones in this bag?'

Doug nodded. 'I put them all in the middle drawer of the TV cabinet, underneath some farming magazines.'

'Hannah has a lot to do and is probably tired, I'm not sure she'll have time for one of your slideshows, dear.'

Hannah held out her hand towards her mother. 'No, it's fine. Actually, I'd like to. And it might give me some inspiration for something I'm working on.'

She was yet to tell them about taking on Luca's job.

'Work? For that company, already?' asked her mum.

'No, actually, I'm going to be helping Luca Antonescu launch his restaurant. In six weeks. Before I move.'

Both her parents raised their eyebrows and their mouths fell open a tad. 'Hannah, honey, please don't overwork yourself. You still have the chooks to care for and packing up years of house stuff is no easy task. How will you have the time?'

'I can manage,' she said. 'I've worked out a bit of a timetable. And the extra cash flow will be good.'

'But it's not needed, you can always ask us for some extra

cash if you need it, and once the sale is all finalised, you'll have some profit to draw on.'

'I know, but I want to do it. It'll be like my last gig as a solo entrepreneur.' She smiled and clasped her hands together. 'Leaving my mark on Tarrin's Bay, with a lovely new restaurant.'

Kathleen nodded slowly and appeared to ponder this. 'Darling, it doesn't have anything to do with that young man, does it? Didn't you take a little bit of a liking to him all those years ago?'

'Luca? What? No, of course not. It's good to see him again, but I just want to help him out.'

She nodded again. 'I do recall him, young Luca,' she said.

'Mum, he's thirty-five now, like me.' She tilted her head.

Her mum sat at the table. 'Oh, I know. How does he look nowadays? I remember he had the most beautiful mane of dark hair.'

'Kathleen!' Doug said. 'What about mine?' He ran a hand over his balding head with an exaggerated smile, raising his eyebrows suggestively.

'Nothing compares to yours, my darling.' She blew him a kiss.

'Oh, you guys, still as corny as ever.' Hannah shook her head and covered her eyes like she used to do as a teenager, then looked back up. 'Don't ever stop.' She placed a hand over her mother's.

Hannah's phone rang. She pulled it from her handbag about to answer it, hesitating on seeing Luca's caller ID.

'Who is it?' her mum asked.

'Just Luca.'

'Well, answer it, dear!'

Hannah wasn't one to answer calls if she was in conversation with others, but her finger pressed the accept button, and she stood. 'Luca, hi.'

'Hey there, HD.'

'Good thanks.'

'Good thanks?'

Oh God, he didn't even ask 'How are you?'!

'Yes. I mean, hi. Hey there too.'

For some reason she felt self-conscious talking on the phone to him in front of her parents... as a teenager, when he would call on the old landline she would extend the curly cord through to the hallway for some privacy.

Luca chuckled. 'I'm good thanks too.'

Her face warmed, and her mum looked at her with a curious gaze.

'Just got back from Sydney, Nathan's out and I don't feel like cooking, wanna grab a casual bite to eat? You know, suss out the competition?'

'Oh. Um.' She glanced at her parents, then the rest of his words sunk in. 'Wait, Nathan? Which Nathan?'

'Nathan Sharp. My housemate. Oh yeah, he mentioned you guys know each other.'

Oh great.

The warmth in Hannah's face intensified.

'What about Nathan?' her mother piped up, standing.

Oh, more great.

Hannah put her fingertip against her lips.

'Yes, we did. Do. I didn't know you were housemates. Well there you go.'

Stop talking, Hannah.

'Ahh,' her mother said, sitting back down now that she understood the connection.

'Let the girl talk in peace!' her father whispered.

'So, dinner?' Luca asked again.

'Would be good, but I'm actually having dinner with my parents tonight, sorry.'

Kathleen stood again suddenly, the chair falling over with a clatter.

Mum! Hannah mouthed as her mother bent down to pick it up, before it fell again with another clatter. *Oh man.*

'No worries,' Luca said.

'Oh dear,' her mum said, loud enough for the person on the other end of the phone to hear. 'Looks like we're going to have *way* too many leftovers, tonight, Doug. Shame there's only three of us.'

Hannah eyed her mum with an irritated glare.

'Sorry, Luca, hang on.' She put the phone near her chest. 'Mum!' she whispered. 'What are you doing?'

'Invite the poor guy over for dinner,' she said.

'No.'

'Oh for goodness' sake.' She walked towards her. 'Ask him.'

'Mum!'

'Ask. It's only polite, and from what I heard he must have asked you.'

'No, it's too... anyway, Mum, do you mind?' Hannah turned to the side, her face as hot as coals.

'Sorry, Luca, it's—'

The phone slipped from her hand and into her mother's.

'It's Mrs Delaney here, Luca, how are you? Long time no see!'

'Mum!' Her jaw clenched.

'Oh, Kathleen!' Hannah's dad buried his slowly shaking head in his hands.

'That's great,' she said, 'a nice classy restaurant is what we need around here. And I hear you're buying our old place, well congratulations! It couldn't have gone to a more worthy recipient.'

Oh God, Mum. What are you doing?

Kathleen waited a while, listening to Luca, then said. 'Funny, I was just saying to my husband, Douglas—you might remember him —that we've gone a bit overboard with tonight's dinner, and put a rather large amount of chicken and vegetables into the slow cooker. We would be more than happy, in fact, we would be delighted if you would join us. You can ask us anything you like about the property, like... a little orientation over a good meal! What do you say?'

Her mother wasn't always this outspoken, only when she really wanted something, and for some reason, she really wanted him to come over for dinner. Oh well, at least she wasn't asking Nathan.

'Wonderful. We'll see you at six. Unit 4, Wattle Lane, Hillview Estate. Although, I must say, I'm a little nervous inviting a chef to dinner!'

Hannah shielded her face with her hand.

'Well thank you, see you soon.'

Kathleen handed the phone back to Hannah, who was now speechless.

Her father stood and approached. 'That was sneaky of you, my dear.' He placed a hand on Hannah's forearm. 'Don't worry. We won't embarrass you. Will we, Kath?' He gave his wife 'the look'.

'Of course not.' She smiled and went to the kitchen, withdrawing two different placemats from the drawer. 'Sunset scene or farmhouse scene?' Her eyes flitted from one to the other.

Hannah shrugged.

'Farmhouse.' Her dad returned to his chair at the table, then rifled through the garbage bag, and pulled out an envelope of slides. His eyes brightened. 'Luca can join us for a slideshow!' he exclaimed.

Hannah's eyes bulged. 'This can't be happening.'

'Relax, sweetheart, it'll be nice for him too. Poor fella, losing his dad so young. What about his mother, is she around?'

Hannah shook her head, and the big picture surfaced in her mind, diluting her immediate predicament. 'She died only recently, actually. So sad.'

'Oh no, poor pet.' Kathleen stilled.

'A slideshow is exactly what this young man needs, then.' Mr Delaney stood with purpose, and went to the TV cabinet, bending his knees first before crouching a little to open the drawer. 'Here we go.' He pulled out a box of envelopes. 'I'll get the best ones ready, and put them in order. Han, can you help me set up the slide projector?'

She sighed. 'Okay, okay.' She could simply explain to him that she wanted to experiment with the slideshow idea for the restaurant launch, get his opinion.

But if her mother hadn't put on her little act, she'd be relaxing with a simple family dinner and a few memories, revelling in her comfort zone for a while, and going home to bed.

As though reading her mind, her mother came over to Hannah as she set up the projector. She gave her daughter a wise smile and said, 'Darling. Sometimes it's good not to wear a life jacket.' She kissed her cheek and returned to the kitchen, and Hannah stood still, feeling like she was floating in a sea of water, not knowing which way the current would take her, and wishing she had something to hold on to.

CHAPTER FIFTEEN

The sky darkened as Luca drove into Wattle Lane. He was a bit nervous, having dinner with the Delaney's after buying their family property.

What if he didn't do it justice? What if he couldn't make it work?

He shook his head quickly, as though to shake away the self-doubt, then took a calming breath. He would be fine. Tonight would be fine. And he got to have a nice meal with Hannah, like he had hoped, even if with the addition of her parents. So they wouldn't be sussing out the competition, but that had really only been an excuse to meet up with her. Truth was, after an emotional but rewarding day making progress at the house with his brother, then giving him some words of wisdom before his big date, he didn't feel like being alone tonight. Yes, he could have responded to one of the Tinder matches and asked to meet up, but he simply wasn't interested.

He parked in one of the available parking bays in the complex, and wandered through the manicured gardens to Unit 4. He was about to knock on the door but footsteps beat him to it and the door opened.

'Welcome to Senior Land!' A man in a woollen sweater, Mr Delaney obviously, stood at the door with arms outstretched and a smile just as wide.

Luca burst into a grin. 'Why, thank you!'

Luca stepped in, smiled at Hannah who had rosy cheeks, and then her mother. 'Mrs Delaney, hello. Nice to see you!'

She approached with hands outstretched, and he kissed her once on each cheek. She held onto his cheeks for a moment with her palms. 'Luca Antonescu, my oh my you've grown into a strapping young man.'

He chuckled, and dropped his gaze for as moment with a bashful smile. 'I don't know about young, but thank you!'

'Of course you're young, both of you.' She eyed Hannah. 'But oh how the years fly by.'

He nodded. 'Tell me about it. I was just saying the same thing to my brother today.'

'Oh, and how is he?' She tapped her chin for a moment. 'Stefan, isn't it?'

Luca was impressed. 'Yes, and he'll be glad to know someone has remembered him. I asked him if he wanted to come and stay down here for a weekend but he thinks no one would remember him.'

'Nonsense. Lovely young boy he was. Did he follow you into the cooking business?'

'No, finance actually. Investments. He's really good at what he does. I'm proud.' Luca smiled.

'Anyway, this lovely lady will talk your ears off, how about we show you around?' Mr Delaney said, gesturing to the other side of the house. 'And then we have a surprise for you.'

Luca held back a gulp. 'A surprise?'

Hannah stepped forward. 'Don't worry, Dad just wants to put on a little show.' She waved her hand dismissively. 'And I thought it might be an idea for your launch, so let me know what you think after we—'

'Ooh, don't give it away now, Han. Keep him in suspense.'

Luca's focus went from Hannah to Mr Delaney, and back again. In the process, he noticed a screen against the living room wall. 'Oh, have you been watching movies on the big screen?' He walked over to it, remembering that his father sometimes liked to show old photos on a screen using a projector. But after his death they sold the projector and screen and never watched one again.

'Not movies, but... slides!' Mr Delaney seemed extremely excited by the fact. 'Although we haven't yet put any up, I guess the surprise is no longer a surprise.' He feigned defeat and lowered his head.

A sense of nostalgia and curiosity welled up inside. 'You're going to put on a slideshow? How cool!'

'See, I knew he'd like it!' Mr Delaney nudged Hannah, whose face was becoming pinker by the minute.

'But after dinner,' Mrs Delaney said.

'Can I check which slides you're showing, Dad, just to make sure there aren't too many, or we could be here all night, and I have a busy day tomorrow.' She reached for the pile of envelopes on the table but her father grasped her hand.

'Uh-uh, no peeking. It's a surprise for you too.'

'Please, no baby photos, c'mon!' she said.

Her father laughed. 'There's nothing embarrassing, I promise.' He winked at Luca.

Ooh, goodie! He was keen to see some good old embarrassing baby and toddler photos. As long as they weren't of himself. He should have done that for Stefan's birthday... maybe next year. Poor Hannah was clearly already embarrassed, but he found it cute. And endearing.

Luca faced the kitchen, where Mrs Delaney was ladling

dinner into some bowls. 'How can I help, Mrs Delaney?' he asked.

'You can start by calling me Kathleen,' she replied.

'And me, Doug,' said her husband.

Luca nodded. 'And how about I carry these to the table?' He gestured to the bowls.

'Well, I won't say no,' she said with a smile.

Luca carried the bowls of steaming chicken casserole to the table. 'This smells delicious. Might have to give you a job at my restaurant.'

'Oh gosh,' she said, 'A family meal I can handle, but a room full of paying customers? I think I'd have a mild panic attack.' She chuckled. 'Oh, that smaller serving is Doug's,' she pointed out. 'He's supposed to watch his portion sizes.'

'Ah, got it.' He placed it down.

'Unfair!' Doug called out.

'So is not being able to look at the slides before the slideshow!' Hannah called out.

Luca smiled, it was nice to see good old family dynamics in action again. He missed it.

When all meals and drinks were served, they sat at the table and began eating. 'Mmm, I taste fresh thyme, my favourite herb,' he said.

'Isn't it great? So versatile. This thyme is from Hannah's garden. Oh, excuse me,' she said, a hand on her heart, '*your* garden, now.' She smiled.

'I can't wait to make good use of what you've all created at Iona.'

'Did Hannah explain how we named it?'

'Yes indeed. And I plan to keep it.'

Kathleen clasped her hands together in delight, and Doug closed his eyes with a grateful nod and smile. 'Thank you, Luca,' said Kathleen. 'That means a lot.'

'Of course. Family history is so important.' He took a sip of water. 'I'd love to visit there one day, the Isle of Iona.'

'Oh you must,' said Doug. 'Magical place. What's your background again?'

'Romanian.'

'Ah yes, that's right. Do you have family over there?'

'I do. Haven't been back for a few years though. I'm about due for a visit. But not yet, I have a few things to do here in the foreseeable future.'

'So, six weeks to open your restaurant, does it have a name?' Hannah's mother asked.

Luca glanced at Hannah with a smile, and at the same time, once again, they both said, 'Home.'

'Oh, how lovely. I already can't wait to eat there. We'll be at the grand opening, that's for sure, won't we, Doug.'

'You betcha,' he responded. 'Can I choose my own portion size there?'

Luca grinned. 'Our portion sizes will definitely be satisfying,' he confirmed, and Doug placed his hands together and bowed in gratitude. Luca then turned his attention to Kathleen. 'While also being moderate and not over-filling.' She copied her husband's gesture.

'Thank you, that was so nice.' Luca dabbed at the corners of his mouth with his napkin, after finishing his meal. 'Let me help you clear the table.' He stood, picking up his bowl and Hannah's and taking it to the sink, while Kathleen brought over hers and Doug's. Doug went to the coffee machine.

'Coffee, tea of various kinds, hot chocolate?' Doug asked.

'Hmm. Tea, thanks. Any is fine.'

'Black tea, or do you prefer herbal: peppermint, chamomile, lemongrass?'

'Ooh, I love lemongrass.'

'Good choice!' Doug got out some teacups. 'Hannah, same for you?'

'Lemongrass it is,' she said. 'So, about the slideshow...'

'Yes!' said Doug. 'Let's get onto that once we have our tea and biscuits. Love, do we have some candles somewhere?'

Kathleen opened a drawer and took a few out. 'It's been a while since we used these, must get back to having candlelit diners sometime, darling.'

'So much for *your* surprise tomorrow night,' he chuckled.

'Ooh, okay, I'll conveniently forget then.' She grinned, then fanned her face. 'Still so romantic after all these years.' She went over to her husband and pecked him on the cheek.

'Sorry for all the schmaltz,' Hannah whispered to him. He hadn't even noticed she had approached, he'd been too busy watching the couple, and remembering his own parents in the kitchen and how they used to flirt and show their love for each other. His mind also went to Stefan and he wondered how his brother's date was faring.

Luca shook his head. 'It's lovely,' he whispered back, giving her elbow a quick squeeze.

Her soft and subtle scent wafted around him, with a vanilla element to it. He wanted to follow her around, breathe in more of it, but when she went to the couch to take her seat, he didn't want to sit until her parents had everything ready. 'Shall I take the biscuits over?' he asked.

'Sure thing.' Doug handed him a plate, and Luca arranged a few of the homemade delights onto the plate.

When Mrs Delaney had asked him for dinner over the phone, saying she'd be *delighted* if he could join them, he'd held back a laugh, recalling his conversation with Stefan about talking like an old man. He hadn't expected Hannah's mother to suddenly appear on the phone, but he was glad she did. The night was proving to be much-needed relief for his sadness and tiredness. And tomorrow the work would begin, once Hannah had her plan ready to present to him, hopefully by the end of the day, or Tuesday. But with the Goldstein kitchen appliances arriving tomorrow, he'd have to be up early to receive them and make sure the kitchen people put everything in the right places. He couldn't wait to have it all set up so he could focus on the rest of what had to be done, and so he could start some menu preparations and figure out what would work in his kitchen in terms of size, space, and how many staff he would need.

'Lemongrass tea is served,' Doug said, placing a teapot on the coffee table. He took a seat with the slide projector in front of him, Kathleen to his right, and Hannah to his left on the other couch. She motioned for him to join her.

Luca sat and was once again swept up in the sweet, warmth of her scent, soon overtaken by the woodiness of the lemongrass as he sipped at his tea.

'Ladies and gentlemen of Senior Land, I present to you...' Doug began, 'the history of the Delaney Family.' The projector came to life with a burst of light.

'Oh dear God,' Hannah whispered. 'Save me now.'

Luca turned his face to look at her and chuckled. 'Not a chance,' he said with a fake-evil cackle.

The projector hummed and made a click sound when Doug flipped on the first slide. A young Doug sporting an impressive thick beard and moustache and Kathleen with hair parted down the middle were at a party, which he explained was their engagement.

'My stylish parents, as you can see,' Hannah remarked.

'And then...' Doug flipped to a wedding photo, this time Kathleen's hair was curled, though still parted down the middle. They were cutting a large, three-tiered cake and smiling at the camera. 'Still as fresh in my memory as always.'

'Mine too.' Kathleen rubbed his arm.

Doug turned to Luca. 'Were your parents married here or overseas?'

'Dad,' said Hannah. 'I thought this was about *our* family history.'

'It's okay,' Luca replied. 'They married in Romania and then moved to Australia to have me and my brother. Dad got work as a chef and Mum did clothing alterations.'

Doug gave a nod.

'After Dad died,' Luca continued talking for some reason. 'When Mum moved us back to Sydney, she resumed doing alterations while working on designs for wedding dresses, eventually making her own collection and setting up a store which became really successful and still runs today, under new owners.'

'Really?' Kathleen said. 'How lovely, do you have any photos?'

'I took some today, actually, of her one-off designs that I brought back with me. The rest are on the Teadora website.'

'I'll have to have a look.' Kathleen leaned over as Luca held out his phone, and swiped through photos of the four dresses he'd taken back today. 'They are absolutely beautiful! Look at that one, with all the little gems.' She pointed to the one he'd taken off the mannequin.

'Yes. That was her favourite, it was displayed in her home office.'

'Lovely, Luca. Really lovely.'

He nodded and put his phone away. Hannah was quiet.

'Now, where were we up to?' Doug flipped to the next slide. 'Oh yes, the honeymoon.'

The couple were on the ski slopes. 'Thredbo by any chance?' Luca asked.

'Indeed. And I came home with not only a wife but a

whopping great bruise down my left thigh, courtesy of a fall and long slide down the slopes.'

'Ouch.'

'I told him to lay on the snow until it healed.' Kathleen laughed.

'I once slipped on a wet pool deck and got a nasty bruise myself,' Luca said. 'While on a cruise ship.'

'Oh, a cruise! Darling, we should do one sometime,' said Kathleen to Doug.

'Easy living, remember?' he said.

'Lounging around a pool deck, no cooking or cleaning, sounds easy to me.'

Doug tilted his head with a 'maybe' expression. 'I always prefer to be on land.'

'Was it worth it, as a holiday?' Kathleen asked.

'Actually I was working, in the kitchen. I did quite a few cruises. Didn't get much time by the pool but when I did, I made the most of it. I think I was rushing to finally relax, and that's when I slipped.'

'Working on a cruise ship, that would be exciting.'

'It was. Gave me a chance to see some cool places and not be stuck in any one spot. Was great.'

'What other sorts of places have you worked in?' Hannah asked.

'You name it, I've done it.' Luca put his phone in his pocket. 'Cafes, restaurants, clubs, bistros, event catering, outdoor-food stalls... until now, I guess. I've never actually owned anything and stayed in the one place for too long before.'

'It must be the right time,' said Kathleen.

'Fingers crossed it all works out.'

'It will,' Hannah piped up. 'With a good events manager on your side, things will get off to a great start.'

'I'm confident they will. And then I just have to continue it and make it last.'

'You can do it, mate,' said Doug. 'We'll put in a good word for you around town. Get people excited about it.'

'That'd be great, thanks.' It was like having his own family marketing team, which he was grateful for, but also wary of, because he wanted to do it *himself*. He wanted to prove that he could, and make his parents proud.

'Anyway, enough chit-chat for now, more slides await.' Doug clicked the projector and another picture appeared.

'Yes, let's get it over with, shall we?' said Hannah, shifting awkwardly on the couch, the sleeve of her jumper brushing against his arm with a warm tingle.

A few more honeymoon photos were shown, followed by some with each of their parents. Hannah's grandparents, who were no longer alive. Hannah's maternal grandmother had lived until Hannah was ten.

'And here we are next to the Tarrin's Bay Town of New Beginnings sign when we decided to make it our *own* new beginning,' said Doug.

Luca remembered driving past that sign as a teenager, believing they would all have a new beginning with the family restaurant, but here he was again twenty years later, hoping for a second chance at that new beginning. It also made him think of how he'd hoped for a sign from his mother, and now here was another. But it was probably just because his mind was focused on it that it seemed relevant.

'And our home. What it used to look like anyway.' Doug gestured to the photo of the large expanse of land with a weatherboard house on it, hardly recognisable from the renovated house it was today.

'You've done a great job with the place since then. And the

original building obviously had a good strong foundation and structure,' Luca remarked.

'Sure did, I didn't see the point in knocking it down and rebuilding, it was so well-built in the first place. So we kept adding to it, and adding to it, over the years.'

'Wow. It's nice to see what it looked like in the beginning.' This was going to be his home, and he was starting to feel more connected to it now that he was seeing how it all began.

'Looks so empty, the land,' said Hannah. 'And the coop was so small.'

'It was a blank canvas waiting to be turned into our own piece of art,' her mother said. 'Fruit trees, herb and veggie garden, a bit of landscaping, and a bigger chicken coop. Wow, I'd almost forgotten how much work we did over the years.'

'Labour of love.' Doug smiled. 'And here is the inspiration for our namesake, Iona.' He clicked to the next slide. 'It doesn't look like Tarrin's Bay, apart from the rock and the ocean views, but as a piece of our family ancestry, it seemed a perfect fit to name it after.'

Several slides showing photos of the Isle of Iona graced the screen.

'Stunning,' he said.

Rocky shores and breathtaking ocean, farmland and fields of flowers, and cute cottage-like houses lining the town. 'And you haven't been, Hannah?'

She shook her head. 'One day.'

He wouldn't mind seeing it one day either. But he would go anywhere, see anything, any place. 'How far does your ancestry trace back to Iona?' asked Luca.

'A few generations. My great-great-grandparents lived there,' Doug explained.

'I might have to add it to my bucket list,' Luca said with a smile.

Doug gave a nod, then a chuckle at the next slide. It was of a pregnant Kathleen, and Doug with a cushion shoved under his T-shirt, making him look pregnant too.

'Oh, Dad,' said Hannah. 'Now how do I know which one of you is my real mother?' She giggled.

'Easy,' he replied, showing the next slide.

Kathleen lay in a hospital bed with a newborn Hannah propped on her chest, Hannah's little mouth hanging open in satisfaction as though she'd just had her first feed.

Luca couldn't hold back a huge smile. 'I believe that is a certain someone I know.' He winked.

'Yeah, yeah. Cute, wasn't I?' Hannah covered half her face with her hand.

'Cuteness overload,' he replied. He went on to explain how her cheeks reminded him of Stefan's and how the kissing tradition had begun, and the family shared a few laughs on discovering Luca's brother was still enduring this tradition even now at thirty-two.

'They grow up so fast,' said Kathleen. 'Hannah was the only child I was blessed with, and although I would have loved for her to have a sibling, she was pretty happy as an only child, weren't you, darl?' Kathleen blew her daughter a kiss from the other couch.

'Of course. My animals were my siblings.' SShe chuckled.

'Speaking of animals,' Hannah's dad said, clicking through a few slides of Hannah as a baby to one as a toddler at the zoo. 'Her favourite were the penguins.' The photo showed Hannah watching the penguins through the glass enclosure with wide eyes and an open mouth. 'She begged us to take some home, "to keep the chickens company", she'd said.' Doug laughed, and Luca grinned. 'When we told her they wouldn't thrive on our farm and needed the cold water, she suggested we take them to the beach for a daily swim. She wouldn't give up on the idea of a penguin as a pet!'

Hannah lowered and shook her head while Luca laughed.

'Maybe you can get one at your new place in Sydney?' he asked. 'A blow-up pool out the back, some ice... could work.' He nudged her discreetly.

'They were cute, okay? I was a little kid, what little kid wouldn't want a penguin for a pet?' She raised her hands.

'You're right. I'm sure I asked for a penguin at some stage.'

'Really?'

'No, but I'm sure someone did. Somewhere, in the world. Like, Antarctica.'

'Oh, stop, you!' She gave him a whack.

Kathleen was quietly giggling, but he noticed her satisfied smile at watching the playful exchange. It was his guess that Hannah hadn't had a man over to dinner to meet her parents for a while. Although maybe Nathan had sat here on this couch once too, though it hadn't sounded like anything much had happened between them.

'Did you know...' he began.

'Wait, another of your random facts,' Hannah interjected. 'Is it... Did you know, that Antarctica is the coldest continent in the world?'

'No,' he shook his head. 'I only mention unique and interesting random facts, when they pop in my head.'

'Go on, impress us all then,' she said with a challenging tone, and another light nudge.

'When a penguin finds a mate, they are mates for life. And a penguin chooses his mate for life by proposing with a pebble.'

'A pebble?' Her eyebrows rose. 'Not a twenty-four-carat gold diamond ring?'

He smiled. 'A pebble. How cute is that?'

'Huh. Never knew that,' she said. 'How lovely.'

'Ohh, that is the most adorable thing,' said Kathleen, clasping her hands together.

Doug cleared his throat. 'Do you mean, after all that money I saved for my lovely wife's ring, I could have simply picked up a pebble from the ground and won her over with that?'

Luca chuckled. 'Well, if she knew about the meaning behind it, maybe?' He held out a curious hand towards Kathleen.

'Oh, my heart would have melted at such a gesture, darling,' she said. 'But... my ring is even better.' She patted her husband's forearm in reassurance, the ring itself sparkling under the candlelight in the room.

'Glad to hear. But as for Christmas... perhaps I can help you start a nice pebble collection?'

She flicked her hand towards him.

'Then the money we save we could put towards that cruise you want.'

Her eyes brightened. 'Now you're talking.'

Doug chuckled again then went to the next slide, and the next, and the next, until they came to one with a man he didn't recognise in the background of a photo of Hannah climbing a tree to put up Christmas fairy lights.

'Oops, didn't look close enough at that one beforehand, sorry love.' Doug clicked to the next one.

'Who was that?' Luca couldn't help but ask.

'No one, just Samuel,' she said quietly.

'Hannah's ex, he was,' Kathleen explained.

'Mum.'

'Well, he was. Anyway, that was a couple of Christmases' ago, all in the past now.' She stood. 'More tea anyone?'

'No, thanks,' he replied. 'Hannah?'

'No thanks, Mum.'

Although something had hit a nerve with Hannah on the

picture with her ex being displayed on the screen, he couldn't help but see why it probably hadn't worked out. The man had been standing awkwardly in the photo, holding the end of the lights cable and trying to appear useful, while Hannah was high up in the tree hooking it around branches, like it was the most natural thing to do, and like she would have done it perfectly well with or without his help. Hannah certainly didn't need a man, but… did she want one?

After a slide showing the family at Christmas time around the tree, Doug said, 'Okay, folks, that's all the best photos I have converted to slides so far.' He clicked the machine off and it whirred to silent. 'But… we do have plenty of normal photos, in fact, Hannah brought some over today, if you like, we could have a photo-viewing session. Yes!' He stood and went to the dining table.

'No!' Both Hannah and her mum stood suddenly.

Luca's gaze flipped from the women to Doug and back again.

'I think that's enough family history for Luca for one night, dear,' Kathleen said.

'Oh, I don't mind, it's been a lot of fun,' he said.

'It sure has,' Kathleen replied, 'but darling, these young people have work to get to tomorrow and things to organise, we better leave them to it.'

'Yes, and I haven't topped up the chook food yet tonight because I came straight here, so I need to do a quick check when I get back and make sure they're all set until morning.'

'Rightio, Han.'

Doug's excited expression weakened a little to one that seemed slightly disappointed, and Luca didn't know if it was because the family photo night was coming to an end, or because he couldn't help out with the chickens anymore.

Luca took that as his cue to stand too. 'This has been a

wonderful evening, thank you Mr... Doug,' he shook Hannah's father's hand, 'and Kathleen,' he shook hers then leaned in close to kiss her on both cheeks. She smiled widely.

'It's our pleasure, Luca. Give our best to Stefan.'

'Will do, thanks.'

He turned to face Hannah, whose mouth stretched into a yawn. 'Would you like me to give you a hand with the chooks before I head home... have a bit of a practice run?'

'Oh no, it's okay, it won't take long, I could do it in my sleep.'

Luca chuckled. 'I'm sure you could. Well, if you're sure.'

She nodded.

'Oh, darling, why not show him how it's all done, perfect opportunity.' Kathleen suggested.

'I already did before, and I know he's a fast learner. He could probably do it in his sleep too now, after just the first lesson, right?' She eyed him.

Luca shrugged. 'Maybe with one eye open at least.' He made his way towards the door.

Doug followed, but closed his eyes and held out his hands trying to navigate his way to the door, bumping into the edge of the dining table on the way. 'Ouch!'

'Oh, Doug,' Kathleen shook her head.

'I don't think I can do much at all with my eyes closed.' He opened his eyes and raised his arms, letting them fall to his sides.

'Dad, be careful now,' said Hannah, who made her way towards him and gave him a goodbye peck on the cheek, then did the same to her mother.

'Night night, darling.' Kathleen opened the door. 'And thank you for your delightful company, Luca.' She gave him another cheek kiss, and he matched it with one on the other side.

'The delight was all mine.' He smiled, and after waving goodbye and walking back outside to the cool night air he quickly checked his phone, which he'd switched to silent, turning the volume back on. There were a couple of notifications from Tinder, but no message from Stefan, so his date must have gone well, or still be going well. He wondered if his brother's new dating resolution had been successful.

Hannah accompanied him to his car. 'Thanks for coming along, hope it wasn't too awkward for you,' she said.

'Not at all. I was going to ask you the same.'

'Ah, it's okay. A few embarrassing moments, but overall, I'm pretty lucky with those two goofballs.' She gestured back to the house.

'Indeed you are.' He unlocked his car, preparing to say goodnight.

Hannah shifted her stance. 'You know, I *could* use a bit of help. A tiny bit.' She pinched her fingers together and squinted. 'Not much. Only because it's late, and well, two hands are better than one.'

He looked at her eyes, weary but welcoming. 'Oh. Sure thing. I'd be happy to, because I really don't think I'm at "doing-it-in-my-sleep" level just yet.'

She smiled. 'Sorry about that, I just didn't want you to feel like you had to help me out to be polite in front of my parents, it's getting late and I don't want to keep you any longer. But if you really want to, I'm happy for you to make a quick detour via Jasmine Road.'

'Done.' He shook her hand. 'And also, since when do we only have one hand each?'

'Huh?'

'You said, "two hands are better than one".' He grinned.

'Oh, did I?' She covered her face with her (two) hands. 'I meant, two *pairs* of hands are better than one.'

He chuckled. 'I know.' Then held his right hand back out to her. 'But we are pretty good at doing a one-handed handshake.'

She laughed. 'Most handshakes *are* one-handed, you know.'

'Yes, but not all *special* handshakes are one-handed.' He tapped her palm with his twice, then curved her thumb around hers and tugged downwards, tapped her palm again. They both made a fist and pushed against each other's, then did a high-five.

'So should we add both hands to make it extra special?' she asked.

He shrugged. 'We could try.'

They made a few attempts at a new and improved two-handed handshake, but kept messing it up. 'I give up.' Hannah stepped backwards with a laugh. 'Why fix what's not broken?'

'That is a wise question, my dear, and you are probably right.' He held out his hand again, and they repeated the handshake, but this time, after the high-five, he wrapped both his arms briefly around her in a quick hug. 'But we could just make that the two-handed bit.'

She smiled, and her eyes sparkled with the light from the moon. 'Deal,' she said. 'But it was too quick, it barely happened. Did I imagine it?' She gave an inquisitive gaze.

'Oh. Let's make sure we both didn't imagine it.'

He tapped her palm twice, but this time slower, making every part of the handshake count, and savouring the comforting sensation of her hand against his. When the clap of the high-five sounded, he slid his arms slowly around her back, savouring the even more comforting sensation of her back against his hands. He stayed there for one deep breath, and she breathed in sync with him, then slowly pulled away.

'Much better,' she said.

Much, much better, he thought. He had really needed some company tonight, and she was here. As she'd always been back at school; Hannah Delaney—there when he needed her, for help with a project, for an imaginative excuse when late for class... but this time, after all these years, he was starting to feel like he needed her in a new way. But she wouldn't always be there. He had only six weeks, eight at the most, to get these memories out of his mind and desires out of his system once and for all, and get on with the task of running his business and the chicken farm, not for a few months, or a year, but for the long-term.

He'd allow himself to revel in the nice, warm, fuzzy feelings of connectedness and family for an hour longer, until the chickens had been fed and he'd had some more practice, and then he would get back to business... Hannah as his launch manager, and together—a productive, professional relationship for the coming weeks.

'Okay, some hungry chickens await,' he said, sliding into the driver's seat. 'See you there, HD.'

'Okey dokey, LR.' She gave a casual wave then walked over to her car.

As Luca went to drive off, he noticed a curtain in the Delaney's unit window flick closed. Had they watched the whole exchange? Or maybe they were wondering why the car engines had not started up until now. Either way, Hannah was right. She was lucky to have those two goofballs. He missed his goofballs, and had enjoyed the company of hers for the night, even if it was nowhere near the same as if being with his own parents. It was still nice, and after the stress of the last few months, nice was a welcome new experience.

Hannah exhaled properly for what felt like the first time all evening as she drove off.

Well, that was an interesting night.

Her mind kept flitting between wanting to get on with moving on, moving forward, and reminiscing the past. If she was always either in the past or the future, then when was she ever in the present?

When I'm with the animals, was the first thought that came to her.

Wasn't that where life was supposed to be? When she worked on events, she was visioning a future moment in time. When she was with Luca, or even her parents, she was drawn back to the past. But where did—*would*—her real life lay?

Would the future she was working towards become the life that would satisfy her, or would the past and the long-held ideas of what *should* be, or should *have* been, hold her hostage?

All she could do was put one foot in front of the other and hope for the best.

She turned the corner into Jasmine Road and opened the window halfway, breathing in deeply the subtle scent of jasmine, which was ever-present, though stronger in spring and summer. This smelled like home, and she had an idea to suggest to Luca that he make jasmine the signature fragrance of the restaurant. It was definitive and welcoming, but shouldn't overpower the delicious food scents that would want their time in the spotlight. He could have jasmine-scented reed sticks and scented candles throughout the place. Not many places of business knew about utilising the power of scent, but it was a subtle yet persuasive way of adding detail and class to any premises, and making it memorable.

Silence cleared the air as she turned the engine off. Luca had already parked. The familiar bumpy sensation of the pebbles underfoot led her to the front steps. 'I'll put my things inside and then we'll head around back to the chooks. Come on in and we'll go via the back verandah door.' She wiped her shoes on the doormat and gestured for him to enter, but he said, 'After you.'

Scarlett stood eagerly pawing at the back door. 'Sorry I'm so late, Scar!' Hannah said, opening the door and letting her in. She bent down and ruffled the dog's fur, then led her into the laundry where she promptly took position on the fur-covered doggy bed. Hannah topped up the water and kissed her goodnight.

Luca patted the dog's head and they left the animal in peace. 'She's your baby, isn't she?' said Luca, as they went to the back verandah.

Hannah nodded as her heart swelled. 'Yep. My very big and old baby.' It would be sad when Scarlett was no longer around. Her fate was inevitable, but for now she was doing well, enjoying her twilight years, happy and content. And for all Hannah knew, at this rate she might be the only *baby* she ever got to be blessed with.

'Right, the other babies await.' Hannah walked outside with Luca, the verandah floorboards creaking underfoot from years of use.

Luca marched towards the silo.

'Somebody's eager,' Hannah chuckled.

'I remember what to do. Don't tell me anything yet,' he said, approaching the silo like it was a giant beast that needed placating. 'Right...' He glanced around. 'Here it is. The hatch thingo.' Hannah stepped forward to remind him of something but bit her tongue when he opened the hatch too quickly and feed fell out onto the ground. 'Oops. Sorry. Wheelbarrow, right, I need the wheelbarrow to, um, *catch* the feed.' He glanced around for it. 'Unless we should get each chicken to line up under the silo hatch with their mouths open for their daily ration?' He offered a feeble smile.

Hannah bit her tongue again, settling for, 'That could take a while. Wheelbarrow's over there.' She cocked her head towards the right.

Luca came back a moment later and placed it under the hatch. 'Fill it all up, or not as much at night?'

'I thought you didn't want me to tell you things.'

'It's okay. Only some things. But the chickens' health and appetite satisfaction are on the line. And as a chef it would be unacceptable to me to think that someone's stomach, human or otherwise, might go unsatisfied.' He smiled.

Hannah chuckled. 'Fill it almost to the top. That should do it. In the morning I heap in a bit more, for days when I'm out and about a bit longer than expected, like today.'

The feed tumbled into the barrow and Luca feigned being unable to lift the handles up.

'You're acting like my dad,' she chuckled. 'Would you like a hand? One of my two hands?' she asked.

'It's okay. I'll see how I go.' He winked, lifting the handles and steering the wheelbarrow to the coop. Some of the chooks were already in the roosting shelves, but many strutted around him, knowing what was coming, even though there was still some feed left in the troughs. There was nothing like fresh feed.

'Let's hope it doesn't end up all over the ground.' Luca tipped the barrow and carefully angled it to let it tip into the first trough, and then the other. 'Ah, that wasn't too hard.'

'Next time, you have to do it with your eyes closed,' she joked.

'You're on.' He held out his hand, but this time she gave it a normal shake. He eyed her curiously.

She'd enjoyed the fun handshake and hug, but the more she let herself enjoy these things, the more she wanted to enjoy them, and to enjoy more things. 'I'll show you how to clean the troughs sometime. And all the other tasks that need doing. But it's all in my manual and is pretty easy to follow. It should be like following a recipe for you.'

Luca gave a nod. 'That's a good way to think of it. Thanks, I'll remember that.'

He must have sensed her reluctance to let the night get too carried away, as he began walking back to the verandah. 'Long day, guess we better get some sleep so the plans can begin tomorrow, huh?'

'Yep.' She walked with him.

They went around the side of the house to the driveway and towards his car. 'Thanks, Hannah, it was a fun and educational evening.' He leaned in quickly and kissed her cheek. On just one side.

Before she could stop herself, she said, 'Why don't I get kissed on two cheeks like my mother?'

Luca flashed a caught-out smile. 'Umm...' He rubbed at his jaw.

'It's okay, you can save those ones for my mum, she likes it.' Hannah smiled.

Luca leaned in and kissed her other cheek.

'Oh. Okay, well, thanks.' She smiled and patted her second-best cheek.

And then he kissed her other cheek again.

Hannah laughed. 'Three? I get three?'

Luca's eyes caught hers like lasers locked on target. 'I only gave you one, because...' He looked away then back again. 'Because, I'm scared if I give you another one, I might not stop.'

Everything around her seemed to freeze in time.

Not... stop? But why...

The scent of jasmine was replaced with the indescribable scent of anticipation, at what would happen next.

'Because...' He seemed to be looking for a way to explain, or deflect. 'I'm reminded of your cute chubby cheeks in that photo, and they're just so squishy and kissable.' He grinned and pinched gently at her cheeks.

Oh. Of course.

'Like your brother's?'

'Guess so. But different too.'

'Just how does the traditional annual cheek-kiss go?' she asked, curiosity hijacking her voice box.

'Like this.' He leaned in, still pinching her cheeks. 'Be warned, it's a bit noisy.' He put his lips to one cheek and a loud squelch sounded as a suction sensation made her giggle. He then moved to the other cheek and doubled the volume, and the suctioning. Her laugh doubled along with it.

'Oh my God, Luca!' She giggled and squirmed, as he repeated his attack.

'See? Just...' he squelched. 'Can't...' he sucked. '... Stop!' He kissed and pinched. 'Oooh, such kissable cheeks!' He stepped back a bit, his fingers still grasping her rounded cheeks as she laughed.

Hannah's cheeks became hot and wet with his repeated kissing, and as he moved from one cheek to the other, his lips accidentally brushed against hers. They both paused, and his eyes found hers again. Her giggles subsided, as did his enthusiastic kissing and squeezing, just for a second before his lips found a new place to stop.

Ohh.

Soft, warm, smooth but firm lips, cushioning hers. She wanted to pull back but couldn't. She had waited twenty years for this. He paused subtly, his soft breath on her face, as though to ascertain her response, and when she didn't back away, he pressed them against her again. Tingles spread everywhere throughout her body, her feet no longer sensing the ground beneath her. As the kiss intensified, his hands left a trail of tingles all on their own... on her back, as they moved from her waist to her shoulders, and to her hair around her neck, and back to her waist.

Her body was still processing what was happening when her mind suddenly kicked back into gear, and she was about to pull away when he beat her to it.

'Sorry.' He stepped back. 'Sorry about that.'

'Um, yeah.'

'I don't know what happened. Sorry, Hannah.'

'It's okay.'

'Okay.'

'Okay.'

'Um.' He turned to look at his car. 'Guess I should...'

'Yeah. Okay.' Her vocabulary seemed to be reduced to only two words, when all it really wanted to say was some kind of Shakespearean response like 'Oh, my Heavenly Creator, what bliss hath presently bestowed itself upon me?'

He got into his car, smiled some sort of apology, then started the engine.

She gave a small wave as he drove off, then went back inside, and sat on the lounge.

A kiss like that had not factored into her plans for the coming six weeks, and the six weeks hadn't even really started yet. How the hell would she concentrate now? How could she be around him and focus on business, when pleasure had just launched itself like a rocket into the atmosphere of her existence?

CHAPTER SIXTEEN

A light breeze floated through the living room window and tickled Hannah's cheeks, making her look up from the six-week calendar in front of her on the computer screen. Her mind catapulted from business activities to last night, and the memory of his lips tickling her cheeks, and then her own lips. She sighed, her wrists softening at the laptop keyboard and her hands falling onto her lap.

It had been a battle all morning to concentrate. Another pulse of breeze met her face and she tied her hair tighter into the ponytail.

Week one: kitchen. Week two: interior design and decorating. Week three: menu planning and staff interviews. Week four...

She sighed again, touching her fingers to her lips. Had his really just been there only hours ago? It wasn't like she hadn't been kissed in too long a time... well, maybe a year was a long time, but she'd had kisses galore before that. But this one... this one was something else. It was like the ones she used to dream about as a teenager. All, tingly and magical and out-of-this-world... like the kiss itself was some kind of bliss-inducing superpower.

She shook her swirling memories and feelings away and cleared her throat, sitting up straighter in the chair. She looked at her notes on the launch and her mind continued the process of figuring out where each task needed to be slotted. She typed away, adding details to each week, and each day, as an approximate guide to determine how long each task should take, and making sure the last week would be mostly about finalising the finishing touches, rather than a mad rush to the finish line. She didn't like mad rushes, as they led to mistakes, and there was no room for mistakes in a restaurant launch… if people didn't have a great experience first go, they would be unlikely to return, and Luca needed return patrons in a small town like Tarrin's Bay. And when tourists asked 'where's a good place to eat dinner around here?', he'd want the locals to say 'Home is fantastic, you must check it out.'

It was his job to make it fantastic, but it was her job to make sure it was all prepared and ready to be fantastic.

At around the same time Hannah's stomach grumbled, indicating it was time for lunch, her phone buzzed with a text message. Her breath caught in her throat as her first instinct was that it might be Luca.

She slid the phone closer and glanced at the screen…

> OMG, I've had to wait three hours to reply to you! I have one hour, tell me all.

Hannah smiled. She'd texted Karen this morning after tending to the chickens, bursting to tell her about the kiss with Luca.

She noticed the time was just after twelve, and closed her laptop.

She sent a quick reply saying *give me a sec*, then grabbed a can of tuna from the pantry, tipped it into a bowl, and added spinach leaves, a cold hard-boiled egg, red onion, and a drizzle of chilli and lemon-infused extra virgin olive oil. Gobbling it up, she texted:

> As I said, we kissed. Accidentally, sort of. But then on purpose. And then we stopped.

Hannah took a breath, her stomach making a weird sensation that made her feel blissfully unsteady.

> Did he initiate?

> Yep. It started with the cheeks, but playfully. It was late, we'd had a nice night, it was probably just the… endorphins? Probably didn't mean anything.

But it did to her.

> Hang on, he wouldn't kiss you if he wasn't attracted to you in that way. See? He did see you as more than a friend back then, but you never believed it.

> Nah, that was ages ago. It's different now, and like I said… endorphins.

> Were his pupils dilated?

> Huh?

> You know, large. Like big black holes.

Hannah chuckled.

> Why?

It means he likes you, if they're dilated. Check
next time.

I don't think there'll be a next time, it was
pretty awkward afterwards. And I'm dreading
having to present my plan to him later.

Her heart beat faster. She might be ready to meet with him
at the end of the day, but maybe she should schedule the
meeting for Tuesday morning... allow some time for things to
settle, and be... forgotten?

Hannah scoffed at her own thoughts... *As if that kiss would
be forgotten.*

Anyway, as planned, she would give him a progress update
mid-afternoon, then arrange the meeting. She still had two to
three hours.

Does your plan include more kissing?

No! I don't know. No!

You should talk to him about it. Get things out
in the open. Clear the air.

What do I say?? Hey Luca, you know how we
kissed? I've been wanting that since we were
fifteen. And now that we've had it, can I please
have some more? I'll sound like Oliver.

Who's Oliver?

Oliver the little kid who... never mind. Anyway,
what I really want is to be able to do my job
properly. I can't let anything get in the way of
that, or of my moving to Sydney plans.
Everything has to stay on track.

> Hannah, sometimes it's okay for plans to go astray. That's how magic happens... In those untethered moments that float between the planned ones.

Hannah sat still and just breathed for a while, absorbing Karen's words, and her own thoughts and feelings.

After a few moments, Karen texted again:

> I could do with some magic too. I haven't been kissed in ages.

Hannah gave a laugh.

> Hun, it's been about two months.

> I know, like I said... ages.

> Well there's plenty of men in Sydney, I'm sure you'll meet another one soon.

> Hope so. But a decent one, I'm sick of the ones who act all keen then disappear, or the ones who can't stop talking about their ex, and then go back to said ex.

Hannah sighed, but this time a different sigh. A frustrated sigh. Finding someone decent *was* difficult, especially in the second half of your thirties. She texted back:

> How about once I'm all settled in your place and at work, we go out on the town like we used to. Live it up a little. Pretend we're thirty. See what happens, you never know who we could meet.

She didn't know if she *really* wanted to do that, she'd rather find someone easily and naturally at a cafe, the beach, or a hiking trail, without all the facades and dressing up and partying. But they did have some good memories of going out on the town together in their younger years, maybe it could be fun.

Okay, sounds like a plan.

Another text came in:

Hang on, what about Luca? Don't you want to see if you two can have a second chance?

We never even had a first chance.

So have one. Take one.

Hannah finished the rest of her salad, dropping the spoon into the bowl with a clang when she was done.

I can't. Can't risk it, can't risk everything.

Romance is a bugger sometimes, isn't it? It's either not there when we want it, or it's there inconveniently and bloody gets in the way.

Hannah smiled.

Too true. Oh well. Moving forward…

She added an arrow emoji.
Karen texted a thumbs up emoji and then:

Chat later, keep me posted. Good luck with the plans.

Thanks.

Hannah slid her phone further up the table to avoid distracting herself when she returned to the table, and went outside for a quick break with Scarlett.

Dogs were easier companions than men. She always knew where she stood, and always received unconditional love and loyalty. Maybe that was all she needed. Kisses were nice, but they were only temporary.

Luca had tossed up repeatedly in his mind the day before whether to 'talk' to Hannah about Sunday night, but when she'd texted quite formally on Monday afternoon to say she would be ready to meet with him about the restaurant plans on Tuesday morning at 11.45am, and suggested a local cafe to meet at (instead of privately at the premises), he figured she wanted to forget the whole thing.

So he'd replied:

Sure. Looking forward to it. See you then.

He hadn't received a reply to that either, so he would have to see how she acted around him today. In fifteen minutes to be exact, checking his watch as he walked down the main street towards Café Lagoon.

When he took a seat at one of the indoor tables near the window, the outdoor ones being a bit chilly, he checked a text message from Stefan, expecting it to say that he had a second date with the woman he'd met on Sunday, which had gone really well, *and* he'd stuck to his resolve to not take things too far.

Women are crazy was all it said.

Luca's eyes opened wide. He texted back:

What happened, bro?

A few minutes passed, then a reply:

> Texted her to ask for another date tomorrow night, or the weekend… giving her a couple of options. But… wait for it…

Luca waited.

A picture of a screenshot appeared. Luca pressed it and zoomed in:

> Hey Stefan! Really enjoyed our date, you're such a nice guy to hang with! 😊 😊 😊 But something amazing happened yesterday on my day off… I met my soulmate! I know, it's so sudden, but it just happened, and we just clicked right away, like we'd known each other for years. We just really… connected, you know? So I'm just REALLY REALLY sorry to have to turn you down, because you REALLY REALLY are such a great guy, and under any other circumstances I would have happily had a second date, but I don't want to mess you around. I just know that Ricardo is my soulmate, and he feels the same. We just can't stop talking and texting and are going to reunite again tonight. I wanted to be honest with you, and I wish you the very best of luck in finding your special woman, because I just know you're one of the good guys. You REALLY REALLY are. Don't give up, gorgeous. Xo

Luca's mouth gaped. He texted back:

Really?! I mean, REALLY?!

> I KNOW, RIGHT!! The woman is delusional.

Sorry man.

It's OK. I'm chatting with a new one now.

You don't waste any time.

I don't have time to waste. Getting old.

He added a grey old man emoji.

Luca laughed, then blew out a breath. Is this what he had to look forward to if he ended up doing online dating? The thought turned him off.

And the only thought that kept popping into his mind now was Hannah, and the kiss, and how different things would be now. He hoped it wouldn't interfere with her work, or his work. But he also hoped that by some magical twist of fate there'd be a way for him to see if there was more between them. Allow things to develop naturally, if they were to develop. Without the barriers of schoolyard politics and other people getting in the way.

But how could it? She was moving out, he was moving in. He was launching a new business, she was launching a new life... away from here.

It was clearly never going to work, and they should just try their best to continue on as friends and temporary colleagues for the next six weeks, then cut ties. He didn't want to hurt her, or himself.

It took him a moment to realise someone was standing by his table.

'Luca?'

He looked up. 'Oh. Hi, Hannah. Sorry, was lost in my thoughts.'

'It's okay. I only said your name about...' She tapped her chin. 'About seven times.'

'Really?' He raised his eyebrows.

'Just kidding.' She gave a quick tilt of her head. 'What can I order for you?' She gestured to the counter, where a young man smiled at her and she gave a small wave of recognition.

Luca went to stand. 'I've got it.'

She held out her hand in front of him. 'No, I've got it. It's a business meeting, so it all goes down as a tax deduction.'

'I can still pay.'

'Luca, you bought my house. That's plenty. Really, it's better if I do it properly, with a receipt and everything.'

'In that case, sure. Thank you.' He sat again.

Yep, as he'd thought, business only. Although she had made an attempt to lighten the mood with her exaggeration about greeting him seven times.

He tapped the menu. 'I'll have the triple turkey sandwich on organic sourdough, please. Extra cranberry sauce. And pepper. Extra pepper. But only a small dash of salt.'

Oops. That was probably too *chef-ish*, he should have just said 'turkey sandwich, please' and be done with it, but after years in the business he couldn't order anything as standard. He'd developed his own tastes, and they liked to be satisfied. Nothing wrong with that.

Hannah gave a nod and turned swiftly. 'Hey, Jonah, how's things?'

'Busy busy,' the young man replied. 'I hear you're moving on? We'll miss you.'

'Gee, news travels fast around here, doesn't it?' Hannah said.

Jonah shrugged. 'I'm usually the first to discover everything in this place.' He outstretched his arms. 'When do you leave?'

Luca listened as she told him of her plans, only further

cementing them into his own mind as well, and dislodging the crazy, magical, twist-of-fate ideas and possibilities that had wafted uninvited into his mind before.

'Luca?' she said again, and he glanced up. 'I said, this is Jonah, he and his parents who own the cafe are customers of mine.'

Luca stood and shook his hand. 'Nice to meet you.' He smiled. 'I hope to be able to continue to provide you with great quality eggs after Hannah goes.'

'I hope so too. We love to support local business, and not everyone does organic eggs around here. Costs more, but we have a lot of customers who come here for our organic omelettes and scrambled eggs each morning, so it's worth it.'

Luca nodded. He was feeling the pressure now, and hoped he could pull this all off. 'Nothing like a good omelette.'

'Indeed. Anyway, guys, your meals won't be long.' He smiled and went to serve the next customer in line.

Luca and Hannah sat at the same time, and as she leaned forward to shuffle her chair closer to the table, his nose took in a light scent of vanilla, and his eyes were drawn to her neck, and then down over her décolletage, bare after she'd taken off her scarf, and the slight line of subtle cleavage. He cleared his throat, forcing his eyes back up to hers.

But she diverted hers. 'Lovely day,' she said, eyeing the street... a few cars driving past, and a couple of people walking past, talking at the same time and laughing.

'Sure is. Bit nippy though, thought it might be nicer inside.'

'Best table in the cafe, you can just watch the world go by here.' Her eyes continued to gaze out the window, and Luca tried to use his mind to pry them away from the goings-on outside and return her gaze to him.

When she did, he said, 'Hannah. I...' and gulped.

Hannah's cheeks pinkened slightly, and she flicked her

hand. 'Hey, it's okay. Today is a new day, let's just focus on what's next.' She clasped her hands together on the table and gave a taut smile.

Luca nodded.

'I'm really excited about what's possible for Home. It's going to be a unique, popular eating place, and with a few special touches to help you stand out, I think you're onto a winner.' She gave the taut smile again, then withdrew a folder from her bag. 'Before I get into the nitty-gritty of each step and our time schedule, here are some visual ideas to let you know what sort of décor and interior I'm thinking of to match the theme and feelings you want to create in the restaurant.' She opened the folder. 'Now, I'm not a qualified interior designer, but I do have a good eye for detail and colour, textures and patterns. You are free to hire a designer if you wish, but with what I have here we can certainly organise the interiors based off ready-made designs from companies and manufacturers I've dealt with before. It will be cheaper in price, but not quality, and faster, and we are on a bit of a schedule, as you know.'

Luca simply watched and listened, trying his best to take everything in. It was like she had stepped out of her chicken coop and into an alternate reality where she was businesswoman Hannah. Which of course she was, but it was interesting to see the contrast.

He eyed the pages as she flipped through brochures.

'This one here has a really nice coastal feel...' she waved her hand over the page as though doing a magic spell. 'But this one here,' she turned the page, 'has a great mixture of coastal and classy. Elegant while still feeling homely. Do you agree?' She raised her gaze from the page to his eyes, and he remembered how close he'd been to those eyes two days ago.

She seemed to be doing a lot better than him at keeping her mind on the job.

'Yes. Yes, I agree. For sure.'

When they'd finished looking at interior ideas and he'd shortlisted a few designs and pieces of furniture as well as a cost estimate for later confirmation on which ones to order, their meals arrived.

He bit into the sandwich, from the middle, making sure to take in a bite with a good amount of cranberry sauce, and said, 'Mmm.' After swallowing, he nodded. 'Really nice.'

REALLY REALLY nice, he joked silently to himself.

'Oh good,' Hannah said, taking a slurp of her soup. 'So, the kitchen should be installed and ready for use, next week?'

'Yes. End of this week they should be finished, but may need a couple of extra days early next week, so once that's all done I can start to work on some menu planning and experiments.'

'Great. The menu will be key, so don't rush it. Make sure you've considered all options, providing food that people will know and love, like their favourite home-cooked meals, but also some unique and different options to give that little something extra to those who like variety.'

'For sure.'

He was getting excited, but he kept having to stop himself from saying something too casual or personal, like calling her HD or Hannah Delannah, even though the words almost jumped out of their own accord. But this was business, and also, with what had happened, their dialogue felt more stilted. He hoped they would be able to get back to their nicknames and their fun banter, and their high-fives and special handshakes. Had he ruined it all by losing control and kissing her? He seriously hoped not.

By the time they'd finished lunch and a coffee, Hannah had explained the overall plan to him and taken notes on certain things to finalise and adjust as needed. When all seemed organised enough to take the next steps, there was an awkward silence.

Luca didn't like awkward silences. He couldn't let one go past without being the first to break it.

'Hannah,' he leaned forward slightly, 'last night was… look, I don't regret it, I have to be honest. But I do regret making you feel uncomfortable, if that is the case. So I just want you to know that if you want to talk about it, I'm all ears, and if you don't want to and would rather forget it ever happened, I'm okay with that too.'

She gave a slow nod.

'The priority is this little restaurant of mine and your moving plans, so I don't want to get in the way of that or of us being able to do our jobs.'

She gave another nod.

'Let's keep moving forward and make this a success. Deal?'

She gave two nods. 'Deal.'

He held out his hand and shook hers, a normal, professional handshake, then they stood and parted ways.

He strode off, feeling somewhat more in control and clear-headed than when he'd arrived. He had a lot to do now, tasks to tick off the checklist, one by one. Starting with deciding on the paint colours and furniture so that Hannah could place the order on his behalf with her industry discount.

By the end of the next day, he'd completed the first few tasks, and with furniture arriving mid next week, he had arranged someone to start painting tomorrow, with completion hopefully before all the tables turned up. He had also set up his Facebook page and printed some temporary flyers using a template Hannah had provided, and handed them out at the markets earlier today. He'd helped out at Hannah's egg stall to watch her in action selling the eggs and chatting with customers. She had introduced him to people and mentioned the restaurant, garnering excitement and anticipation among the locals.

And now here he sat at Nathan's kitchen table, eyes on his laptop, sorting through logo ideas for Home.

'That one's pretty cool,' Nathan said, pointing at one with a white swirly H and italic font, engraved on a background picture of weathered timber.

'Yeah, not bad.' Luca scrolled through some more options in the online logo sampler he'd found on a graphic designer's website. He simply had to select three of his favourites, using his business name, then send through and they would do up a unique design based on them. Once that was sorted he would be able to get a sign made for the front of the premises, a logo to put on the menus, and the website.

After more time than he'd planned, he'd selected his three favourites, filled out the online design brief, and hit send. His request would be answered within twenty-four hours and they would let him know the time frame to expect for the design, plus the total cost, with a deposit payment required for beginning the work.

'Done.' He ticked it off the checklist and updated Hannah via text. She simply sent a gold star emoji.

'Guess I should get a proper logo for my own services,' Nathan said.

'Why not. That was kinda fun,' Luca replied. 'Though you seem to be getting enough work as it is?'

'Yeah, basic flyers and word of mouth have worked well enough. Besides, when swimming season kicks in in a few months I'll be needed back at the surf lifesaving club.'

'Oh yeah. I'm looking forward to swimming season. Probably best I moved here now in the winter, no time yet for those things unfortunately.'

Nathan gave a nod. 'Time flies. It'll be here before we know it.'

Time flies. It sure does.

He didn't want time to keep flying without having made some sort of progress towards a proper future, one where he had created his own life, not just moved around taking whatever jobs seemed fun at the time.

By this time next year, things could—would—be a lot different. He had to remember that, keep his eye on that future point in time. No letting self-doubt step in, or doubt from others stepping in, and no chickening out of his plans. He chuckled at the pun that popped into his mind, then stood and blew out a tired breath. 'Time for an early night, I think. Have to let the painters in bright and early tomorrow.'

'Sleep well. I'm gonna chill with some TV for a while, I'll keep the volume low.'

'No worries, I think I'll be out like a light in two seconds flat.'

And he was. He'd had a few restless nights since Sunday, thinking of the launch, and of Hannah, and needed to catch up on sleep.

'Night, Scar,' Hannah said, patting her dog and closing the laundry door. She plugged in her phone to charge and flopped into bed. She really needed a good night sleep, having not had one for the last few nights, and her body was feeling the groggy effects.

Before turning out the light she took one last look at her phone, and at the gold star emoji she'd sent Luca. Her finger hovered over the text window.

He'd said if I wanted to talk he'd be all ears...

She pressed the letter H and then I, but then deleted it.

But he'd also said let's move forward...

There were thoughts and feelings inside that she needed to express, but didn't know how. And didn't want to rock the boat. The kiss they'd shared felt complete and yet unfinished all at the same time. He'd said he didn't regret the kiss, but that was the only insight she had into his feelings about it. He could have just meant that he enjoyed the physical pleasure of it... but that didn't mean that it meant anything more to him.

It meant more to me, she thought. *So, so much more...*

She put the phone back on her bedside table and switched off the lamp, before she allowed her unexpressed thoughts and feelings to get carried away... again.

CHAPTER SEVENTEEN

The following Thursday arrived, and Hannah had barely stopped to catch her breath. She shook her head as she got in the car, disbelieving of the fact a week had passed by already.

'Oh!' She got out and dashed back inside, grabbing the photo frame from the island bench and getting back in the car.

As she drove towards town, she used the time to process the progress. Luca was on schedule, his logo was done, the finishing touches of the kitchen had been done on Monday, and the painting had been completed Tuesday. She had scheduled all the next tasks into her calendar, fitting everything in around the chooks, markets, and sorting and packing. The latter was taking the longest, as each time she'd go through a box or a drawer, something would trigger her memory and the next thing she'd be texting her mum... 'remember when this happened?', and 'hey, check out this old photo I found!', and 'what on earth do I do with this?'. She wouldn't have as much space in Karen's house, and had to simplify. She even downloaded an eBook on it to help with some ideas and motivation. Problem was, so many things held sentimental value to her, and so many things were useful... so how could she get rid of them?

Anyway, she had made progress. More boxes were packed and ready to move to Karen's, and more bags of donations delivered.

Hannah returned her thoughts to the present moment as a gush of cold air awakened her senses when she stepped out of the car. She crossed the road and pushed open the door, which now had a temporary computer-printed sign on it saying 'HOME—new restaurant opening July 22!' It had Luca's phone number for any enquiries.

The smell of fresh paint awakened her senses further, but then something different... garlic? Onions? And was that... thyme?

She wandered towards the kitchen and entered. Steam rose gently from a pot, and Luca stood there ladling something into a bowl.

'Ah, perfect timing!' he said. 'I know I wasn't going to experiment with the menu until next week, but I couldn't resist these shiny new appliances calling out to me... "Luca... Luca... We need you!"' He spoke in a high-pitched voice.

Hannah chuckled. 'You're hearing things? Should see someone about that.'

'It's okay, the voices have stopped now that I've given the kitchen its initiation. Here.' He held out a small bowl. 'Try some.'

The scents intensified, and with added sweetness. 'Pumpkin?' she asked.

He shook his head. 'Sweet potato. A little cauliflower, garlic, onion, turmeric, and some of the best local...'

'Thyme,' she said. Luca had collected some from her yesterday at the markets.

He dipped the spoon into the soup and lifted it to her lips. She parted them slightly and let him slide the warm liquid into her mouth.

Heavenly...

'Good?'

She nodded. 'Mm-hm.' She opened her mouth again for another sampling, as Luca laughed.

'My first happy customer.' He gave her the bowl and spoon so she could continue, then ladled some soup into a plastic container. 'Take this over to your parents for me? Would love their opinion.'

'Sure. Thanks, they would love that.'

Hannah finished her soup as Luca turned off the stove and gave her a tour of the kitchen.

'Oh,' she said, retrieving something from her bag. 'Almost forgot.'

She handed him the photo frame.

His eyes brightened and he held the frame up high. 'The view from upstairs!'

'Yep.' She smiled. 'Consider it a kitchen-warming present. Now, when you're hard at work, you can still look up occasionally at the view.'

He took his eyes off the picture to look at her. 'Thank you, Hannah. Wow, you really do think of everything.'

She shrugged with a smile. 'Just a little something. The finer details can make all the difference, and with all this stainless steel and man-made shiny stuff in here, I thought it could do with some outdoor inspiration.'

Luca held it up in a few different spots on the wall. 'Here,' he said, choosing a spot on the far wall, above a power point. 'I'll see it every time I walk into the kitchen, and every time I turn off the appliances on this side.

'Oh,' Hannah said a second time. 'I also have this, if it helps. Or do you want to wait till the paint has settled a bit more?' She held up an adhesive picture hanging hook.

Luca laughed. 'No time like the present.' He accepted the hook and stuck it to the wall. 'Perfect.' He glanced at her. 'Do you also have the furniture in there?' He gestured to her handbag.

She tipped her head back with a laugh. 'No, unfortunately, but it's arriving shortly, and I do have... let's see...' she rummaged through her bag, 'a nail file?' she said as she pulled it out. 'And a... measuring tape?'

'Well that could come in handy. I keep losing mine.'

She placed it on the countertop. 'Take this, I have another in the car.'

He nodded a thanks and they left the kitchen when a knock sounded on the door.

Two bulky men stood there. 'Delivery for Luca Antonescu?'

'That's me,' he said, signing the electronic device.

'We'll bring it all in,' he said with a quick smile. 'Just let us know where you want it all.'

They helped the delivery men for the next thirty minutes or so, bringing in the tables and chairs, and a few other pieces.

'How exciting,' Hannah whispered to Luca, as his eyes scanned the premises with eagerness.

'I know, right?' he said back, as though he'd just had a delivery of a year's supply of his favourite potato chips.

It reminded Hannah in a way of the excitement of decorating the old doll's house she had as a kid which her dad had built, and which she'd found on the weekend hidden away all dusty in the shed. Except this was real, and life-size. And it wasn't hers, but still there was excitement, for the fun in setting things up, and for him, knowing how fun it would feel for him.

By the end of the day they had all the tables in their places, as well as the reception counter, and a rough seating plan drawn out which Hannah would do up properly on the computer later and print out, for staff to learn the location of all the table numbers and for reservation planning.

'Looks so full now, yet so empty,' Luca said.

'It will be full of people soon enough,' Hannah said. She glanced up the stairs. 'I think for the opening night, let's do pre-dinner drinks and hors d'oeuvres upstairs, people can mingle and you can give a speech...'

'I have to give a speech?'

'Yep. And everyone can take in the view at sunset, with the warmth from the fire pit, and then make their way downstairs for the main meal and dessert at the tables.'

'I guess I can whip up a speech.' He shrugged. 'Or do you write that for me too?'

'No,' she chuckled. 'You're not the prime minister.'

'Okay, I'll just have to come up with something. And yes that does sound like a good idea. Let's say five pm start for a six thirty dinner.'

'Sounds good. We'll start organising the flyers and the social media campaign shortly, so we can take advance bookings. You'll need to come up with a price per ticket though if you want a set menu?'

'Set menu would be best for the launch I think, easier to prepare and arrange pre-paid tickets.'

'So, you have your launch menu to design, and your ongoing à la carte menu.'

'Correct.'

'Let's get cracking.' She rubbed her hands together and they sat at one of the tables, discussing his ideas for both menus, and working out ingredients lists, and as day became evening, Luca served up some of his soup along with crusty bread he'd grabbed from the nearby bakery.

'I better get home!' Hannah said, standing. 'Looks like we did a bit of overtime.'

'And I'll have to pay you accordingly,' he said.

She gave a flick of her hand. 'Consider this free dinner your overtime payment.'

'Oh, don't forget the soup for your parents.'

'Oh yes.' They went to the kitchen and she took the container from the fridge. 'It was delicious, thank you.'

'Thank you for all your help, it's looking much more like a restaurant now.' He smiled, glancing around. 'Wish my parents could see this,' he spoke softly.

Hannah lightly touched the side of his arm. 'Maybe they can. Somehow.'

She connected with his eyes, and they held a mixture of sadness from his grief and satisfaction from what he was accomplishing.

'Maybe they can,' he said. 'Anyway, won't keep you any longer. Thanks again and I'll see you tomorrow to work on the...' he got out his phone and checked the schedule, 'interior decorating, hanging artwork etcetera, and oh, delivery of all the cutlery and utensils is due. And advertise for staff.'

Hannah smiled. 'By this time tomorrow it'll look even more like a restaurant. And more like home.'

'I feel at home already.'

Hannah smiled wider. *Me too*, she thought. *Me too*.

Although she was tired after getting home and tending to the animals, Hannah was still filled with inspiration. If she hadn't become a chicken farmer and an events manager she probably would have gone into interior decorating. It was one of her favourite parts of the job, setting up the visual space to create a theme and a feeling. Making it inviting and enticing.

She put on a jacket and boots and went outside with a torch to the shed.

There it sat, in the corner, dusty and forgotten, until now.

She wiped away some of the dust from the roof of the doll's house, then shone the torch inside. Wrapping paper she'd stuck on the walls for wallpaper peeled at the edges, and some of the furniture had fallen over, along with the dolls. She opened the doors that formed the front of the house and a tender emotion swam up from deep inside her. Happiness at the memories? No, it had a hint of rawness. Nostalgia? It was both, but also loss, strangely enough. She hadn't lost anything, yet that's what it felt like. Lost opportunity? She'd always loved the idea of passing this onto her own daughter one day, if she had one. Or a boy, it didn't matter, as long as the child could get the same joy from it as she had.

She picked up one of the dolls, a girl, and at the touch of her soft woollen dress and the musty scent, Hannah's eyes became moist.

'Jasmine,' she whispered. She smiled on remembering naming the doll after the scent of jasmine in her street. She would pretend Jasmine was her little sister, and they'd play together in the house, hiding little things secretly around the doll's house from the doll brother. She would make the boy's arms extend out to the side, as if to say 'Where is my toy car?' or 'Where has my favourite book gone?' And then Jasmine and Hannah would giggle together.

She held the doll to her chest and a few tears rolled down her cheek. Her first thought on seeing the doll's house the other day was to donate it, but her dad had made it, and had probably assumed she'd pass it onto her own children, and so on. Even if she never got to have a child, she couldn't get rid of it. She just couldn't. But she couldn't keep it here and couldn't bring it to Karen's.

Hannah picked up the house and took it to the car, then she went inside and retrieved the soup from the fridge, before texting her mum:

> Just dropping a couple of things over if that's ok. Won't take long.

Her mother replied, saying *sure*, and she got in the car and drove off, window open as her nose searched for the scent of jasmine. When spring would arrive and the scent would intensify, she wouldn't be here. Maybe she should consider growing some indoor star jasmine at Karen's.

When she arrived at Wattle Lane and her mother greeted her at the door, mentioning that her father was in the shower, Hannah burst unexpectedly into tears.

'Oh, sweetheart, what's wrong?' Her mother hugged her, then held her at arm's reach and studied her face as though it would reveal the answer to her question.

'Nothing, nothing at all.' She sniffed. 'Probably just hormonal.' She held out the soup. 'Here, compliments of the chef.'

'Oh, lovely.' She took the soup and placed it on the kitchen counter, but Hannah stayed at the open door. 'Come on in and let's chat.'

'There's something else I have to bring in.' She gestured to the car. 'Be back in a sec.' She wiped her eyes and went back to the car, lifting out the doll's house and carrying it inside.

Kathleen Delaney covered her mouth with her hand, then helped Hannah place it on the dining table. 'Oh my, I'd forgotten about this!'

'Me too.'

'I remember asking you as a child if you wanted a house like this when you were all grown up, but you said, "No, Mum, I want a house just like the one we're inside right now!" pointing to the ceiling of Iona.'

Hannah nodded and smiled. 'Well, I got to have the house for many years.'

'You don't want to keep it?' Kathleen opened the front of the doll's house. 'The doll's house, I mean.'

Hannah shifted from one foot to the other, and scratched her temple. 'Yes, but I can't really bring it to Karen's, there's not much space. And besides, a grown woman with a doll's house in her bedroom?' She raised her eyebrows.

'So? Your father is a grown man with a train set in the spare room.'

'True, but this is different. And anyway, I always thought...' the words got stuck in a lump in her throat.

'That you'd give it to a child of your own, yes, I know, dear.'

Her mother knew her too well. And Hannah knew her mother too well, knowing that sometimes she didn't have to complete a difficult sentence, as her mum would do it for her. She also knew that her mother had tried unsuccessfully to have more children after Hannah, but wasn't able to. Hannah still had time, but who knew how much, and if she was even capable of it. Her last check-up said all her hormones were fine so there shouldn't be an issue in that regard, but there were other issues that could affect fertility, and she hoped she wasn't one of the unlucky ones.

'It doesn't look like that is happening any time soon.' Hannah sighed. 'So, can I keep it here for now? Otherwise, we could donate it. I know Dad made it and all, but... maybe someone else could put it to good use.'

'Nonsense. I'm keeping it right here, thank you very much.' Kathleen went to carry it into the spare room, narrowly missing a collision with Doug as he came out of the bathroom.

'Whoa. Is that what I think it is?' He ruffled what was left of his wet hair.

'Yep. Keeping it here for now.' She went past him into the room and placed it down. 'Looks like I've still got a few muscles on me.' She lifted her biceps and gave them a squeeze.

'You've had an active life, Mum, of course you do.'

'Would you like me to clean it up a bit? The doll's house?' her father asked.

'Umm.'

'I'll make it my Sunday project.'

'Love, you already have about seven Sunday projects.'

'So make it eight.' He gave a nod. 'I'll remove the wallpaper, give it clean, sand down and re-oil the exterior...'

'Dad, thanks, but would you mind leaving the interior as it is? Just a dusting is fine, and the exterior. Maybe one day I'll have a go at redecorating.' She smiled. But in reality, she mostly just didn't want her memories to be gone. Didn't want it looking different. Not yet. She was saying goodbye to a lot of things but this one she wasn't ready for.

'You sure? I can make it all modern and fancy, maybe add a disco ball too...' He made a twirling movement with his finger.

'Doug, just the exterior. Thanks, love.' Kathleen patted his arm.

'Rightio. I'll, ah, just go get changed.' He went off to the bedroom.

'Thanks, Mum.'

She gave her mum a quick hug.

'Some things take time, don't they. In the letting go, or even in the receiving. You just have to trust in the unknown big picture of life sometimes, see how it all unfolds.'

'Yep, I know.'

Kathleen turned to the kitchen counter. 'Pumpkin soup?'

'Sweet potato. Among other things. Oh, and keep July 22 free from five pm. Luca's restaurant launch. I'll get you one of the best tables.'

Kathleen whacked her hands together. 'Oh, yippee! Can't wait. Haven't eaten anywhere new in this town in forever. How's it going?'

'All on track. Busy, but good.'

'Well make sure you get enough sleep. Do you want some tea while you're here? An episode of some comfort television perhaps... *Bewitched? I Dream of Jeannie?*' She gestured to the couch where they had sat for the family history slideshow.

It did sound comforting. But what she really wanted was to get home to her bed. 'I'll pass tonight, but thanks. Been a long day.'

Her dad came back out in his pyjamas and dressing gown and slippers. 'Did someone say *Bewitched?* That show never gets old. And Ms Montgomery, can't go past a classic beauty like her.'

'Oh, Doug.' Kathleen shook her head. 'What about this classic right here?' She gestured with her hands down the length of her body.

'You can bewitch me any time, my dear.' Doug approached and gave her a kiss, then switched on the kettle.

'Oh, all right. Maybe one episode,' Hannah said. 'Half an hour, then I'll be off.'

She sat on the corner of the couch with her feet tucked up underneath her, and pulled the throw blanket around her. It was comfortable, and homely, and she wouldn't get as many opportunities like this after she moved.

When the opening music played, she smiled and allowed herself to drift into nostalgic euphoria as she realised once again how lucky she was. And at the end, she found herself wondering what Luca was doing right now, and what he was feeling. She wanted to help him bring as much of these comforting feelings into his restaurant as she could. She would make this launch the best one she'd ever done, and would give nothing less than one-hundred per cent.

CHAPTER EIGHTEEN

On Sunday afternoon, after spending the night at Stefan's in Sydney and the day at their mother's house sorting through more of her belongings, Luca grabbed a takeaway mocha from Café Lagoon.

'Enjoy, mate,' said Jonah, the friendly and competent barista.

'I'm sure I will.' Luca smiled, then put his hand in his pocket where he'd put a few stray coins he'd found at his mother's house. 'Here,' he said dropping them into the container at the counter. 'Have a tip. It's not much but you deserve it.'

Jonah eyed the container. 'Awesome, thanks, man. Every bit counts, that's for sure. Especially now I'm saving for my next overseas trip.'

'Oh yeah? Where and when?'

'The when will be decided once I have enough funds, and then I might get some work overseas for a year or so, see how it goes. I did it once before. As for the where... I'd like to go back to Europe, that was great. But I'd also love to see America. I reckon I could bring some great Australian coffee their way.' He grinned.

'Hope you get to go asap,' he replied. 'And if you happen to visit Romania, send me a postcard.' He winked.

'Oh, do you have relatives there?'

'Yep.'

'Then you'll have to let me know where I can find them and I'll personally bring some great coffee over to them.' He gave a nod.

'Ha, they will love that. My aunt will fill your stomach with her fabulous *gogosi*.'

Jonah raised his eyebrows. 'No idea what that is but I already want some.'

'It's a little bit like a doughnut. Without a hole. But extra special, and nothing beats homemade.'

'Romanian doughnuts? I'm sold.' He patted his stomach.

Luca was filled with a craving for one right now. He made a mental note to add his aunt's *gogosi* recipe to the dessert menu. 'And if you don't end up over there, I might be able to satisfy your cravings just a few hundred metres up the road.' He pointed towards Home.

'Ooh, yes please. When do you open?'

'Sunday July 22, our launch starts at five pm with dinner at six thirty. We'll be selling tickets soon.'

'Put me down for one. I can get off work by five on a Sunday, I'll get one of our casuals to do the evening shift.'

'Great. I'll let you know when the bookings are open. Organise a table with friends or family if you like. There's plenty of room.'

'I look forward to it. Have a good one.' He waved, as Luca walked off.

So, with Jonah, Hannah and her parents, and Stefan, that would be five people at least, he thought with a chuckle. He hoped the launch would be all booked out, or eighty per cent full at least. He was glad to have Hannah and her rapport with the locals on his side.

He wandered across the road, through Miracle Park and past the Wishing Fountain, finished his mocha and tossed the cup into a bin. Then walked down the adjacent street where the terrace shops were. Some were closing up, but a few remained open.

Homewares, tourist souvenirs, gift items, candles...

Candles. Hmm.

He walked into a shop called April's Glow, recalling Hannah's suggestion of having jasmine-scented reed sticks and candles in the restaurant. It wasn't a huge priority yet, as they would do the finishing touches in week six, but... there was no time like the present.

And speaking of present...

He wanted to get one for Hannah. Not only as a small token of appreciation for her work, but as a farewell gift, and a new house-warming gift for when she moved to Sydney. Something to hopefully remember him by, and also the town. And as she'd lived on Jasmine Road her whole life, he figured the jasmine scent meant something to her. Reminded her of home.

'Hi there, how's your weekend been?' the pretty, smiling woman behind the counter asked.

'It's been busy, that's for sure. But great. How's yours?'

'Oh, same as usual. But great. Day off tomorrow though, can't wait to flop on the couch and binge-watch something on Netflix.'

'Sounds good.'

'You happy to browse or can I help you find something in particular?' Her hands spoke as much as her voice, and his eyes were drawn to a tattooed ring on her left ring finger.

He'd sometimes check women's fingers for wedding or

engagement rings, out of habit, but he'd never seen a tattooed one before.

'I hope someone else has a matching one?' he asked, pointing to the tattoo.

'He sure does. I love jewellery, but the tats were cheaper. And we figured it was more unique, more... us.'

'I think it's great.' He smiled. And now he could rule her out as a potential date in future. He looked up at shelves. 'Jasmine.'

'Jasmine? No, I'm April,' she said.

He looked back at her. 'Oh, no, I mean I'm looking for jasmine candles. Sorry! Hi April.' He held out his hand and she shook it. 'I'm Luca.'

'Oops, hi Luca. And I should have realised.' She shook her head. 'I always say the first thing that pops into my head.' She grinned, and he grinned back.

'Sometimes I do that too.'

April came out from behind the counter and showed him to the corner shelf where some soft, white coloured candles in various jars and tins and containers sat around a vase of jasmine flowers, fake, but realistic looking.

'Oh, I should have noticed them. A bit obvious.'

'Not at all, you'd be surprised how many men come in here and have no idea what jasmine looks like, or other flowers for that matter.'

'My parents loved their garden, so I've learned to recognise many.'

'Wonderful. Well it's nice to have a customer who knows what they want. I've had a few... *interesting* male customers who've turned up and said things like, "Give me something that smells good," or "What's something a chick will like?"' She shook her head.

'Charming.'

'Indeed. So, how many were you after and what size?'

'Actually, just one or two for right now. But I wanted to order in quite a few, if I could?'

April's eyes widened with eagerness. 'Absolutely! Orders only take a couple of days usually, depending on the item.'

'I'll start with thirty small ones, and I think… two medium ones, and two large ones… of these.' He pointed to the ones in the embossed glass jars that reminded him of his father's old-fashioned Scotch glasses.

'Wow. Okay, sure. And vintage style, nice choice.' She grinned again. 'Large house?'

'It's for my new restaurant, Home. Up near the harbour where the beauty salon used to be.'

'Oh! Fab. Can't wait to check it out!'

'Our launch is Sunday July 22 from five pm, we'll be selling tickets soon.'

'I'll be there. And I'll bring my tattooed other.'

'Great! I'll let you know the details asap.'

Make that seven people now. Hannah would be proud of the networking he was doing… maybe he should just go into each store in town, buy something, and casually mention the launch, like he'd just done without even thinking about it.

'And which would you like for today?' She held her hand towards the display.

Luca scanned them again. He didn't want to get the same ones as the restaurant, something that was purely for Hannah. 'This one here, please.'

April picked up the triple-wicked frosted glass candle with silver lid embossed with a twirling vine pattern. 'It's a lovely one.'

'And a jar of the reed sticks too, please.'

Hannah had suggested reed sticks for the reception counter. He hoped it wouldn't be overkill and that his restaurant wouldn't reek too much of jasmine and cause everyone to hold their nose or run for the door.

'Not a problem.' She took the items to the counter and he made payment, as well as a deposit for the large candle order. 'I'll give you a call when they're in. And here's my card if you need anything else.' She handed it over with a smile, followed by a gift bag with the store's logo on it containing the items.

'Thanks.'

'Thank you for supporting a local business. And all the best with yours!'

'My pleasure, and thanks again.'

Luca walked out with a smile. This new beginning would be good. Things were moving forward, he was meeting the locals, and hopefully soon, people would be leaving his premises with a smile on their face, and on his too.

But one thought struck him... when it came time for Hannah to leave, he couldn't help but imagine that his smile would only last until she was out of sight. If he could have everything his way, he wouldn't want to watch her walking out, he'd want to see her, a smile on her face, walking in. Over and over again.

CHAPTER NINETEEN

'You sure you want me to help you interview candidates?' Hannah asked, as Luca welcomed her into the kitchen on Tuesday for some menu practice, wearing a black apron over his clothes.

'Yes, I interviewed three for chef positions yesterday, and another two coming this afternoon plus two for wait staff. The online ad has got a lot of hits so far.' He laid out some ingredients.

'Great stuff. How did the first three go, do you think they fit the bill?'

'Not sure yet. One I could put on as casual, the other two have a fair bit of experience, but I'm also looking for someone with at least a decade of experience and good references to take over my role on the nights I'm not here. Which won't be many, but I will need the occasional day off.'

'You will. Don't burn yourself out.'

'I won't, I've spent too many years doing that. Things might be a bit crazy at first, but hopefully once things are settled here I'll be able to get into a good routine that works for me, and spend some quality time with those chickens.' He smiled.

'Yes, very important.'

'Anyway, next interview is at three, so if you're happy to hang around, would love to get a second opinion, someone to discuss the options with.' He raised his eyebrows.

'Sure. It'll be interesting. But ultimately, you have to choose who feels right to you.'

'I know. I just hope I get some stayers. Finding staff when a restaurant is already open and busy is an extra time pressure, so I'd love to get it right first go, at least to kick things off for the near future.'

'Once they see what a great place it is to work, people will be lining up to work here.' She gave a confident smile. 'And what are we taste testing today?' She leaned towards the oven, and a folder with pages of notes and recipes on the benchtop next to the ingredients.

'Capsicum *cassolette*, with chicken. I've finished roasting the capsicums and need to peel the skin off soon.' He gestured to the cling-wrap covered bowl with the steaming red peppers in it. 'And I'm about to prepare the *cassolette*.' He rapidly chopped two red onions, minced three garlic cloves, and added them along with some olive oil to a saucepan. 'Would you like to add the thyme?' he asked.

'Yes. That I can do.' She picked up one thyme sprig and ran her thumb and forefinger down the stem, releasing the leaves into the pan. She repeated it with the remaining two, then Luca gave the pan a stir. 'Are you going to make me peel the capsicums though? I've never done that before.'

'In that case, yes.' He grinned. He slid the bowl towards her and took off the plastic wrap. 'These should be ready. See how the skin has lifted?'

She nodded.

He took one and pinched the corner of the skin, peeling it downwards. 'Ah, so rewarding, feel that baby slide right off.'

'Let me try.' Hannah took another and followed his movements. The first part slid off easily, the second got a bit stuck. 'Hmm.' She picked at it, and Luca gave the pan another stir.

'Be gentle with it. Some parts will naturally peel more easily than others. Just glide it with even pressure and don't yank it off.'

'Yes, Chef.'

She continued, and soon all three capsicums were as naked as a baby's (red) bum.

Luca scooped out the seeds in a flash, and handed her the vegetable to slice into thin strips.

'All set. Now here are some tomatoes I prepared earlier.' He slid over a bowl.

'You sound like you're on a cooking show.'

He chuckled. 'I doubt I'll end up doing that. But cooking classes I could do, maybe some workshops of various kinds?'

'I think that would be great. I had envisioned different themed nights too, for guests to dine, but you could do something similar with cooking workshops.'

'Yeah,' he said, stirring the onions in the pan. 'Like one for soups, one for desserts, one for egg recipes, for example.'

'Definitely. And each person can not only watch you do your thing, but help with the recipe, and then everyone gets to eat what's been made and maybe take some samples home.'

'*Home* Cooking 101!'

'Yes!'

Without thinking she held up her hand and he high-fived it. They hadn't done that since before their kiss.

'Okay, let's add all the red things to the pan now.' He picked up the bowl of diced tomatoes, and she picked up the sliced capsicums.

'Red things... is that official kitchen terminology?'

'It is in my kitchen.' He smirked.

She added her contribution and he stirred the pan, then reduced the heat to low.

'While this simmers for about twenty minutes, we'll do the chicken.'

He browned the boned pieces for a couple of minutes each side, then placed them into the oven. 'And both should be ready around the same time. Voila!'

'And that's it?'

'I'll season it to taste and add some Cajun spice. Garnish with fresh herbs and *then*, voila!'

Hannah licked her lips. 'This is the best job in the world.'

'Ha-ha, hungry, eh?'

'Just a bit. I wasn't before, but now I am. How did you do that?'

'Magic.' He clicked his fingers.

Hannah remembered something. She ducked her head out of the kitchen doorway. 'Did I smell something else enticing when I walked in?'

'Ahh, you noticed?'

She went to the reception counter. 'Jasmine,' she said.

'Indeed. You like?'

She turned to look at him. 'I love.' She twiddled the reed sticks for a moment and lifted her fingers to her nose. The scent brought her back home instantly. 'Oops, I should have washed my hands first. Sorry, Chef. Now it might smell like capsicum and thyme.' She flashed an apologetic smile.

'Nah, it's okay. Jasmine will outdo it.' His head disappeared behind the kitchen again, followed by the sound of water flowing from the tap.

She noticed the cut-out squares and rectangles of paper stuck loosely but purposefully on the wall rising up alongside the stairs. 'Ah, you're getting ready to hang the frames for the photo wall. Positioning looks great,' she said as he returned and stood beside her, shaking his hands dry.

'Yes, I followed your suggestion. Now I can see how it'll look *before* I hang up the picture hooks.'

They walked around the premises and discussed a few more things, and soon enough the meal was ready.

'Shall we take it upstairs today?' he asked, spooning the *cassolette* into bowls and topping each with chicken and herbs.

'A table with a view?'

'Best in the house. I mean Home.' He smiled, and they each carried their lunch up to a table beside the glass doors opening onto the deck, and the magnificent view that graced a small part of his kitchen thanks to the magic of modern printing.

Hannah checked her watch. 'Ah, plenty of time before your next interviewee arrives.'

'Yep, so let's sit back and stuff our faces and enjoy this view and some peace and quiet.' He got comfortable in the chair.

'Does that mean I have to be quiet? And peaceful?'

'Nah, you can talk as much as you want. Listening to you is still quiet and peaceful. But no business for a little while, how about that? A proper lunchbreak.'

'Deal,' she said, digging into the moist chicken resting atop the *cassolette*. 'Mmm, another winner. Seriously,' she said as she gulped down her mouthful, 'you don't even need to practise, you know perfectly well what you're doing, Mr Antonescu.' She offered him a curious gaze.

He shrugged. 'But one can never get too much practise.'

'Especially when it comes to practising the eating part.' She covered her smiling mouth a little as she ate and spoke at the same time.

'Well there is that.' He smiled and ate another mouthful. 'And feel free to take some more to your parents for me.'

'Really? Thanks, Luca, I think you are their new favourite person. They practically have their own personal chef.'

'It's nothing, really. There's nothing I love more than making people's bellies satisfied.'

'I can see that.' She patted her own, and he held his hand to his chest and bowed as if greatly rewarded by her satisfaction.

'If you weren't a chef, what would you do?' she asked him. 'Hypothetically.'

'Hmm, maybe a gardener. Nathan's job is pretty interesting to me,' he said.

'Ah yeah, he is good at it,' she said, then quickly changed the subject. 'I would have been an interior decorator, I think. But I get to do a bit of it anyway in events management.'

'You'd be great. I mean, you are great. But what else, apart from that, what other skills have you developed over the years that I'm yet to be made aware of, HD?'

She realised that was the first time he'd called her HD since their kiss also. Maybe the tension between them was softening somewhat and they were almost back to being old friends.

She breathed deeply and sighed an uncertain sigh. 'I'm not sure. What do you think?'

'Maybe a gardener too?'

'I kinda do some of that already. But hmmm, what about... a vet?'

'Oh yes, a vet. Perfect for you.'

'Oh, but I'd get way too sad.' She pouted. 'It'd be nice to see animals get better, but to see animals suffering... that would be so hard for me.'

'Yeah, me too. Okay, a big no to the vet career then.'

'Agreed.'

'Dog walker?'

'Possibly.'

'You'd also be good with kids, I bet. How about day care, or early childhood teaching?'

Hannah's heart fluttered. She gave a slow nod. 'Now that would be rewarding actually.' If she couldn't have her own, she could help contribute to the lives of others.

She changed the subject again. 'While we're talking hypotheticals... let's see... another question.' She tapped her spoon against her lips. 'If you had to... choose between having a million dollars upfront in a lump sum, or one-hundred thousand dollars given to you once a year for ten years, which would you choose?'

Luca swallowed his mouthful then said, 'Lump sum for sure. Pay all bills and loan, then invest the rest and let the interest pay me each year. At least, that's what I think my brother would recommend.'

'It would be good. Though I kind of like the idea of having the one-hundred K regularly, to take the pressure of living expenses and allow me to have freedom to do whatever I want for a while. I'd invest also, but I'd worry that with a lump sum I wouldn't have the willpower not to overuse it.'

'Hannah Delaney with no willpower? I don't believe that. You're the strongest, most disciplined person I know.'

She shrugged. 'Guess I am disciplined, but maybe part of me sometimes doesn't *want* to be. Maybe I want to know what it's like to be undisciplined for a while. Unplanned. I dunno.'

Luca eyed her for a moment. 'You need a holiday,' he said. 'A change of scenery. When was the last time you took a holiday? Like, overseas?'

'Never been overseas.'

'No? Oh man, you have to change that sometime. Make a promise to me you'll go overseas sometime, finances permitting, within the next...'

'Ten years?'

'Um, no. Two years. That gives you enough time to settle in Sydney, earn some dough, and make some plans. Deal?'

'Umm.' She shifted in her seat. 'It's a big thing to agree to, and to plan. And if I'm going to live in Sydney I should keep working towards having my own place, and you know how shocking the prices are there.'

'Two years,' he repeated. 'Promise me.'

She hesitated.

'And if you haven't planned anything by eighteen-months' time, I'll do it for you and I'll take you there myself. Deal?'

'You would come with me, overseas? Just so I can have a change of scenery and get out of my predictable routine?'

He nodded. 'I promise. So if you don't want me tagging along, organise something within eighteen months, or I'm coming with you. And I could either be a great help or a pain in the arse, who knows.' He held out his hand.

She squirmed a little, then slowly, slowly reached out her hand.

He tapped it twice, tugged down on her thumb and they did the handshake.

'If definitely definite now. We've done the handshake. Can't go back on a special handshake deal.'

'Guess not,' she said, her stomach doing a little somersault. He may have satisfied her belly, but he had also given her belly butterflies. Just like she used to get around him, all those years ago.

With three and a half weeks to go, she didn't know how many more butterflies she could take.

CHAPTER TWENTY

Luca studied the woman sitting across from him. Black hair pulled tautly back into a bun like a ballet dancer, eyes focused and unblinking, hands calmly folded in her lap. First impressions told him she would be an efficient worker, ambitious, but cool under pressure.

'Six years at the one restaurant... and why are you keen to change?' he asked, pen poised to paper, and Hannah mirroring him.

'We all need a change sometimes. I'm satisfied working at the Vietnamese restaurant, but keen for more variety, in food and working environment. I understand you'll be serving a variety of dishes from different cultures?'

'Correct.' He felt like he had to speak more formally, being the interviewer. Though the un-formal Luca would probably say, 'Yup.'

'I like that.' She smiled.

Luca returned the smile. 'And as you live a good two hours away, are you prepared to travel or move closer if given a full-time job?'

She nodded with enthusiasm, like one of those bobbing

head dolls often seen in the back window of a car. 'The Northern Beaches are nice, but every time I've visited Tarrin's Bay I've felt so... welcomed. Comfortable. At home.'

Luca nodded.

'And would you be moving a family down with you?'

'No, just me. I've recently gone through a divorce.' Her fingers intertwined on her lap.

Ah, looking for a fresh start. A new beginning. And as he knew, Tarrin's Bay was the place to go for one of those.

'Lea, can I ask,' Hannah said. 'What is your favourite ingredient?'

Luca held back a grin. He was focused on the business and career questions, the logistics, the likelihood of hiring a stayer, and she was curious about favourite foods.

Lea smiled and her hands relaxed. 'Garlic.'

Oh. Nice work, Hannah. She was probably just lightening the mood. Must be a woman's intuition or something.

'I know it gets a reputation for causing bad breath, but to be honest I'd rather enjoy it and face the consequences.' She gave a small chuckle. 'It's such an important ingredient in so many dishes... without garlic, so many meals simply don't work.'

Hannah nodded, and Luca added, 'True.' He then asked, 'Lastly, what does "home" mean to you?'

Lea glanced upwards, her lips twisting to one side. 'It means... feeling somehow... *right,* wherever you are.'

Luca jotted down a few notes. 'Thank you, Lea, pleasure talking with you. Thanks for coming in.' He stood.

'Pleasure. Thank you for your time and the opportunity.' She held out her hand. For a moment he wondered whether to try the handshake on her too, as an added component of the assessment criteria, to suss out how well they'd work together with his playfulness. But he resisted, for now.

She left and he turned to face Hannah.

'You wanted to show her the handshake, didn't you?' Hannah grinned.

He shrugged. 'Maybe.'

'Definitely.'

'Maybe definitely.'

'Definitely definitely.' She laughed. 'Well whoever you choose to work here will eventually find out, but I think you'll have to come up with a new, special Home handshake.'

'Yes, good idea. I should keep ours just for us.' He didn't want to downplay the sentimentality of their special greeting. 'So, score out of ten?'

'Hmm. Nine. She was pretty good.'

'Agreed.' He nodded. 'Let's see how contestant number two fares,' he said, as the next subject wandered in.

And when the interviews were over for the day, they had a nine, an eight, a ten (instantly hired as waiter), and... a four (probably not hired as waiter).

At just before five, after Hannah had left, he received a call. He didn't recognise the number.

Might be another job applicant.

'Luca, hi. It's April from April's Glow. Your thirty candles have arrived nice and early.' Even her voice smiled.

'Oh, fantastic. I'd forgotten about them.'

'Well you won't be able to forget them once you fill that restaurant with their beautiful fragrance. Would you like me to drop them off at your premises after work if you're there, or would you like to come and get them?'

'I can get them, no problem. I'll be leaving soon anyway. What time do you close?'

'Fifteen minutes, but I'll be here for another hour closing up, so just knock on the door.'

He was there at five.

'You got a bonus,' she said when he walked in. 'My supplier

had a special for those who order more than twenty of the same item. An extra candle. It's not jasmine though, it's vanilla.'

Luca smiled, but more so on the inside. 'Vanilla will be wonderful. I might keep that one at home for myself.'

To remind me of Hannah.

'Great, it's always nice to get an unexpected bonus.' She smiled. 'Well, here we go.' She slid the box on the counter. 'And let me just sort out the remaining balance.' She tapped at the computer register, and gave him the final amount to pay, which he did.

'Tomorrow I'll be setting up the bookings for my restaurant launch,' he said before walking out. 'All going well and there are no technical disasters, it should be live by the end of the day. Home at Tarrin's Bay dot com,' he said.

'Fab! I'll check it out. See you around.'

He smiled and gave a wave, and the door jingled as he exited the shop, leaving behind the delicious scents.

Vanilla.

He could smell it already. He had cravings of vanilla custard, vanilla milkshakes, and vanilla ice cream. He put the box of candles into his car then stopped by the ice-cream shop to buy a vanilla cone. It didn't matter that it was close to dinnertime. He often ate dessert first, it was more satisfying that way; that rush of sugar into the bloodstream, those eager tastebuds soaking up the sweet flavours, and his hungry stomach making plenty of room for more.

He walked through Miracle Park with his ice cream, the sun dying away behind the clouds, and the water of the Wishing Fountain still and serene. He stopped and glanced at his reflection. He chuckled. A grown man looking like a happy child. It was good. He didn't want to get bogged down in the seriousness of adult life all the time, and the consequences of getting older, and family getting older. He wanted to remember what it was like to feel that childlike wonder, to believe anything was possible, and to feel limitless.

When his ice cream was finished, he opened his wallet and took out a two-dollar coin. So it wasn't the official day of the Wishing Festival, but there was no time like the present. He took a breath and tossed the coin into the water. With a plop it sank to the bottom, ripples radiating out from its landing spot to the edges of the fountain, his reflection going wobbly.

Wish made.

He had initially decided on a simple wish for his business, but as the coin was in the air, he suddenly knew what he wanted more. He didn't know if he even believed if it were possible. But in that moment just before the coin descended to its watery new home, he knew he had to wish for it. Even if wishes were a load of rubbish. But if somehow they weren't, well, it was always nice to get an unexpected bonus.

After Hannah fed the chooks and Scarlett, she went through the interview applicants again in her mind. They'd all been great candidates, except the last one. He would need to learn not to infuse every sentence with an array of swear words if he was to impress a potential boss. Luca had been kind to give him a four, for her it was a three.

As she did some basic housework, she found herself scoring all the men she'd dated in her life, giving herself a few laughs.

Samuel was an eight, until he left suddenly and downgraded to a five.

Matthew was a six. Nice enough, though a bit too eager, and simply not the one for her.

Liam had been a perfect ten on the first date, a nine on the second, an eight on the third, gradually working his way down the scale of suitability, until she'd realised at level six it wasn't going to work.

Her phone buzzed.

How's things?

Hannah typed in a quick reply to Karen.

Pretty good, how about you? Just about to make dinner. Actually, make that not-make dinner. I got leftovers, yay!

And by leftovers she meant Luca's chicken *cassolette* from today.

Lucky you! I made eggs on toast.

Yum. You'll have to give me the recipe for that ;)

Ha-ha. So, will we get free eggs when Luca takes over?

Hmm, not sure about that.

And it's definitely still all going ahead?

Yep, contract signed, sealed, delivered.

So excited for you. For us.

Me too.

Hannah smiled. It'd be like the chance she never took at age twenty to move out and live a life of freedom.

So, I started online dating. Tinder, mostly.
Sheesh, most of the men on there so far are
weird!

Hannah had never tried that before. She preferred to meet men the organic way.

In what way?

They either have photos of themselves with
giant fish they've apparently caught, tigers
they've managed to sedate with the power of
their mind and charm, or cover their face with
their phone while taking their profile selfie.

Images flashed in Hannah's mind.

You'll have to send me some screenshots.

A few moments later, a few such pictures appeared.

I vote for the fisherman.

Oh but wait… this is his NEXT picture…

It was a photo of him slouching on a couch, empty beer cans on the coffee table, playing a video game with a lot of mess in the background.

Young at heart?

Or lives in his mother's basement.

Can't judge a book by its cover.

True, but a picture tells a thousand words.

Also true.

She went to the box on the living room floor that had some more photo albums she'd set aside from last weekend, and plucked out the old school one. The Year Ten student group photo brought smiles and giggles to her face. Oh, the hair. The goofy grins. Luca's dark locks dangling over his face, but not obscuring his beautiful smile. The picture was taken at the height of their friendship, when all things seemed possible. His family setting up a restaurant in town... Hannah and Luca growing up together as Tarrin's Bay locals... the possibility of more... Who would have thought that by the end of the year things would change so dramatically, and they would not meet again for twenty years.

Her phone chiming again brought her awareness back to the present.

Check out this charming convo I had with one guy...

She sent screenshots... it started out nice enough, until it rapidly escalated into a raw and direct suggestion—make that a demand—of what he would do with her when he met her. And it wasn't the most appealing scenario.

Yikes. I hope he's one of few.

Actually, more like ninety per cent.

Yikes x 2

Oh well, I'll keep trying. I have no expectations.

No expectations. Hannah had always had expectations, for almost everything... career, house, farm, family, goals... knowing what to expect gave her a sense of security at what was to come. A direction, a purpose, an outcome to work towards. But she'd never expected anything to happen with Luca, not back then, and not now. But she had expected that he would at least still be in town and she'd be able to see him and hang out with him... that was often enough. But now, she still couldn't believe he'd actually kissed her. And her heart, her lips, wanted more of that.

Good plan, my dear. Meet in a public place if you decide to meet any of them in real life.

Will do.

Hannah put the leftovers in the microwave, even though she was sure Luca would insist on heating it up the proper way without radiation. But she was starving, and as soon as the meal was ready the enticing scent brought her back to earlier in the day... she'd enjoyed being there in the kitchen with Luca, the outside world a world away. She could see why cooking appealed to him, it allowed him to be in his own world, away from the grief... gave him a sense of purpose, a satisfying outcome to work towards. Expectations. With cooking, there had to be an expectation, but with one's love life, not so much.

Hannah knew that the only way to avoid a repeat of her heartbreak from the past was to have no expectations with Luca. She'd enjoyed a long-awaited kiss, but that was it. She'd have to carry it in her memory and leave the past behind.

'Hannah, something's wrong,' Luca said into the phone when she answered next morning.

Hannah's body tensed. 'What?'

'My website, it says unavailable.'

Oh. Her tension subsided.

'Let me check, it's probably something simple.' Hannah opened her laptop and went to the domain url. 'Hmm, same message.'

'Bookings go live today! What do I do? Should I have hired a professional web designer?'

'Too late for that, have you asked your brother?'

'Left a message but no reply yet.' Keyboard tapping sounded over the phone. 'It all looks good from my end, but doesn't appear on the internet.'

Hannah's mind ticked over. 'Um, Luca?' she asked. 'You've saved the pages, right?'

'Yup.'

'But have you published the pages?'

'Publish?'

'There might be something to click on to make the pages go live, I had to do that with my previous business website.'

More tapping sounded at the keyboard.

'Um, Hannah?' he said softly.

'Yup.'

'You're much smarter than me.'

'I know,' she said with a grin, loading the webpage and seeing it appear as it should, the welcoming logo for Home displayed along the top banner. 'See... something simple.'

'Sorry to bother you, got a little worried there for a minute.'

'No problem. Good luck with the bookings. I'll share the link now with my network.'

'You have a network?'

'You know, friends, family, industry colleagues.'

'Okay. Cool. Thanks.'

For the next few hours, Hannah's phone buzzed at regular

intervals with a high-five emoji symbol from Luca for every booking that the website had received for the launch, until after a few too many Luca texted:

Guess I'll stop now. But how exciting!

She chuckled.

I understand your excitement. High-five away!

He replied with about ten rows of high-fives, then added:

They aren't really bookings, just got carried away. Okay, NOW I'll stop. Promise.

She replied with a thumbs up.
He replied with a thumbs up.
She replied with two thumbs up.
He replied with three. Then a laughing emoji. Then:

Back to work for both of us, I think.

Agreed.

And she returned to her work with a smile.

CHAPTER TWENTY-ONE

Just over a week later, on Sunday afternoon, after a dusty and emotional day cleaning out the shed and garage, Hannah stepped inside the liquor store and eyed the glossy bottles carefully. She grabbed two bottles of organic locally made champagne.

'Big week ahead?' the young store attendant asked. She didn't know him, as she didn't often drink and when she did, it was usually while out at a restaurant or a function, she never had to buy the alcohol herself.

'And a big one just gone,' she replied. The bookings for the launch were gaining traction, more stock had been delivered for the kitchen, and Luca had hired some staff.

'Can I recommend the organic red too? Filled with antioxidants to get you through the week ahead.' He pointed to his right.

'It's not for me, actually. A gift. Well, two gifts.'

'Ah,' he said with a backwards tip of his head. 'Why not make it three and gift yourself too. I bet you need it. We all need a little stress support from time to time.'

'I'm good,' she said, a little unsure of his overt (though

completely appropriate considering his job) encouragement of using alcohol for stress therapy. She placed the bottles on the counter and retrieved her purse from her shoulder bag. She had seen this particular brand of champagne at a local function and the guests had seemed impressed by it, so she assumed it must be good. It even had an award sticker on it. Karen would love it, and maybe they could pop it open together in celebration on the night she moved in. And hopefully Luca would love it too... a little congratulations gesture for his restaurant. She would give it to him the day before the launch, as she didn't want its impact to be diluted among the crowd on launch night. It would also, she mused, be a sort of... goodbye gesture. Something to remember her by, although it wouldn't last forever, unless he had a champagne bottle collection habit she wasn't aware of.

'Can I interest you in a couple of gift bags to accompany your purchase?' The store attendant magically produced two rectangle paper bags with gift tags, shining and glittering under the lights as he held them up.

Hannah shrugged. 'Why not.'

She paid for her purchase and resisted his attempts to upsell her to a monthly wine club, then returned to her car where she stored the bottles in the boot.

She sat in the driver's seat and couldn't resist texting Karen:

I have a surprise for you!

Her reply came right away:

Oooh, do tell!

Nope. You'll have to wait till I move in.

She replied with a frustrated face emoji.

How's your weekend going?

Not bad. A bit of chatting on Tinder, but it's getting on my nerves.

So why do it?

I'll give it till end of month, if there are no decent catches who can hold a proper conversation by then, I'm giving up.

Okay, well good luck.

She texted back, then put on her seatbelt.

Thanks. Why don't you try it too, then we can swap screenshots and be Tinder support buddies!

Ha-ha. TBH I don't really want to date. I just want to find a partner who'll stick around, and be done with it. Is that unrealistic?

Sorta, you have to date before you find the one you want to be your partner, you know.

Hannah sighed.

I know, but I'm just over the disappointment and uncertainty. And right now I need to stay focused on my own life anyway.

Yes you do. And a great one it is, and will be. A fresh start.

It will. Anyway, gotta go. Have a great rest of the day!

You too!

Karen added a kiss emoji.

Hannah drove down the street alongside the terrace shops, realising she hadn't wandered around the local shops for a while and would have to do it sometime before leaving, as a goodbye gesture to the town. See all the sights again, talk to the shop owners, revisit her memories...

She also realised she was going in the opposite direction to her house. But still she drove, letting her subconscious take her wherever it wanted to go. Somewhere not in her plans. She pulled up alongside the road near the first beach in town, not far from Serendipity Retreat. She got out of the car, the strong breeze greeting her with enthusiasm like a long-lost relative rushing up to embrace her suddenly.

Hannah tightened her button-up sweater around her neck and walked to the sandy shore, her feet tensing above the crumbly terrain to keep her balance. She stopped, arms crossed over her chest, and gazed out at the wide expanse of ocean, dark blue in the distance and bluey-white as it bubbled nearby onto the shore. With a deep breath, she inhaled its effervescent presence.

She walked closer, and had it been spring or summer, she may have rolled up her jeans and waded in the water, but the water would be icy today. But she was filled with an urgency to move, to feel, to be awakened. She looked down the length of beach and started walking, picked up her pace, and sped up into a jog. Her shoulder bag strapped diagonally across her chest bounced up and down but she didn't care, each bounce like a slap on a horse's back from a jockey, urging her forward. She ran, her hair leaping backwards in the wind and her skin feeling alive, her muscles warming up and her smile stretching wide.

She didn't know whether it was exercise she needed, or the

rush of adrenaline, or the intense sensation of the wind against her body as she pushed through it, but whatever it was, it felt good, and she needed it.

When she neared the end of the beach she slowed to a walk, her chest rising and falling rapidly, her lungs squeezing air in and out.

'Holy moly,' she said with an exhalation, bending forward to catch her breath. 'I should do some preparation next time I plan on a spontaneous run.'

She glanced up to make sure no one was around and could hear her talking to herself, and her eyes latched onto a sight not too far in the distance, on the wharf.

A man sat on the edge, fishing rod raised up in the air and the line trailing into the water.

Hannah squinted, and adjusted the bag on her shoulder. *Luca.*

She couldn't turn around, he might see her. Had maybe seen her already, though he was faced at right angles to where she was. She wandered towards the wharf, purposely breathing slower to recoup her normal breathing pattern.

By the time she reached the end of the wharf where he sat, he had turned around.

'Hey there, looking rosy.' He smiled, moving his tackle box aside and gesturing for her to sit.

She flicked her hand. 'Ah, just went for a run.'

'So it appears.'

She sat next to him. 'I might smell all sweaty, just warning you.'

'I might smell like fish. Just warning *you.*'

She pinched her nose and said, 'Eww,' then chuckled. 'Caught anything?'

'Nothing worth keeping.'

For some reason his remark made Hannah think about the

analogy of fish in the sea representing available women... *nothing worth keeping.*

He clearly hadn't found any woman worth keeping either... was that the way he thought about her? A good old friend, but nothing more? So they'd shared a kiss, but that was a spur of the moment thing, it probably didn't mean much—to him, anyway.

'But maybe my luck will turn.'

Was he also thinking of the analogy, or just fish?

'... And get to cook some fish for dinner tonight.'

Oh. Fish.

Hannah cleared her throat. 'Yes. Hopefully.'

'Dad used to take me and my brother fishing. *Male-bonding time*, he'd call it.' Luca reeled in the line and added a new piece of bait, then cast it out to sea. 'Want to help?' He gestured to the handline in the tackle box.

'Sure.' She picked it up and unravelled it, then added half a prawn. 'My dad used to take me too. But it was *father-daughter* bonding time, not *male*.' She smiled.

'That's nice,' he replied. 'When was the last time you went?'

Hannah thought back a while, before her dad's heart attack. 'Geez, I think it's been a good few years.'

'Sometimes we get caught up in life, huh? It can be easy for things to change, but when we look back, it's hard to comprehend how much time has passed.'

Hannah nodded, giving the line a few light tugs to check if any fish had caught on.

'Sorry, fishing makes me nostalgic and sentimental,' he added.

'Nothing to apologise for. It's good to be nostalgic and sentimental on occasion.'

Luca's line became taut. 'Ooh.' He reeled it in, but then it slackened. 'Damn. Lost it.' He added more bait and tried again.

'"Never give up", my dad would say when fishing, when I'd

lose patience. "Give it time. Only stop when you absolutely have to, or your dinner is ready and family are waiting", he'd say. He'd tell me that the biggest catch could be just on its way, and if you give up too soon, you could miss it.'

Hannah's mind visualised beautiful little female fish swimming below, waiting for Luca to catch them, and Luca getting up and walking away just before the most amazingly beautiful and exotic and enticing fish swam by.

She wasn't *amazingly* beautiful and exotic and enticing, but she was a good catch. Sensible, smart, organised, active and healthy, caring and kind. But had she given up too soon on Tarrin's Bay? On the idea that someone could just appear and somehow slot into her life at Iona and be right for her? Someone amazingly beautiful, exotic, and enticing...

Like Luca.

But he wouldn't just slot in anyway. He would be taking over. Making his own way, his own rules. And he wasn't one for patience, despite his determination with his business. Personal matters were completely different.

Hannah pulled in the line and added more bait when the previous bait had been sneakily eaten without consequence by some fish below.

'Sounds like he was a wise man, your dad,' she said. 'I do remember him, but not much.'

'Yes. He was always busy, not one for lazing around. Fishing was his only relaxation.'

'Do you feel close to him when you fish?' she asked, and immediately regretted it when Luca's eyes became grey and he rested his elbows on his knees. 'Sorry, I didn't mean to bring up the past.'

He gave a weak wave of his hand. 'It's okay.' He gazed into the distance. 'You're right. I do,' he said. 'How did you know?' He turned to face her.

She shrugged. 'A hunch.'

'You *get* people, you know,' he said. 'You're very understanding and intuitive.'

She shrugged again. 'Oh I don't know, some things just seem obvious to me. I state what feels right at the time.'

'Well it's a special talent.' He pulled at the taut line a little, but it slackened again. 'I also feel close to him when I cook. So I guess I feel close to him a lot of the time.'

'True. And I'm sure he's always around you... I mean, if you believe that sort of thing.'

'I do,' he replied. 'And Mum too. I've been cleaning out her house on weekends with Stefan. Not sure what to do with the wedding dresses I brought back but I can't get rid of them. I think I'll just store them in honour of her memory.'

'How lovely. I'd love to see them properly. I had a little look when you were showing photos to my mum but didn't look close enough. Anyway, I don't have to, only if you... if it's...'

Oh man. Here she was, bringing up the past to a grieving man, and asking to see his mother's wedding dresses.

'Sure. I'll wait till my hands are clean and show you the photos again. And maybe I'll show you them for real sometime.'

Hannah exhaled, relieved that he didn't seem to be overly affected by her inquisitive nature and suggestions. And as often happened, when an idea or suggestion stood forth in her mind, another usually followed. 'What about displaying them in the restaurant? In the upstairs section, somewhere they won't risk getting damaged... or you could have a different one on display each month.'

Luca's lips turned downwards with a few slow nods of his head. 'Hmm, that could be a nice idea. Actually, I thought of something similar, with my father's chef knives. I've never used them, even though he left them to me. I've kept them safely stored away in a box, but was thinking of having them displayed in a window box somewhere, maybe in the kitchen itself... not sure it's a good idea to have sharp implements around the customers. Might create an insurance issue.'

Hannah nodded, tugging her line and reeling it in to find a small bream attached to the end.

'Oh, well done!' Luca moved aside as she removed the hook from the fish and placed it into the esky filled with some water. 'Looks like it's just over the minimum length to keep.'

'Some dinner for you.' She smiled.

'Oh not for me, for you. You caught it.'

'I'll have to catch another one then. Ooh, the pressure is on.' She attached bait and dropped the line into the water.

'Ten bucks says I beat you to it,' Luca said.

'Only ten? Twenty.'

'You're on.'

They sat and chatted sporadically, eyes focused on the water and hands holding gently but firmly to sense any resistance. They discussed a few minor matters relating to the restaurant, and when discussing staff training for the coming week, Hannah sensed a stronger tug on her line.

'Oooh, I think it's holding...' She kneeled and carefully pulled the line, and hanging on the end of it was another bream, much bigger than the first. Pride swelled within and she almost found herself saying 'Look, Dad!'

'Oh, man!' Luca shook his head. 'Nice catch, though, Miss Multitalented.'

Hannah removed the fish and put it in the esky. 'I'd say there's enough dinner for both of us.' She realised then that it sounded like they should have dinner together. 'I can give you the bigger one if you like, I don't mind. I can just take home the smaller one and grill it.' She gave an indifferent shrug.

'Of course not. I'll grill them both at Home. As in Restaurant Home. Unless you have to rush back?'

She shook her head. 'As long as the animals get fed sometime in the next couple of hours.'

'No problem. Hmm, might even batter these babies up and fry them. Care for some gourmet fish and chips?'

Her eyes opened wide. 'Oh, yum. Do you have potatoes in the kitchen or…'

'I do indeed, though a few days old. Was trying out some rosti last Wednesday when you were at the markets.'

'I love rosti. And chips.'

'Then we must have both.'

She smiled. 'Luca, you don't have to keep cooking for me, I'm sure you've had enough practise and know what's going to work for the menu.'

'Yes, but it's the least I can do, with you helping me out like this when you have so much else going on.'

'You're paying me for my services, that's plenty.'

And I'm getting to satisfy my inner teenager a little, which is a nice bonus.

'Either way, we have fish and it mustn't go to waste. Fresh is best.'

'If you insist.' Her stomach grumbled at the thought.

As he packed up his fishing equipment, Luca said, 'Thank you. For your company. It was a nice surprise.' A smile softened his jawline. 'And I didn't know you were a runner.'

Hannah let out a burst of laughter. 'I didn't either.'

He eyed her curiously.

'Spur of the moment thing.' She shrugged. 'I've walked on the beach, but never run.'

Yet another one of those things…

'Who would have thought that after twenty years of adulthood, we can still have things we haven't done in life,' he said. 'Like running for example.'

'There are so many possibilities, so many things to try and

experience, I bet most people only experience a fraction of what is possible in their lifetime.'

'Hmm.' He nodded. 'What do you think you've learned most, over the last two decades, Hannah?'

'Learned most? As in, what has life taught me?'

He nodded and held out his hands to the side. 'See... fishing makes me philosophical.'

She looked to the sky to try and retrieve an answer. 'I would have to say... that life doesn't always turn out the way you think it will, so sometimes you have to take hold of it more directly and do your best to shape it into what you want it to be.'

'Like a piece of clay.'

'Yes. Metaphorical clay,' she clarified. 'What about you?'

'I think I've learned that "one day" doesn't always turn up. You have to decide when your one day will be and make it happen.'

'That's so true. Similar to mine, in a way.'

'But without the metaphorical lump of clay.'

'Yes.' She smiled. 'And your one day is coming up very soon.'

'I can't wait.' An excited smile flashed onto his face, and he stood, along with Hannah. 'So, apart from jogging on the beach, is there any other simple thing you've never actually done that you'd like to do? Today?'

Kiss my teenage crush all over again.

'Umm... nope.'

'C'mon, there has to be something. Something you haven't learned but would like to, like... surfing?'

'Today? It's almost dinnertime.'

'Cartwheels?'

'Done them.'

'Handstands?'

'Done.'

'Become a human sandcastle?'

'Ah, I seem to recall having sand piled on top of me when we were all at the beach one day?' She crossed her arms and narrowed her eyes.

'Ha, just checking that you still remember.'

Hannah adjusted her bag across her chest and thought of Luca's kitchen, and of hers, and of her chooks. 'Actually... there is something. It's a little embarrassing though.'

Luca leaned a little closer. 'Yeah? Well, spill it, HD.'

'Nah, it's silly.' She flicked her hand. 'Not important.'

'Of course it must be if it came to mind. What is it?'

It wasn't really much to be embarrassed about, but she still felt awkward with him being a chef and her being a chicken farmer.

'Despite me dealing with hundreds of eggs on a daily basis, I've never actually been able to successfully...'

'Successfully what? Collect them all without breaking one?'

'Nope, that's not it. Poach one. Poach an egg.'

Luca laughed.

'See? You're teasing me!'

He laughed again. 'No I'm not, I'm laughing because it's cute that you're embarrassed about it.'

'Well,' she said, her cheeks warming up, and her hands starting to take over some of the conversation by circling around as her words formed. 'I've done all the tricks, used fresh eggs of course, but all I've managed to serve up each time is a sloppy mess.'

'Well we can't have that! No sloppy messes allowed on my menu.'

'I'm not going to be cooking at your restaurant though.'

'I know, but I can't possible acquaint myself with someone who serves up a sloppy mess, now, can I?' He winked. 'Let's rectify this situation immediately!'

'Rectify? Situation?' Her inability to poach eggs was a *situation* that needed *rectifying*? 'It's fine, it'll be a waste of time as I'll just mess it up. I'm happy to continue frying or boiling my eggs, thanks anyway.'

'Forget that,' Luca said. 'I'll teach you right now. And soon you'll be a pro.'

She laughed. 'If you can teach me to poach eggs within no more than thirty minutes, I'll be very surprised.'

'Prepare to be surprised.' He did a magician-like flourish of his hands.

'Okey dokey. We'll see. By the way...' She put her hands on her hips, straightening up. 'I think you owe me twenty bucks.'

'Oh yeah.' He wiped his hands on a rag then slid one hand into his pocket.

Hannah held out her hand. 'It's okay, you don't really have to pay me. It was just a bit of fun.'

He took out a twenty-dollar note and folded it into her hand. 'Take it. I want you to buy something interesting with it. And I don't mean adding it to your grocery bill or buying petrol.'

'Luca.'

'Uh-uh. It's yours. I want to find out this week what you bought with it. Or see the evidence firsthand. Something you've never bought before.'

'Can it be over twenty dollars in price?'

He shook his head. 'Twenty dollars or less, that's the challenge. It can be one item or two at the most.'

She sighed her resignation, though secretly keen to see what she could find in the shops. 'Okaaay. If I must.' She put the money in her purse.

'Now,' Luca said. 'Let's show you how to poach some eggs!'

CHAPTER TWENTY-TWO

H e'd probably poached tens of thousands of eggs in his career, Luca thought, as he entered the kitchen and switched on the bright lights. He got out a medium saucepan and took out a carton of eggs that he'd received from Hannah on Friday.

'The fresher the better, as you know,' he said. 'In your case, at least for the next few weeks, you can make them straight from chook to table!'

Hannah offered a nervous smile. 'Hmm, we'll see.'

He'd planned to just fish until he didn't want to anymore, but her unexpected presence changed all that. And he was hungry. So after the poaching lesson, he would cook up the day's catch and have an early dinner with her, before getting back to work tomorrow.

'Right,' he said, putting on an apron.

She chuckled. 'You need an apron for egg poaching?'

He glanced down at his chest. 'Force of habit.' He shrugged. 'Oh well, it's on now. Want one?' He gestured to a rack where he'd stored some spare aprons and chef whites.

'Why not. With my sloppy eggs, I'll be needing it.'

'Ha! Rest assured, you will not get one little bit of egg on your apron. I promise.'

'Okay then, so, we fill about half with water...' She picked up the pan and filled it.

'Yes, now let me take over from here.' He nestled in beside her and she stepped slightly to the side. 'Let's bring it to boil first.' He upped the temperature, then grabbed some sea salt and white vinegar. When bubbles formed, he sprinkled some salt into the water, then a tablespoon of vinegar. 'There are other ways without adding vinegar, but this is the method I prefer.' He turned the temperature knob. 'Next we lower the heat, and then we're going to move the pan to one side so it's half on and half off the heat.' He did as he said.

'Oh, I've never done that before.'

'It's the secret,' he whispered with a smile, leaning towards her a little. 'See how it's boiling on one half and forming a current?'

'Uh-huh. I always tried swirling the water instead.'

'Yeah, this way is easier.' He picked up an egg. 'You can crack them into a bowl or cup first if you prefer, but I'm just going to...' He cracked it on the edge of the pan and slid it into the non-boiling half of the water.

'Cool.'

'The current should keep the egg rolling and the vinegar assists in keeping it together. Voila.'

'Okay, so just a few minutes?'

'No more than three or four. Then gently scoop it out.' After the required time, he lifted the egg from the pan and placed it onto a small plate. 'One poached egg, just for you.'

'No, you have it. I'm determined to not eat one unless I've successfully poached it myself.'

'Awesome.' He popped most of the egg into his mouth in one go. 'I'm starved,' he mumbled.

'And I thought you were going to say, "Here, have half," at least.' She laughed.

He held up his hands. 'Oops.'

'So, now to put the water back on the boil?'

'Yep, repeat the steps and see how you go.'

He watched as she waited for it to boil fully and then moved it to one side. She cast a knowing glance his way. 'It's the secret you know.' One corner of her mouth turned upwards.

'Oh really? Uh-huh, uh-huh. Show me more.' He put on a voice of overt enthusiasm.

She cracked the egg and was about to put it in the centre when he intervened. 'Wait... on the non-boiling side.'

'Thanks. Phew, almost stuffed it up.' She slid the egg in, perhaps a little too carefully as it elongated a bit too much, but the current took hold. 'Is it working? Did I do it?'

'Wait and see,' he said. 'Not too bad.'

After the cooking time, she lifted it out on the slotted spoon and placed it down, though a few small bits floated in the water still. 'A little sloppy, but not too bad.' She used a fork to take a piece, unlike him. Yolk oozed out. 'Oh, maybe a bit runny?'

'Depends how you like your eggs. You can leave them in a bit longer if you prefer a firmer yolk.'

She ate her egg and then prepared the pan again. 'I think I can do better.'

'You can always do better.'

'Gee, thanks,' she raised her voice slightly.

'I mean, *we*, us, humans in general, can always do better.' He winked. 'You can't become blasé in the kitchen, it'll show in your food. A good cook should always strive to learn better ways of working and continue to stimulate their creativity.'

More words of wisdom from his dad.

He glanced at the framed picture of the outside view, and wished his dad could see it. Maybe if he displayed his knives next to it, somehow it would be a way of saying, 'Hey, Dad, check this out! My view. From my restaurant. My new home.'

By the third egg, Hannah had done it. 'You have my permission to serve that one,' he said. 'Chef-worthy.' He held up his hand and she high-fived it.

'Yes! How cool.' She snapped a photo of it on her phone. 'Facebook-worthy too.' She held up the fork and it hovered above the egg. 'Hmm, guess I should share, since I ate the other two.'

'Your egg, your choice.'

She took a clean fork and sliced the egg in half, giving one to Luca. 'Bon appétit.'

'Or as we say, *se bucura*. Enjoy.' He smiled and slid the egg into his mouth. 'Mmm, perfect. Well done. See? Within half an hour.'

She held her arms to the side and shook her head. 'Yep, you did it. You taught me. And to think I've been missing out all these years.'

'You have indeed.' He eyed her satisfied smile as he flashed one of his own. He felt like somehow, he too had been missing out all these years. Not on poached eggs of course, but on her. Her delightful charm. Her comforting companionship. Her... everything.

Her smile softened as he found himself leaning closer. Only slightly, then a little more. He wanted that smile to be part of his. He wanted those lips more than her perfectly poached egg.

Her warm and earthy scent unsteadied him for a moment and he lost sense of space and time, but when she stepped aside reality came hurtling back.

No, I should not kiss her. Not again.

'Sooo,' she said, turning away from him and clearing her throat. 'I believe there is fish to be cooked as well? Should we poach them too?'

'Huh? Oh. Of course, I mean nope. Let's fry them.' He bent down to the esky and lifted it to the sink.

Whoa, a moment of weakness. Get a grip, man.

Luca spent the rest of their food preparation time trying not to look at her again for fear of not being able to resist pulling her into his arms and feeling her against him, tasting her lips and experiencing the connection and pleasure he had not had for a while and hadn't realised he was craving.

They ate their battered, fried fish, and deep-fried chips, with a side of sweet potato rosti and tartare sauce at one of the tables next to the upstairs view, chatting about nothing too deep and meaningful. The grey sky darkened and rain began its descent, dampening the edges of the outdoor deck that weren't protected by roofing.

'Looks like the main part of the deck will be okay in wet weather,' he said.

'Unless it gets really windy,' she replied. 'Those coastals can be pretty strong up here.'

'I bet.' He studied the rain as it pelted down. 'Where is your car parked?'

'Oh,' she held a hand to her forehead. 'Way up near Serendipity! I forgot I parked there to go for my spontaneous run.'

'Mine is just near the harbour, not too far. I'll drive you up there.'

'Thanks. I didn't even bring my umbrella. See, this is what happens when I'm not prepared, chaos ensues.' She grinned.

'And sometimes chaos leads to learning a new skill and

having an awesome seafood dinner.' He gestured to their dirty plates.

'Well, that is true. Thank you. It was a nice afternoon,' she looked at her watch, 'evening.'

'T'was, my dear.'

Hannah looked at the plates too. 'I'll help you clean up, I'm in no rush to get out there into that weather. And my chooks can wait a while longer as I don't fancy heading out into the wet paddock in my gumboots and raincoat just yet either.'

He chuckled, imagining her in that outfit, bright yellow raincoat, oversized gumboots leaving huge muddy footprints. 'Okay then, let's get to it.'

They made their way back to the kitchen and rinsed the plates, then Luca filled up the sink with detergent. There wasn't enough to bother putting on the dishwasher, and he didn't want to rush the process of her going home.

'Nothing like a good handwash sometimes,' she said. 'It's kind of therapeutic.'

'For the dishes or for you?'

'For me, of course. Though I'm sure the dishes appreciate the extra pampering.' She smiled with an amused shake of her head.

'Everything done by hand is always best,' he said, and was reminded of the delicate handiwork his mother did on her dresses. 'Oh,' he got out his phone, 'I was going to show you the photos of my mother's wedding dresses, the ones I'm keeping.'

She leaned in. 'Oh yes, please do.'

He opened his camera roll and the family category, then pressed on one of the dresses, the one he'd taken off the mannequin.

'That is absolutely beautiful,' Hannah said, her eyes scanning all over it.

He zoomed in to the details. 'See the embroidery and

beading over the bodice… all done by hand.' He scrolled down. 'And on the hem too.'

'Wow. Truly amazing.'

He smiled and flicked through to the others, receiving the same amount of praise.

'What a talented lady,' she said. 'Honestly, I bet she made lots of women extremely happy.'

'And their husbands,' he chuckled.

'I bet. It's so great that you're keeping these, I'm sure she would appreciate that.'

'Yeah. It's really comforting sometimes, to know that her hands touched this very fabric, that her eyes focused on each minute detail with so much passion and dedication.' He cleared his throat and rubbed at his jaw, though his hands weakened and trembled a little.

She gently touched his arm. 'It is. It really is.'

When she'd finished having a good look, he quickly put the phone on the kitchen counter, next to the drying rack. 'Anyway, you wash, I'll rinse and dry.' Luca handed her the dishwashing brush.

Mesmerised, he watched her circling the plate with the brush, spreading the lemon-scented bubbles over it and removing the remains of their dinner. It was therapeutic, hypnotic. Gently, she handed the plate to him and he rinsed it, then wiped a tea towel over both sides and positioned it on the drying rack while she began washing the next one.

They worked silently, slowly, peacefully, and with a subtle sense of anticipation of something yet to come, or something not quite… addressed, as yet. The handing over of each plate, glass, or piece of cutlery was accompanied with a soft smile, and one from him in return.

She scratched her cheek and a small blob of bubbles remained.

Luca reached over with the tea towel and wiped it off. She flinched a little.

'Sorry, you had a bit of...'

'Oh. Thanks.' She lifted her forearm to dab it as if his wiping hadn't removed it, but it only added more.

He chuckled. 'Hang on,' he said. He dabbed at her cheek with the tea towel again, his eyes captivated by the dewy sheen on her rounded cheeks. When he placed the tea towel back down and looked up, she was still looking at him.

Something rumbled in his belly. And it wasn't his dinner. A warmth spread throughout his torso and he lifted his hand back up to her cheek, this time without the tea towel. He glided his thumb across her cheek, so slowly, as if stopping the gesture would end the heightened feeling of connection of the moment.

No words would form. He could only touch. Feel. Breathe.

The dishwashing brush fell into the soapy water with a light splash, but her gaze didn't budge from his. His awareness fell to her upper chest, rising more sharply, more quickly than before. Like it had been after her run, only... different.

His did the same.

And then both hands were on her cheeks, their soft warmth spreading down his arms right to his core. In a matter of milliseconds their faces were an inch from each other, and he breathed her in as she did him, his lips unable to avoid hers... he pressed them onto her, then gathered her bottom lip between his lips and her hands met with the back of his shoulders, one climbing slowly to tangle sensually in the back of his hair, the other putting firm pressure on his back to pull him closer and closer.

The rumbling inside built to an intense rush of pleasure, a need, where everything else disappeared from his awareness and she was the only part of his world.

As the kiss intensified along with the sensations, his arms

wanted to lift her, to gather her up… and so they did; with one swift manoeuvre he propped her up onto the counter and her legs slid firmly around his thighs, but his phone toppled to the floor.

He broke away for a moment. 'Oops,' he said, bending to retrieve it from the floor, luckily unbroken thanks to his protective cover. He placed it next to her on the counter, then looked back up at her… her eyes baring her soul and her lips parted and pink.

He smiled and moved in towards her again, but his phone chimed and he glanced towards it. So did she.

It took a second to recognise the sound, and then another one chimed. It was a Tinder notification.

Oh my God, of all the times…

A woman called Madeline had sent him a message. Two by the looks of it.

It chimed again.

Make that three.

'I'll turn this off,' he said, putting his phone on silent, but when he brought his hand back to her cheek, she removed it and slid off the countertop back to standing.

'Hannah,' his hand sought hers.

'Luca,' she breathed. 'Whoa. I think I should get going.'

'Hannah, wait.' He reached his arm forward but she was walking towards the kitchen entrance. 'You still have your apron on,' was all he could manage to get out.

She stopped and turned, lifted it off over her head and placed it on the rack. 'Luca, we can't complicate things. We only have two weeks left, and this is a bad idea.'

It had felt like a damn good idea to him.

'It doesn't have to be complicated,' he replied.

'Exactly,' she said with a sigh. 'You don't want what I want, and you have to focus on your new business right now, and me with my move. I can't deal with these emotions right now.'

'How do you know what I do or don't want?' He crossed his arms.

She shrugged. 'I know you. And...' She gestured to his phone.

'What... Tinder?' He turned briefly away and shook his head. 'Bloody Stefan. My brother signed me up for it, I haven't even been using it.'

'Doesn't look that way.'

'It's some random message from some woman I don't know. I don't even want to use the stupid app.'

'Then why didn't you just uninstall it?'

He shrugged. 'I dunno, didn't get around to it. Busy opening a restaurant. Anyway, this has nothing to do with what just happened between us. What's *been* happening between us.'

'What's happening is that we've had lots of catching up to do, and we're in close proximity because we're working together, so it's natural for some feelings of closeness to arise. That's all.'

'It's more than that and you know it.'

'Do I? You've never talked about it. You've never mentioned it.' She placed one hand on her hip with a huff.

'You didn't seem to want to.' He walked up to her and grasped her arms gently. 'Look... I know it's a strange feeling, reuniting after all these years, but I like you. I really do. Always have.'

'You liked everyone, Luca, but never me.'

'What are you talking about?' His eyebrows drew together and an ache spread across his forehead. 'Anyway, I don't know what's happening but I know it feels good. I'd like to just go with it... enjoy it.'

'I have a lot to handle right now, as do you. I can't do

uncertainty, Luca.' She went into the restaurant, towards the door.

'Then let's talk about it some more, open up, see how we feel.'

She turned for a moment and looked at him, and all he could see was her innocent teenage eyes staring back at him. 'You're twenty years too late, sorry.' She picked up her shoulder bag and he watched her leave the building.

CHAPTER TWENTY-THREE

'Y'ou sure everything's okay, love?' Doug Delaney eyed his daughter with curious concern as he was about to farewell her at the market stall and go for a wander.

'Yes, all good. It's just been a busy six weeks and the launch is in five days. Sorry if I seem a bit preoccupied.'

'As long as you're okay.'

'Yep!' She probably said it with too much enthusiasm.

Her mother hitched her handbag on her shoulder. 'Can't wait for the evening, I'm really looking forward to sampling Luca's food in the environment for which it was intended to be enjoyed.' She smiled. 'He's been so kind, to give us all his samples. I've barely had to cook.'

'I know, he's fed me well too,' Hannah replied.

And given me a taste test of something else...

'Can we get you something to eat or drink while we're here?' her mum asked.

'Actually,' Hannah eyed the portable coffee stand, 'I'd love a mocha, but would you mind manning the stall for me while I go get one? I wouldn't mind a few minutes to walk around and have a break, and I wanted to pick something up too.'

Kathleen Delaney was behind the stall in a flash. 'Thought you'd never ask! I miss doing this, don't you too, Doug?'

'It does bring back memories,' he said, glancing around the markets. 'Rightio, anything new we need to know?'

'No, but do you remember how to use the card machine thingy, in case they don't have cash?'

'Just hold it out to them and they scan their card, right?'

'Yes, but you need to type in the cost first.' She gave him a quick demo.

'Ah, got it. Okay, love, off you go. No hurry.'

She smiled a thank you and took off towards the coffee stand.

'Good thing that rain held off,' the barista said as he made her coffee.

She nodded. 'It's been a wet week and a half.'

'Got some helpers, I see.' He gestured to her stall.

'My parents. They haven't done the markets for ages. Today is my last day, actually.'

'Oh?'

'Moving to Sydney, so I need the next couple of weeks to get organised, and then hopefully the person taking over my farm will take over the markets too.'

The person... it felt so weird to talk about him like that. But every mention of his name brought back the butterfly sensation from his kisses, followed by the uncomfortable but necessary resolve she'd made and tried hard to stick to so she could get through the next few weeks.

'I'll keep an eye out and make sure the person you speak of does it justice.' He winked and handed her the mocha.

'Thanks.' She took the coffee and walked the long way around the stalls, having a look at the other produce on offer. There were a few other types of stalls scattered among the food. She waved at Maria in her running gear who was behind the handmade baby-clothing stall, and pretended to look carefully at some homewares to avoid going over and facing the fluffy knitted things and feeling that sense of loss-in-advance again, should her time never come.

But then she did a double take at something on the corner of the display table. A collection of small, painted rocks. She wouldn't have really taken any notice of them, colourful rocks with words like 'love' and 'peace' and 'happiness' painted on them, except that one said 'home'.

She picked up the slightly oval-shaped rock. It was cool on her skin and seemed to mould to the shape of her palm, nestling in comfortably as though it was a baby and her hand was the cradle.

'They're lovely, aren't they?' the older woman behind the stall said. 'My daughter paints them.' She gestured to the rosy-cheeked younger woman also behind the stall.

'Oh, really? They're lovely.' Hannah picked up another couple, but she was only interested in one.

'Fifteen dollars each or two for twenty,' the older woman said.

A metaphorical light bulb lit up in Hannah's mind. She opened her purse and unfolded the twenty-dollar note she'd tucked securely behind her reward-card collection. 'I'll just have this one, thanks.' She paid for the 'home' rock and received it in a paper bag stamped with the stall's logo. That left her with five dollars to buy something else different. Although the rock was for 'the person', so perhaps she should buy something else for him to go with it, since he didn't really have to go and pay her the bet money anyway, but had insisted. She had a few days to find something, if she wanted to get it all out of the way before the launch. Or she could keep the change and say the rock had cost twenty. But she never lied. Even small, white lies. She sometimes blurred the truth, like when she'd told her father everything was all good, but never an actual lie. Because everything *was* all good, it was just that there was also the slight matter of having feelings for someone even after twenty years, but timing once again sucking big-time. She had decided to take control over the timing of her life, starting with the move. Her decision, her plan, her timing.

She walked with renewed clarity, sipping her mocha, holding her purchase, and taking in the atmosphere one last time.

She gave one more glance at the baby-clothing stall and did another double take. She noticed something she used to love as a kid.

She couldn't help but wander over.

'Hi, Maria, you're looking great.' She smiled.

'Aw, thanks, hun. Lost about eight kilos so far.'

'Pretty soon you might fit into some of these,' Hannah joked, pointing to the tiny baby clothes.

Maria laughed. 'Knitted adult clothes... hmm, maybe a new business idea for me.'

Hannah felt the need to keep the mood light, hence her joke. 'You never know.'

She picked up one of the plastic tubs of Play-Doh, only it wasn't branded, it was called Fun-Dough. 'Do you make this?'

Maria nodded. 'Saves a lot of time for the parents, and those store-bought ones are getting a bit pricey, so I figured a little side income for me, since most of my customers have older children too.'

'I used to love it. Mum used to make it too.'

'Easy to do, but mine all have natural food-grade dyes in them, so if the little ones happen to eat them... you don't have to worry.' Maria smiled. 'Hang on, something you're not telling me?' She eyed Hannah's stomach.

Hannah's hand flew instinctively to her stomach. 'Oh, God,

no. Not at all.' She put the tub down. 'Just getting nostalgic with my upcoming move.'

'Of course, hun. We'll miss you here.'

'Thanks. And lucky we have Facebook, huh?'

'Honestly don't know what I'd do without it. Keeps me sane. Love knowing my worldwide friends are there to chat to at the touch of a button.'

She nodded, and picked up the sample piece of dough. As it formed shapes in her hand, she was reminded of what she'd told Luc—*the person*—about shaping life into what you wanted it to be, like a piece of clay. 'How much for these?'

'Small tubs are two dollars, large are five.'

Hannah smiled at the exactness. 'I'll take the large one. For a gift.'

'Wonderful! I hope the lucky little one will love it.'

'Oh, I'm sure he will.' She held back a chuckle.

A rock, and some Fun-Dough. Not a purchase she ever thought she'd be making, especially as a sort-of gift. Sort-of, because technically he had paid for it. And hopefully it would help clear the air a little after the tense past week and a half, which could only help the launch go more smoothly.

She finished her mocha and popped it into a bin, then returned to her parents where she put her purchases into her backpack underneath the table.

'Thirty-six dollars so far, all paid with the little scanning thingy,' her dad said proudly.

'Nice work.' She gave a nod.

'And it's been nice chatting to a few people,' her mother said. 'We're happy to stay longer, you know. If you want us to.' Her mum put a warm hand on Hannah's arm, and even though it was her last day and part of her wanted to say no so she could just do her thing one last time, most of her wanted to say yes, to being lucky enough to have her parents living and breathing and standing right beside her, supporting her as she tied up one more loose end of her life in Tarrin's Bay.

'Yes,' she said with a smile, though her chin quivered and two tiny tears formed in the corner of her eyes. 'I would love that, Mum.'

The next day, after confirming the launch details with a photographer and journalist from the local newspaper who would be in attendance on the night, and scheduling a few social media posts to generate marketing buzz and encourage reservations for the following week and beyond, Hannah opened the door to Home with a confident push.

Luca and one of the chefs were chatting, and their conversation grew louder as they both exited the kitchen.

'No sleeping on the job, okay, I got it,' the chef said, as he pretended to sleepwalk.

'Look at him, will you?' Luca said to Hannah with a chuckle. 'Barely even started the new job and he's already got one over me in the joke department.'

'Oh?' She raised her eyebrows, clearly having missed something.

'Don't worry.' He flicked his hand. 'Just a joke about being overworked and working while asleep. Anyway, you had to be there.'

Yet another case of bad timing.

'Okaaay.' She waved off the chef awkwardly as he (sleep)walked out the door with a grin on his face.

'You've basically hired another Luca, I see.'

'Isn't it great?!' He grinned too.

Despite the recent awkwardness, it was nice to see him

happy and excited. It made her feel like she'd done a good job, professionally speaking.

'I'm glad you found the right staff.'

'Me too. Hey, did you know that you can't really work while sleeping... I mean, dreaming?'

'Sorry?'

Oh, random fact time.

'We're paralysed when we dream. Have I mentioned that before? When we dream, our muscles become temporarily paralysed so that we don't act out our dreams. Pretty cool, huh?'

Hannah shuddered. 'Pretty scary actually. What if there's an emergency?'

'In your dream or in real life?'

'In real life!' She chuckled.

'Then the brain wakes your muscles up. Haven't you ever had that experience when you're just waking up but your body won't move for a second? That's the leftover effects of the paralysis.'

'I may have... ew, that's not a nice thought. What if the brain forgets how to wake the muscles up?'

'Then you're in a bit of trouble.'

'Indeed. Wow, makes you realise how lucky we are to have working limbs, doesn't it.'

'You bet.' He wriggled his arms. 'Anyway, all set with the newspaper?'

'Yep, they'll cover the launch in their community pages next week.'

'Fabulous. Thanks, Hannah.'

'My pleasure. Have you finalised the pictures you want to show in the slideshow?'

'Done. Will email them to you later this afternoon, and we'll do a run-through tomorrow on the screen.'

'Great. And all the food is stocked up, barring the fresh produce we're getting on Sunday?'

'Yes, next two days will be nonstop prepping, we'll have a full kitchen, can't wait. I've missed the adrenaline.'

'I best leave you professionals to it then. I'll be in on Saturday of course to prepare the tables and the decorations and all the last-minute things, so Sunday will be a final polish and a double check out here while you lot get everything ready in the kitchen. Fresh flowers are coming too.'

Luca rubbed his hands together. Looked like he'd forgotten about their second kiss and her rejection of continuing it or discussing it any further.

'Hey, I ah, did what you suggested.' She held out a paper gift bag.

His eyebrows rose, partially obscured by his hair dangling on his forehead.

'The twenty dollars you gave me. I bought two *different* things. Both for you.'

'Oh, really? You didn't have to buy anything for me.'

'It's just a novelty, really. Nothing much.' She handed over the bag.

He pulled out the tub of Fun-Dough, and his face morphed into a different expression of curiosity, as though made of Fun-Dough. 'What's this for?'

'Remember what I said, about shaping life into what you want it to be? That day we went fishing?'

He nodded his understanding.

'That's to remind you. And I figured you and the staff would probably have some fun with it on break time. I bet Mr Sleepwalker,' she cocked her head to the door, 'will make something funny out of it when you're not looking.'

Luca laughed. 'Ha, how cool! Thanks.' He placed it on the reception counter. 'And what's this?' He pulled out the tissue-paper wrapped rock and unwrapped it. She watched as his face changed once again, this time... softening. 'Home,' he said, caressing the stone with his fingers. 'Hannah, this is... wow, nothing much? This is beautiful. How did you find this?' He looked up at her and his eyes connected with hers.

'Came across it by accident.'

'"There are no accidents", my mother used to say.' He ran his hand over the rock again. 'It's perfect. I'm going to put it right here.' He placed it beside the fragrant jasmine reed sticks at the reception counter, where every customer would see it. 'Ha, you just gave me a pebble.' He winked.

'Yes. Well, it's a rock. Pebbles are smaller.' After she'd spoken she remembered the night he'd had dinner at her parents' house and had mentioned the random fact of how penguins chose their mate for life by offering them a pebble. 'Ahh. The penguins.'

He nodded.

'Oops. In this case, I assure you, it is most definitely a rock. A stone even,' she confirmed.

'Pebble, rock, stone... all the same.' He chuckled. 'No, seriously, it's great. Thank you.'

'You're welcome.'

Please don't hug me. Don't, because I'll have to start all over again resisting you.

'I ah, won't hug you...'

What the heck? Can he read my mind?

'Because I probably smell like fennel. And fish. And... and... beetroot.'

She held back a burst of laughter. 'Fennel, huh? And beetroot?' She wafted a hand around her nose like she'd scented something vile. 'I'm getting out of here while I still can.'

He chuckled. 'I'll see you Saturday.'

She gave a nod of agreement, then turned to face the door.

'Oh, Hannah?'

She turned back.

'Hang on a sec...' He stood behind the reception counter, only visible from his shoulders upward, his gaze looking down while his hands did something. 'There,' he said a few moments later.

She stepped forward and peered over the counter, and he held up the Fun-Dough.

She covered a delightful giggle with her hand.

It was shaped like a penguin.

CHAPTER TWENTY-FOUR

Luca washed his hands and gave them a thorough dry, then shook the hands of each of his staff members. 'Well done, team. Thank you and I'll see you all tomorrow for the launch, it's going to be... what's it going to be?' He pointed at Lea first.

'Awesome,' she said.

'What else?' He pointed at Tom.

'Amazing,' he said.

'And...' He pointed at Amy, feeling like he was the host of a game show.

'Memorable,' she said after a few moments thought. 'Sorry, I tried to think of an A word but couldn't.' She chuckled.

'*Absolutely* fantastic,' Lea added.

Luca gave a thumbs up. 'That's what I like to hear. Now go! Get some sleep, people.' He clapped his hands and shooed them out of the kitchen.

'Hannah, you're still here?' he said as the staff filtered out. Hannah was sitting in the corner flipping through her folder.

'Yep. Just double-checking everything, making sure nothing's been missed. I had someone come to the house to help with the animals this evening so I didn't have to rush.'

'Hannah, everything's all set. All on schedule. Thanks to you.' He smiled. 'Make sure you get a good sleep, we'll need it.'

She nodded and closed her folder.

'Oh,' he said, raising his finger in the air. 'I have something for you. Just a sec...' He dashed into the kitchen storeroom and got it from his bag, returning to Hannah. 'Here. A small thank you for all your effort.'

She held a hand to her heart and mouthed a silent 'Ohh'.

His cheeks warmed.

She opened the wrapping and revealed the jasmine candle, bringing it to her nose and closing her eyes as she breathed in the scent. 'Oh, Luca. It may be small but it means a lot. It...' She nudged her nose with the side of her finger and sniffled. 'It...' Her eyes became slightly red and glossy.

Oh no, have I made the wrong decision?

He stepped closer to her.

'It... smells like home,' she whispered.

'Yes. Jasmine Road. I thought it might be a nice reminder. But if it's too emotional, I can—'

She held up a hand. 'It's perfect,' she said. 'Thank you. I love it.' Her smile reached her eyes, and he knew she appreciated the gift. Hannah dabbed at the corners of her eyes with her sleeve. 'Actually, I have something else for you too. But damn it, I left it at home. My home. Your home. Iona,' she explained.

He never thought his restaurant name would make things so confusing sometimes.

'That's okay, bring it tomorrow,' he said, not even expecting another gift after all her hard work and then the Fun-Dough and 'home' rock.

'No, I wanted to give it to you earlier, like a good luck present. And not among the crowd of people.'

'Oh.'

She glanced outside, and he followed her gaze, at the dark sky and the moonlight reflecting off the water in the harbour.

'It's at the house. If you like, drop by before going back to Nathan's and I'll give it to you quickly. Or I can bring it to Nathan's, although he might be asleep, and...'

'Sure. I'll come by. If you're sure that's okay. I'll just grab my present and run.'

They laughed together. 'Sounds good,' she said.

Luca went back to the kitchen and grabbed his bag, switched off the lights, then before switching off the lights around the restaurant, he took a good look around.

Tables clean and shiny and ready to be draped with tablecloths tomorrow... small candles on each... chairs all neatly arranged at equal distances behind the tables... framed prints hanging on the walls, various decorations here and there... they had transformed this place into not only a place to eat, but a place to feel at home. It was just as Hannah said it would look.

His eyes warmed and he blinked as his vision blurred from unshed tears. He scratched his temple to distract from it.

'It looks great, hey,' she said.

'It feels great too.' He nodded. 'Thank you.' He looked at Hannah, her honest and caring eyes looking back at him.

Instead of nodding and saying 'you're welcome', she held up her hand.

He smiled and high-fived it.

'Nice work, Hannah Delannah.'

'Awesome stuff, Luca Antonuca.'

And then he hugged her.

***

'It's just in here, give me a minute,' Hannah said, switching on the light to the kitchen. The house was cool and quiet, except for a few murmurs from Scarlett as she settled into the laundry-room bed.

'I'll wait by the door,' Luca said.

'It's okay, come on in.'

He joined her near the island bench and she held the tall sparkly gift bag out to him. 'Congratulations on your new business.' She handed it over with a smile.

'Thanks! Wonder what this could be...' He smiled back, peeking into the bag. He lifted the bottle out. 'Organic champagne. And local too. *And* award-winning, awesome! Thank you.'

'My pleasure. I thought what better way to celebrate than with some bubbles. Whenever you wish to celebrate that is. But I wanted to give it to you today.'

'How about now?' Luca stepped behind the island bench. 'Where are your wine glasses?'

'Oh, it's okay, save it, Luca. For when you can make the most of it.'

'No time like the present. To make use of my present.' He winked.

Hannah's insides went all unsteady.

Maybe he sensed it, because his smile softened and he said, 'Of course. It's late and we have a big day tomorrow. And I shouldn't impose on you. I'll let you get some sleep. Thank you again, for everything.' He popped the bottle back in the bag with an apologetic smile.

But at that gesture, she felt an urge to take it back out. To take back what she'd said, to find her wine glasses, and say to hell with plans and just let the moment be whatever it will be.

As Luca went for the door, she came up behind him and placed her hand on his elbow. 'Wait.' It came out as a whisper.

He turned around, his eyes seeking hers.

'I haven't had a glass of champagne in ages,' she said.

'And why ever not?'

'I haven't had much to celebrate.'

Luca turned and stepped closer. 'Then let's change that.' He took the bottle from the bag. 'There's no one I'd rather share these celebratory bubbles with than you, Miss Delaney.' He waltzed to the cupboards. 'Now where are those glasses?'

Hannah smiled at his actions and showed him where they were, and within moments they were sitting outside under the night sky, on a picnic blanket and cushions on the grass, blankets around each of them. The fire pit on the nearby paved BBQ area was lit and sending light and warmth their way.

'The rain clouds have cleared,' he said. 'Can see the stars tonight.'

Yes, the clouds have cleared. For now at least.

Who knew what tomorrow's forecast would be, metaphorically speaking, but for now she was going to enjoy the moment.

'To new beginnings,' Luca said, holding up his champagne flute to hers.

'To new beginnings.' She clinked her glass with his, then took a nice long sip. Bubbles tickled her throat and warmth awakened her tastebuds. 'Ahh,' she said.

'Ahh indeed.'

'And to new... *homes*,' she added.

'To new homes.' He clinked his glass with hers again. 'Anything else?'

'To... to starry skies.'

'To starry skies!'

Clink.

She sipped and admired the silhouette of the big willow tree in the distance, stars sparkling between the branches.

'And to life,' he said. '*Viata.*'

'*Viata!*' She hoped she pronounced it correctly, as it just flowed without effort from his voice box.

Clink clink.

She sipped some more, until soon they were onto their second glass. The delicious taste and sensation relaxed her mind and body.

'This is great stuff,' Luca said. 'Organic things taste so much better.'

'Of course they do. You're preaching to the converted here,' she said.

'It's always better when everything is organic, don't you think?'

'Again, Luca... preaching... converted.' She waved her hand at him in a 'duh!' way as though the alcohol had gotten to his head already. Or maybe it had gotten to hers.

'I mean, not just with food.' He looked her in the eye.

Tingles spread through her body, from the champagne or his gaze she wasn't sure.

'When everything in the moment just flows... naturally... perfectly... no force, no pressure, nothing holding it back. Allowing it to be what it is. Organic.'

She took a long, drawn-out sip of her champagne, as she tried to find a way to resist what he was saying, and what she was feeling. But it only relaxed her further, softened her resolve from a tightly-knitted ball to a loose and unravelled clump of tangled emotions.

The blanket became too warm around her shoulders, and she nudged it off.

'I'm so glad I'm here. That you're here.' Luca put down his wine glass and nestled it into a patch of ground.

She took another sip, though it was empty now.

An amused smile escaped onto his lips, as he reached his

hand forward and gently took the glass from her. 'More? Or have you had enough?' he whispered.

'Enough. I mean more.'

'More champagne?'

'Enough champagne. More... this.'

Luca's eyes widened, deepened, connected more intensely with hers.

'This,' he echoed. 'This is...' He looked up at the sky for a moment. 'Whatever this is, I love it.'

'Me too. I don't want to but I do. Right now, in this moment, I do.'

He took her hands urgently. 'Hannah.' He brought them together and up to his mouth, his lips meeting her skin and spreading more tingles throughout her body.

Oh how she'd waited for this. Longed for this. Yearned for this.

A spritz of air cooled her face as a breeze went by, and Luca moved closer, gently dropping her hands in favour of her cheeks. 'It feels so right when we're together. That's all I know.'

She closed her eyes, and a built-up breath fell from her mouth as he ran a hand through her hair and kissed her softly on one cheek, then the other.

'Luca,' she murmured. 'You know if we start, we'll... never stop.'

'Then let's not stop.' He ran his thumb across her lips then kissed them gently, firmly, then passionately.

Oh what the hell...

Hannah wrapped her arms around his back, then let her hand run through his smooth, thick hair, and he pulled her up onto his lap. Their chests touching, she could practically feel his heart beating in time with hers, his lungs breathing rapidly with hers, and his desire warming her whole body as hers warmed his.

His hands travelled around her body, massaging and holding her firmly, dormant sensations awakening and overtaking her whole awareness.

With his arms around her and holding her tight, he lowered her down on the rug and lay half sideways and half on top of her, which sent her newly awakened sensations into overdrive. She kissed him with an urgency that matched his, and as he adjusted the blankets around them, she slid her hands underneath his top and caressed the firm shapes of his chest and torso. His hands came up underneath the back of her top and her skin became hot and needy for more of his touch.

His pockets dug into her hips and he lifted himself off for a moment to remove his wallet and phone. She smiled and resumed kissing him, touching him, exploring him, as he did her.

When the blankets were all they had covering them and the heat from the fire pit no match for their own, Hannah's desire built from simmering to boiling, and her pleasure blossomed into a hot, summery, bliss.

The more she surrendered and enjoyed, the more passionate he became in response, as though her pleasure was his pleasure. She had never felt so satisfied and empowered.

By the time their bodies became one, it was as though they already had been, long before, and this moment was simply a culmination of what already existed. That inner connection and attraction she'd always felt for him had been tended to... finally, and anything more was a bonus.

'You're the most amazing woman I know,' he whispered, as he rolled gently to the side, his hand caressing her face, his other on his rapidly rising and falling chest, which soon calmed to a satisfied rhythm.

'I'm just... me,' she said softly.

'Amazing you.' He kissed her forehead, then held her close.

For a while they did nothing but simply breathe together, as they held each other, their bodies calming down and cooling down.

The soothing crackle of twigs in the fire pit, along with the occasional sprinkle of kisses, nourished her body and soul, as she lay there completely exposed yet protected in the arms of the man she'd always longed for.

This wasn't what heaven felt like. This was home.

CHAPTER TWENTY-FIVE

L
ight pried open Luca's eyes and he sat bolt upright at a sudden sound intruding on his sleep. 'What the hell was that?'

'Huh?' a gentle murmuring sounded.

He glanced next to him. Hannah lay there with the blanket over her eyes.

The roosters crowed again and he chuckled.

Of course. I'm on a chicken farm.

'Hannah, wake up,' he whispered, placing a hand on her blanket-covered arm. 'We accidentally fell asleep.'

'Huh?' the murmuring repeated. She was clearly immune to the sound of roosters signalling morning light. And clearly needed more sleep. But sleep would have to wait, they had a lot to do today.

He found his clothes on the grass, checked for stray ants or spiders or whatever insects roamed around out here, then got dressed. He did the same for Hannah's clothes, but held them towards her.

'Here you go, my dear. Your clothes.'

'Huh?' This time she rolled over and her eyes slowly

opened. On seeing him, her eyelids flicked wide open and she sat upright, holding the blanket to her chest. 'What? Oh my God. We slept outdoors.' She looked at him, and he smiled at her wayward bed hair sticking up at all angles. 'Luca, we slept here. We're outside. In winter. We slept...'

Together.

It was like she'd just remembered. Her cheeks brightened with a subtle peach hue.

He kissed her forehead. 'It's okay. No one else out here but us.'

A rooster crowed.

'And that annoying alarm clock I'll have to get used to.'

Hannah buried her face in her hands. 'Oh man.' She scrambled for her clothes and got dressed discreetly under the blanket.

Luca grabbed his belongings and the remains of last night's late-night picnic, and gestured to the house with a tilt of his head. 'Mind if I... deal with these and use your bathroom?'

'Go ahead,' she said. 'I need to feed those chooks.' She stood. 'Actually, bathroom first.'

He felt like taking her hand but his hands were full.

'Okay. Let's ah, go inside, and... let's go inside.'

Disorientation confused him. He wasn't sure what to do or what to say now.

'Yep. Inside. Bathroom. Then chooks. Then...' She scratched her head. 'I need to find my schedule for today. What day is it? Is it... oh. The launch. Oh my God, we have to get organised!'

'It's okay, we're still on track. Might even have time for breakfast.' Hannah looked as confused as him. 'If you want to, or I'll just ah, go back home and eat there, and ah, see you later on.'

She didn't respond, her mind appearing to be ticking over

with a million things, and, he presumed, one of them probably being him and the situation they'd gotten themselves into.

After using the bathroom, he checked his phone. A text from Nathan:

> Hope you didn't get cold feet on the launch and do a runner, mate.

> Not at all, got carried away with so much to prepare. Slept at work. Be back soon for a shower.

He felt a bit weird giving a white lie, but there was no need to invade Hannah's privacy, especially when it came to Nathan.

There was also a text from Stefan, which had come in late last night:

> Hope you're all set for the launch. I have an afternoon coffee date with someone new and will then make my way straight to Tarrin's Bay after.

> So not ALL women are crazy?

> Hopefully not this one ;)

He smiled, and hoped Stefan wouldn't get carried away and be late.

Hannah came out of the bathroom with her hair tied back in a tiny ponytail, and her face with a few droplets of water left on it. 'Have to feed Scarlett.' She went into the laundry room and left the door open. As she prepared water and food, Scar walked slowly into the hallway and looked at him. Just stared. Like, 'what on earth are you doing here at my breakfast time?'

The dog began eating and Hannah gestured outside. 'Chooks next.'

'Do you want me to help?' he asked. 'Or maybe I can make breakfast while you do that, so it's ready when you're done. Save some time.'

'Oh it's okay, I can manage, I'll just...' She looked at her watch. 'Okay then. Thanks, that would be good.'

If it were any other day, perhaps they'd bring their breakfast outside for another leisurely picnic, and spend the day talking, laughing, and loving, surrounded by nature and birds and animals.

But it wasn't. It was one of the biggest days of his life, and he had to make it a success. Processing, or talking about last night's interlude would have to wait.

As he prepared some zucchini fritters he watched her outside the window, carrying the wheelbarrow to the coop. Her foot tripped on something and the barrow tipped sideways.

He went out to the verandah. 'You okay?'

She turned to face him, and held up a hand, in between trying to scoop up some of the feed that had escaped. 'All good. I've got it.'

He nodded and returned to the kitchen.

Soon, this would be his. He would be cooking here every day, as well as the restaurant. But as she disappeared from view when she went into the coop, a loneliness crept into the room.

It would be just him.

No noise of city hustle and bustle, no brother around to poke fun at, no parents, and no Hannah.

He shook the thought away and let the oil heat up in the pan.

He'd be fine. He'd get used to the chooks as companions and he'd be busy at the restaurant most of the time anyway. And the peace and quiet here would be a welcome change.

The breakfast was ready before she was, so he found some smoked salmon in the fridge and added it on top of the zucchini fritters, along with a dollop of lemon mayonnaise he found in a jar in the fridge.

It just needs some dill...

He checked the spice rack, and was about to go outside to search her herb garden, but she stepped through the door, a couple of cartons of eggs in her hands.

'The rest are in the storage chest. I'll deal with them later. Here, take one back home with you.'

'Thanks,' he said.

'Oh yum.' Her gaze dropped to the dining table. 'Thank *you.*'

'Hope you'll still have an appetite for tonight's food after this bountiful breakfast.'

'I think I've gained a few kilograms since you've been in town, Luca.' She chuckled. 'So much great food.'

'Life is for living, and to live we need to eat. So dig in.' He pulled out a chair for her and she sat.

As though she hadn't eaten for days, she devoured the fritters quickly, stopping briefly to give a thumbs up.

'I can make more if that's not enough.'

She shook her head, then after swallowing her mouthful she said, 'It's plenty. It's really nice.'

'Wait till tonight.' He winked. 'Though you've already tried most of the meals. Except my *gogosi.*'

'Gogo what?'

'*Gogosi.* A Romanian doughnut type of thing.'

'In that case, I'm definitely saving my appetite so I can fit in dessert.' She finished her breakfast, as did he, and he took the plates to the dishwasher.

'Anything I can do here to help before you come over to Home?'

She shook her head. 'I'll just freshen up then come over and see how things are getting on, make sure we're all good to go, then I'll come back here to get dressed for the evening and make my way back before the guests start arriving.'

'Sounds like a plan.'

'It is. All planned.'

Unlike last night.

Hannah stood and exhaled a deep breath. She looked him in the eye, as though she wanted to say something. 'Luca, I...'

He gave an anticipatory nod. 'Yes?'

'I'll see you later on.' She flashed a smile.

'Oh. Yes. Indeed.' He pocketed his phone and wallet, found his keys, and went for the door. She met him at the doorway but kept her distance. 'Hannah,' he said. 'I know things are probably a bit confusing right now. But last night was... perfect. I know we'll have to talk about it sometime, but...' He wanted to talk about it now, or better yet, forget the talking and share more of what they shared last night, but he regained his focus. 'Today is a big day. We've both worked hard. Let's go make this a raving success, shall we?' He challenged her with a determined gaze and a winning smile, at least he hoped it looked like a winning smile from her point of view.

'Huh, HD?' He nudged her with his elbow.

'Let's do it.' Her face became strong and determined. She held out her fist.

He tapped her fist with his and smiled.

Today was the day, and he would make his parents proud.

CHAPTER TWENTY-SIX

HOME—Opening Night Set Menu

Appetisers

Salmon and Quail Egg Bites ~ creamed avocado on French bread topped with smoked salmon and quail egg

Polenta Rounds ~ crispy polenta mini-pancakes with macadamia pesto and sun-dried tomato

Garlic and Chilli Prawns ~ with aioli dipping sauce

Mini Frittatas ~ with Mediterranean vegetable and goats' feta

Honey Beef Chipolatas ~ certified organic and grass-fed mini sausages

Main (choice of)

Organic Chicken and Capsicum *Cassolette* with cauliflower rice

Poached Barramundi in lemongrass, chilli, and ginger-infused coconut broth

Rosemary Lamb Meatballs with Napolitana sauce and spaghetti

Ratatouille with organic local vegetables and fresh herbs, and
toasted olive bread

Dessert (tasting plate of mini desserts)
Gogosi ~ traditional Romanian doughnut
Coconut and Mocha Mousse
Chia Cup with fresh seasonal fruit
Fig and Walnut apple crumble
Red Velvet cupcakes with white chocolate ganache
Salted Caramel Pudding with ice cream

Hannah smoothed down her black dress, a new one she'd bought just for the occasion since most of her good clothes were packed away, and exhaled slowly to help herself relax. She took three more deep breaths and paused to take in her surroundings, to ground herself, to become aware of the present moment instead of rushing to the next and the next. A little pre-event ritual she'd developed over the years.

All the candles on the tables were lit, the old-school jazz music was playing in the background, and the restaurant smelled like jasmine, with a subtle hint of the ingredients being prepared in the kitchen behind closed doors.

Luca emerged from the kitchen, adjusting his button-up silvery-grey shirt. 'Okey dokey, my job is done for the time being. Finally out of my chef whites and into my evening attire. Now I can greet everyone and mingle before dinner gets underway.' He rubbed his hands together, and his gaze stopped on Hannah. 'You look gorgeous, you know.'

She lowered her gaze a moment, then looked up. 'I know, right?' she said, waving a hand around her body, then chuckled. 'Who would have thought I could pull off a dress, huh?'

He approached, leaned in and whispered, 'I can pull it off later.'

She gave his arm a light whack. 'Luca!' she whispered.

Her insides tingled with anticipation like they had the night before, but they also tingled with uncertainty. The night *had* been perfect, and today was shaping up to be a huge success, but after tonight, she didn't know what was going to happen. And that unsettled her. The only way she could be certain was to take control. To decide what she wanted to happen afterwards and make it happen. But he wouldn't like her decision. So for now, she would have to keep things light-hearted, and stay professional to ensure a smooth running of the event.

They walked upstairs briefly to check on the wait staff who had platters and drinks prepared. They stood there at the ready, like toys waiting to be wound up before they could move, or actors in a stage show waiting for the curtains to part. 'Looking good, folks,' Luca said. 'But relax a bit, okay?'

They nodded and pretended to look a bit busier.

They returned downstairs, just in time to see two people walking towards the restaurant.

'It's Stefan!'

'It's Karen!'

They both spoke at the same time, then looked at each other, then back at the couple.

'Huh?' Luca said. 'Do they know each other?'

'No, unless she remembered him from high school, but he was two years below us.'

Hmm, Karen had said she was chatting to someone online who seemed decent and would hopefully meet them on the weekend, but Hannah had been so busy with the launch preparations and last night that she hadn't checked in with her. Was it Stefan she had been talking about?

Hannah caught Karen's eyes with a welcoming but questioning glance and Luca opened the door.

'Welcome, my brother!' Luca gave Stefan a hug.

'Hi!' Hannah said to Karen, hugging her too. 'Luca, remember Karen?'

'I do indeed, long time no see! How are you?' He gave her a quick hug and a kiss on both cheeks.

'I'm great, thanks, Luca.'

'And you might remember my brother Stefan, Hannah?'

She smiled at him, a younger and chubbier version of Luca, and just as endearing. 'So nice to see you.' Hannah received the double-cheek kiss from Stefan.

'You haven't aged a day,' he said.

'Oh, thanks.' She held a hand to her cheek. 'So, I see you two have already met?' She alternated her gaze between them.

They both grinned.

'Did you meet each other in the harbour car park?' asked Luca.

Stefan shook his head, then eyed Karen as though asking her a silent question. She gave a nod. 'We only just met today for coffee, in Sydney. We've been chatting for a couple of weeks online.'

Hannah's eyes widened. 'Small world!'

'Yes. And here I was thinking I wasn't having any luck,' Karen said, 'then along comes someone who can finally hold a decent conversation and who shows a woman some respect.'

Stefan slid an appreciative arm around Karen. 'I thought *I* was the one not having any luck. But looks like today the tables have turned.' He smiled, and they smiled at each other, and Hannah could feel the chemistry between them. She exchanged a quick and curious glance with Luca.

'What a coincidence,' Luca said. 'And when did you realise the connection, with me, and with Hannah?'

For a moment she thought he meant the connection between her and Luca, but then realised what he really meant.

'I told Karen I couldn't stay too long as I had to attend an important function,' Stefan explained.

'And then,' Karen added. 'I said "oh really, I have an important function on too, where's yours?"'

'And I said "Tarrin's Bay" and her mouth dropped open... *so* cute, by the way... and she said—'

'Me too!'

They looked at each other again and smiled.

'I said "It's not a restaurant launch by any chance is it?" and he said "my brother's!" and I said "my friend Hannah is the event manager!"'

'How amazing is that!' Luca said, giving his brother a light touch on the arm.

'Wow.' Hannah exchanged a happy smile with Karen.

'So it looks like I have a date for the evening,' Stefan winked. 'Can you, ah, make some adjustments to the table seating at last notice?'

'Onto it!' Hannah raised a pointed finger, and dashed to her table where her parents and Karen would also be seated, and swapped one of the other randomly allocated placings with Stefan's, who was supposed to be sitting on Nathan's table, along with a few other locals. Part of her process was to always have a few contingency plans in place for cases of no-shows, cancellations, unexpected extra guests, or situations requiring changes to seating. 'I hope you don't mind listening to my parents talk about our family history all night,' she said.

'I would be *delighted* to learn about the family history, Hannah,' he said in a posh voice, then exchanged a look with his brother as though they were sharing a private joke.

'Oh speak of the devil.' Hannah pointed outside. 'Here they are, ten minutes early as usual.'

Heads turned.

'I haven't seen them in so long,' Karen said. 'I really should get down here to visit more often.' She glanced at Hannah. 'Although, I won't need to, now that you'll be my roomie!'

'Yes!' They gave each other a little squeeze, and Luca seemed to have developed a slight itch on his neck. She couldn't wait to tell Karen what had happened last night, get everything off her chest and out of her system... she really needed to debrief, but now wasn't the time.

'Karen, dear!' Kathleen Delaney held out her arms for her daughter's best friend. 'You look lovely, how nice to see you.' They hugged and Karen complimented Hannah's mum on her haircut and gemstone jewellery.

'Mr Delaney, glad you're doing well.' Karen embraced Hannah's father.

'Fit as a fiddle,' he said. 'Though how a fiddle is fit I have no idea. Maybe fit as a finch? Light and free as a bird?'

'That sounds better,' Karen agreed.

Her parents greeted and congratulated Luca then her mother did the most embarrassing thing...

'Stefan, dear. It's lovely to see you.' She hugged him. 'What a charming and handsome young man you are. Can I give those gorgeous cheeks a squeeze?' She held out her hands and Hannah almost fainted.

'Mum!' she whispered, even though everyone could hear.

Luca just laughed. 'Sorry, bro, I told them the story.'

He didn't seem to mind. 'Squeeze away, Mrs Delaney. Though my brother usually gives them a disgusting big kiss.'

'Shall I do that tonight during my speech?'

'Don't you dare!' Stefan pointed his finger at Luca's chest, then raised his face for Kathleen to give his cheeks a squeeze.

'I'm getting so much female attention today from two lovely women, how lucky am I?' He stretched his arms out to the side.

Hannah tried to usher them towards the stairs to put an end her warm cheeks.

'Okay, peoples, the fun all starts upstairs, I need to greet some more people so up you go and we'll be up there shortly. Our team up there will take good care of you.'

They nodded and had a glance around as they went. 'Looks absolutely gorgeous,' said her mum on the way up. 'And that scent... oh my it smells like home.'

Hannah caught Luca's eyes and they smiled a knowing smile.

They welcomed several more people in, a few Hannah recognised and knew, including Jonah DeRae and his parents from Café Lagoon, Nancy Dillinger who sometimes bought eggs at the markets arriving with a happy-looking older man attached to her elbow, plus some new faces. And then Nathan entered with a couple of friends.

'Hey, roomie,' said Luca.

'Not for long,' he replied. They shook hands.

'Hannah.' He gave a polite nod.

'Nathan. Welcome, thanks for coming.'

'Wouldn't miss it.' He looked around. 'This looks bloody amazing. You've both done a great job.'

'Thanks, mate. Mostly Hannah's hard work.' Luca gestured his open palm towards her.

She appreciated him playing her up, especially in front of Nathan. But funnily enough, as she shook the hands of Nathan's friends and more remarks were made about the place, she didn't feel as awkward as she thought she might. Perhaps it had dissolved and been replaced by her feelings for Luca, but now she would be left with that awkwardness after tonight's event. Would every scenario with a male leave her with an uncomfortable sense of failure and incompleteness?

It seemed almost everyone was arriving as a couple... Olivia from Mrs May's Bookstore and April from April's Glow entered the restaurant with their men by their side, both incredibly toned and muscular. If superstar singer Drew Williams had been able to make it with his gorgeous wife Chrissie they may have had to roll out some red carpet.

But the red seat cushions on each chair, and on the armchairs and bench seats upstairs, would have to do.

'Hi, Dr Greene, welcome,' Hannah smiled softly at her GP as she arrived with her husband Mark, and they made their way upstairs. It was always a bit awkward to see the health professional who did your pap smears and breast checks in a personal context, but that was what you got from being in a small town. And she would see her next week for an appointment to check up on everything and get a summary letter to take to a new doctor before she moved to Sydney in two weeks.

As others arrived and were greeted, the ambient chatter of voices echoed from above, a good sign that people were settling in.

'Is that everyone?' Luca asked.

Hannah checked her list having done a mental headcount. 'I think there's still...'

'Sorry we're late,' a woman said as she entered, a man by her side.

'Emma, isn't it?' Hannah asked. She recognised her from around town, and had seen her at the beach and caravan park on occasion when she'd been there for walks with Scarlett.

'Yes, hi, and this is James.' Her partner, or husband she realised on noticing their rings, shook both her and Luca's hands. 'We would have been earlier but our son decided last minute he really wanted to come along. So we ah, had a bit of difficulty settling him down with the grandparents.'

'Oh not a problem at all, plenty of time to mingle and enjoy some appetisers upstairs. Shall we?' She held out her hand with a flat open palm like she'd been taught, towards the stairs.

'Looking forward to it, haven't been out for dinner for ages.' Emma smiled widely.

With each step she took, the sounds of chatter increased, and the scent of delicious hors d'oeuvres enticed her, although she was more interested in making sure everyone had a good time.

'Great food, bro.' Stefan clapped Luca on the back. 'Why don't you make this stuff for me?'

'I just did, man.'

'I mean like, on a regular basis, say... a few times a week?' He winked.

'You'll have to come down for regular visits then.'

'Me too,' said Karen. 'Maybe a monthly "Home" cooked dinner.'

'I'd be honoured to accompany you.' Stefan winked at Karen, and she blushed.

So she was moving away, and now everyone wanted to come visit?

Anyway, back to the purpose of the night...

Hannah mingled and chatted with the guests. It was a great distraction to the conflicting emotions pushed deep inside now for later retrieval.

After a while, the sound of high-pitched tapping took Hannah's attention away from Nancy Dillinger's discussion of her twilight-years love life and towards Luca, who stood in the corner near the outdoor deck, a view of the rising moon behind him through the window. He tapped a wine glass with a spoon, and the chatter gradually lessened as everyone's attention turned to him.

With a microphone in hand, he spoke...

'Welcome, everyone... welcome to Home. Or should I say, welcome Home.' He smiled, and a few in the crowd called out 'thank you'.

'Wow, what a turn out. I'm so grateful to have you all here for the opening night of my brand-new restaurant. I hope it'll become a popular and well-respected part of the Tarrin's Bay community, as I start my new beginning here in this beautiful town I've been so lucky to be able to return to.'

He took a small sip of wine, only one allowed tonight as he was technically working, and scanned the people in the crowd. How he'd love to see his parents' faces among the smiles. His eyes searched, as though by some bizarre occurrence they would appear, or at least his mother, and he'd realise that she hadn't really died, it had all been a big mistake or a bad dream. But the only part of his mother that was visible was one of her dresses. It was displayed on a mannequin in the corner opposite to him, protected between two slightly touching armchairs and a small round side table, the moonlight reflecting sparkles off the bodice and hem.

And in memory of his father, apart from his chef knives in a framed box in the kitchen... on the wall near the wedding dress was a framed old painting of a garden that they had received from Romanian relatives on their wedding day. A sign of the abundant blossoming and growth that would occur through their union over the years.

It wouldn't be a restaurant without some part of their presence.

'Some of you may know that I lived here for a couple of years in my...' he put on his best teenage swagger impersonation, 'wayward youth.' Some chuckles sounded in the crowd. 'It was a fresh start then, but, well, not everything always turns out as planned.' He lowered his gaze a moment. 'My memories of the two years spent here will always be with me, and it seems, they have drawn me back, to start fresh again.'

He smiled and caught eyes with Hannah, standing a couple of metres away from him to his left.

'My parents had planned to start a restaurant in town, but it was cut short unfortunately when my father...' he hated saying it, 'passed away.' He swallowed a lump in his throat. 'So back to Sydney we went, where I trained as a chef, like my dad, and where my mother became an award-winning wedding-dress designer...' He gestured to the corner. 'One of her *Teadora* designs is over there.'

A few 'oohs' and 'ahhs' sounded from the crowd, and a few photos snapped. He also noticed the newspaper photographer taking a few photos of him and of the crowd.

'So when my mother recently passed on to join my father, I knew it was now or never to honour their dream and create my own by starting a restaurant.' His hand trembled slightly on the microphone, and he brought his other hand up to steady it. 'The premises here becoming available made it a no-brainer for me. I mean, how lucky are we to be here tonight with this amazing view, huh?' He gestured outside and people clapped. The older lady he was introduced to as Nancy blew him a kiss, and he pretended to catch it.

'So not only did I want to create a restaurant in the town they'd wanted to call home, I wanted to create a sort of... second home, a place where people can feel comfortable and know that they are welcome, no matter who they are, where they come from, or what their food preferences or requirements might be. I wanted to be able to cater for everyone and provide a tantalising array of multicultural food, including modern Australian, using fresh local produce wherever possible.'

'So far so good,' Stefan called out.

'That charming chap there is my brother, Stefan,' Luca pointed out. 'And I'd like to thank him for his contribution to helping make this a reality, and to putting up with me over the years.' He raised his glass to Stefan who raised it back. 'Love you, bro.'

'Aww,' people said, and Stefan covered his grinning face.

'I'd like to thank everyone, all of you, for being here and helping me kickstart my dream. And I hope to see many of you in the coming weeks. We'll be open for lunch seven days a week, and dinner Wednesday to Sunday. I plan to have regular themed nights as well, where we'll have a specific set menu, a bit like tonight, but with different themes such as a specific culture, local seafood nights, special holidays, or even old-fashioned nights to step back in time to different eras like the nineteen-twenties... costumes essential.' He winked.

'I'd like to thank my new team of staff who have been working hard to prepare for tonight, some as we speak and who won't even hear my speech, but I'll thank them later. And to all the local businesses who've contributed to the restaurant in some way, providing décor, furniture, and candles.' He smiled at April whose arm was firmly entwined with Zac's. 'Each business is listed on the back of your keepsake menu booklets, which are on each table downstairs.'

Luca glanced back at Hannah. 'And lastly, I have someone very special I'd like to thank. Without her help, I probably wouldn't be standing here tonight giving this speech. She's worked tirelessly to plan not only tonight's launch but my whole business plan for beyond this day, and all within six short weeks. Seriously, she's amazing, and I couldn't have done it without her. So I'd like you all to raise your glass to Hannah Delaney.' He held up his glass, and smiled as she flashed a proud yet humble smile, and her dad lifted up her arm suddenly and called out, 'That's my daughter!'

He chuckled, also grateful for them and their indirect contribution in not only raising the amazing Hannah, but also creating the beauty of Iona, which he hoped to do justice to from this day on. 'Doug, Kathleen, cheers to you too,' Luca said, raising his glass higher.

Everyone clapped, and Hannah glowed under the praise. She looked at him and mouthed 'thank you'. Then, she walked up to him and took the microphone from him.

This hadn't been in her plan, and she hadn't warned him about this. Could she actually be doing something spontaneous?

'Thank you, everyone. It's been a pleasure working on the launch of Home. And I'd like to thank Luca for his vision, his patience, and his... persistence.' She cleared her throat. 'He lives and breathes what he does for a living, it's his passion, and I promise you, you'll be well looked after when you come to eat here. So let's all give a round of applause to the man who, without him, I wouldn't be standing here tonight either.' She held the microphone out to him and clapped it with her free hand, creating an amplified sound as the crowd applauded.

A warm flush rose throughout his body, and pooled in his heart. He was glad he'd stuck with his determination to follow through, to give it a good hard shot. Now the real work would begin, in maintaining Hannah's hard work and keeping the place running, but it would be exciting, fun, and rewarding. He loved nothing more than to see people happy, and if just one person left his restaurant with a smile it would be worth it.

He accepted the microphone back again. 'Thank you, thank you. Now, I hope you've been enjoying your appetisers and drinks, but I also hope you've got enough room left in your stomachs for our main meal followed by our dessert platter. I figured why should you have to choose between one dessert when you can have all of them?'

'Hear, hear!' someone called out.

'And you'll get to taste my aunt's traditional Romanian *gogosi*. If you're a fan of doughnuts, you won't know what hit you when you taste these, believe me.' He patted his stomach. 'Okay, folks, enough talking. Before we head downstairs to take our seats, I have a little show for you all.' He gestured for Hannah to start the projector. 'We used to have family slide nights when we were younger, and I know some of you may do or have done the same thing, so let's get a bit nostalgic, as I share with you some of my roots and make a little tribute to my parents.'

Hannah switched it on and ushered some of the crowd to the side, so that the far wall lit up with the first slide... a photo of him as a baby, devouring *gogosi*, sugar and crumbs all over his face and hands. 'This, my friends, is how it all began...'

And as he watched the slideshow along with everyone else, background music playing, the scent of jasmine in the air... he knew that somehow, somewhere, his parents were watching too.

CHAPTER TWENTY-SEVEN

'Food was superb,' Hannah said to the chefs as they finished up their late dinner after everyone had left. 'I for one will definitely be back at some stage in future.'

They thanked her and filtered out together, tired and yawning, checking their phones after a full-on few days of work.

Hannah closed the window blinds and switched off some of the lights, blew out the candles. The only light remaining was the one over the reception counter and by the table in the corner where Luca sat, as still as a statue. 'What a success it was,' she said, walking over to him. He didn't move, except to run a hand through his hair.

'It's done. We did it.'

'We did.' Hannah smiled, and as she sat, Luca covered his eyes with one of his hands as his elbow rested on the table. 'Luca?'

A small sound emerged, and his upper body trembled a little.

'Luca?' She placed a hand on his shoulder.

He wiped away a couple of tears and sniffed. 'I'm sorry.'

'Hey, it's okay. What for?'

'For getting emotional. We should be on a high.'

'It's normal to be emotional after a night like tonight. After the past six weeks.' She gave his shoulder a light rub.

'It's just…' He looked up, his eyes slightly red and glossy. 'It's all finally happened, you know. It's all real to me now. Up until tonight I was working towards something, making preparations, and distracting myself from my grief.'

She nodded.

'I just miss her, that's all.' He lowered his face again against his hand and sobbed. 'I know she's still with me, I feel it sometimes. But it doesn't make it any easier.' He exhaled and shook his head.

'I know, I know. It's hard as hell, but you'll get through it. Day by day. One step at a time. And you've taken a lot of steps already. You're doing great, Luca.'

He looked up at her. 'Thank you.' He curved his hand around hers. 'For everything.'

'My pleasure.' She smiled, and offered him a tissue.

He chuckled. 'Always prepared,' he said.

'Of course. Tissues are an essential item for functions. There's usually some kind of emotion going round.'

He took the tissue and dabbed at his eyes. 'I can't seem to hide anything from you. You make it so easy to… to just be real. Raw. Honest.'

'That's the best way to be.' She shifted her position and crossed one leg over the other, knowing she'd soon have to practise what she preached. Seeing him like this just made everything so much more difficult.

She bit her lower lip. 'It's getting late, so maybe it's time for a good night's sleep, huh?' She patted his shoulder. He nodded.

They both stood, and glanced around the room.

'This is it. My restaurant.' A small smile appeared. 'I can hardly believe it.'

'Well, believe it, because right here is the vision you had and the one we planned for. Dreams become reality when you work at them and don't give up.'

'I've learned so much from you,' he said, turning to face her. He collected her hands in his. 'I've enjoyed this time so, so much.'

She smiled. 'Me too.'

'And it got me thinking... maybe there's a way we can still enjoy this, see what happens. Make some effort to give things a shot.'

Hannah's stomach plummeted. 'Luca, you've just started a business. You're going to be super busy, I'm going to be super busy, and we'll be two hours away from each other... it's not like we can just pop in to see each other after work. It would mean four hours travel each time.'

'I know, but... there's gotta be a way,' he said, and she'd never seen him so insistent about something, least of all about her.

'I just can't see one,' she said. 'And believe me, it's in my job description to see how things are going to work logistically. I just can't see it here.'

He lowered his head again and kicked gently at something non-existent with his shoe. 'It's gotta be worth a shot.'

It took all her willpower to resist him, she steeled her nerves and stood strong. 'I can't do shots, I need certainty. I'm all or nothing, remember?'

'I know.' He looked her deep in her eyes. 'Hannah. Oh, Hannah. How can I be so happy yet so heartbroken at the same time?'

She could hardly believe what she was hearing. Luca, the man who could get any woman he wanted, who'd never been without a girlfriend, pining over her like a lonely teenage boy.

He leaned closer to her and held her cheek in his hand. She

let it rest there and closed her eyes. One last beautiful moment. Something to hold onto.

He leaned closer and brought his lips to hers, but she knew all too well what would happen if she didn't resist, so she put her hands on his chest and pressed firmly. 'Luca, no. What's done is done. I'll always remember this time, but I can't risk my heart right now, I just can't. Let's leave things on good terms.'

He stood back.

'Time to move on. To move forward. You're going to love it here, I know it.' She offered a small smile.

'I guess this is the goodbye we never got to have, then,' he said.

'Guess so.' Hannah breathed out a sigh.

At least she would have closure, maybe that's all she needed.

'But I'll still be around the next two weeks, so there'll be another goodbye just before I go.'

He nodded. 'In that case, I'll bid you goodnight, thank you again, and farewell, beautiful amazing Hannah.' He held out his hand.

'Farewell, charming and talented Luca.' She held out her hand.

Their skin touched, gently at first, and then she tapped his palm.

He smiled, and tapped hers back. Then tugged down on her thumb, tapped her palm again, gave her a fist pump, a high-five, and then... held her in the tightest, longest hug she'd ever experienced. As though all her body morphed into his and they became one being, one soul. He still felt like home, and so did Tarrin's Bay. But sometimes you had to leave home and step out into the big, bright world in order to find that home within.

It was her time.

CHAPTER TWENTY-EIGHT

'That wasn't too bad, was it?' Karen asked as she and Hannah stepped out of the office building and into the noisy city street, trying to find a gap in the moving crowd.

A rushing woman brushed past her and Hannah's shoulder was pushed backwards, dropping her handbag. She bent to pick it up and then bumped into a young man wearing earphones and not seeming to look where he was going. 'Sorry.' They stopped at the pedestrian crossing and Hannah revelled in the moment of peace while they waited. 'Um, no, it was fine. Everyone seems nice. And I get a cubicle for an office, that's a bit exciting.'

'It is, and we can have lunch together each day and send instant messages via the office computer system and still look like we're working.' She chuckled. 'Only one week to go!'

Hannah had attended a morning meeting with her new boss, along with Karen, for an orientation to the company and her new role. She'd been on a tour of the office, met everyone, and introduced to their brand and the daily tasks that would make up her job description. She would have to buy a new wardrobe. And heels. Five days a week, plus evening and weekend events as needed would require more than her small, standard array of outfits.

The rapid beep of the green pedestrian light sounded and they crossed the street, the lights turning red and flashing before they'd gotten halfway, making Hannah speed up. 'They don't give you much time to cross, do they,' she said, scurrying and stepping up onto the safety of the pavement.

'Gotta be quick around these streets. No idea how older or less mobile people go, a bit hard for them.'

'Sure is. So where shall we eat?'

'Up here. They have nice wraps and salads, unless you want something more exotic?'

'I'm easy.'

'It's probably no match for Luca's food, but a work lunchbreak requires efficient planning to make the most of it.'

They took a seat in the small cafe and soon their plates arrived. Hannah got out her notepad and pen.

'What are you doing? Not working I hope.'

'Just jotting down some numbers for my budget. I need new clothes and shoes for starters. There's the rent, the other household expenses, my phone and internet...' She tapped the pen against her chin, then jotted down a few more.

'Did you add Pilates classes?'

'Pilates?'

'Yeah, I go on Monday nights. Tonight. You should come!'

'I'll think about it. Once I get settled.' Hannah poked the fork into her roast lamb salad. 'How's the past week been with Stefan, still chatting?'

'Yep, and I've seen him twice since the launch. He's so adorable.' She smiled and giggled. 'He sends the funniest messages and pictures, you know, those meme things. Makes me smile. I like him.'

Hannah grinned. 'You look smitten. I'm glad. And I know

he comes from good stock, so I'm sure I can trust him with my best friend.'

'He hasn't even tempted me into bed yet, so either he's just not into me in that way, or he's trying to be a gentleman.'

'I think he's pretty into you, my friend. From what I saw.'

Karen sipped her mineral water with a smile. 'And what about you and Luca, you two worked so well together that night. It was like you've been doing it for years.'

'Doing what?' Hannah still hadn't told her about the night they'd spent together.

'Working together.'

'Oh. Yeah, well we did do a lot of that in high school I guess.' Hannah munched rapidly on her salad and pointed outside. 'I really like that woman's top, I wonder where she got it.'

'Hannah?'

'Do you like it? I should get one like that for work.'

Munch, munch, munch.

'Ah, Hannah?' Karen leaned closer across the table. 'What are you not telling me?'

'Telling you? Nothing really, not important. What's important is right now. The moment.' She pointed outside again. 'That one's nice too. Wow, people here have such nice fashion sense.'

Karen took the glass from Hannah's hand. 'Talk to me.'

Hannah sighed, and told her about the night with Luca, his suggestion that they try and work something out, and her rejection of the man she thought she would always do anything to have.

'Oh, Hannah. How did you get into this situation?' Karen shook her head.

'I can't do anything about it. He bought my place, I got this new job, I'm ready to move in with you. I've packed up the house. Everything's all set and ready.'

'But are *you?*'

She flicked her hand. 'Is anyone truly ever ready for anything? Just have to stick to a plan and follow it through.'

'Han, this isn't an event, this is your life. Your future. There aren't always set plans for that, you have to listen to what your heart says.'

'My heart's only ever led me to disappointment. And anyway, it's time I spread my wings and... I don't know, *find myself.*' She made quotation marks with her fingers.

'You're the most "found" and together woman I know, Hannah Delaney. Strong, capable, independent, authentic.'

She closed her eyes briefly with an appreciative smile. 'Thank you. I'm lucky to have you as my friend. I have to stick to my decision though. My promise to myself. This whole thing with Luca was probably a test, a challenge, to determine how strong I really was, and also to give closure to something that never got a chance to start, let alone end.' She sat tall. 'It's good. All good. It's been good. Everything will be good.'

'Good. If you're sure.'

She nodded.

'Well I shall look forward to seeing you on the weekend to help with the move. It's been good for me too, knowing you're coming. Made me do a big clean out and declutter. You know, I was reading about how when you declutter and simplify things, you can attract more of what you want into your life. It creates a kind of vacuum effect. Maybe that's how Stefan came into my life.'

'From cleaning out your drawers and cupboards?' Hannah chuckled.

'Yep, I think there's something to it. Made me feel lighter and clearer.'

'Actually, I think the clean-out helped me too. There were some things I needed to let go of to help me move forward I think. Do you know I still had that bracelet Samuel gave me, in my bedside drawer? I decided to donate it. Felt good.'

'See, there you go.' Karen held up her glass. 'Here's to decluttering. Our houses and our lives.'

'To decluttering!' Hannah held up hers and they clinked them together.

And to new beginnings.

'Be there in a minute, Scar!' Hannah called out to her dog's lonely murmur from around the back verandah as she walked through the front door, shopping bags in her hands and her ringing phone to her ear.

'Hello, Luca?'

'Hey, how you doin?'

'You sound like Joey from *Friends*. I'm good thanks, and you? How's the first week of business been?'

'Better than planned actually. Flat out making sure everything runs smoothly, but that's to be expected.'

'Excellent. Just got in the door, hang on a sec.' She unhooked her handbag from her shoulder and placed down her shopping bags. 'Okay.'

'I just got home too after the lunchtime shift. Anyway, ah, I won't keep you, I just wanted to say a couple of things.'

'Oh?' She stood and rested a hand on the island bench.

'Seems silly now after all these years, but I wanted to get it out of my system, and just so you know that this whole thing... the last few weeks, hasn't been random or meaningless.'

Hannah's heart throbbed. She thought they had already discussed everything, and after today, was just about ready to leave things behind.

'Back in school...' he began, 'I did like you, you know. I mean, I was attracted to you. In a different way than the others.'

'Luca, you don't have to say all this. I know, you liked me differently, as a friend.'

'No, I mean yes, I did. But more than that. I liked you differently as in *better* than all the others. In a special way that I didn't understand until now. I think I was too young back then, we both were, to recognise what it was.'

Hannah had to take a seat.

'What I felt back then was everything, all wrapped up into one. Not just lust, or temporary attraction, or friendship, but everything.'

Once again, she couldn't believe what she was hearing.

'I think I...' he breathed loudly, 'I think I loved you.'

The phone slipped from Hannah's grasp onto the bench with a thud. She scrambled to pick it back up again.

'Hannah?'

'Yes? What? I'm here.'

'I think I still do.'

Hannah's breathing, heart rate, body temperature, and everything that could possibly increase *increased*.

'I... I didn't think you liked me in that way... I don't know what...'

'It's okay, I don't mean to put you on the spot. I just... really needed to say it. I'm still figuring things out, but that's what I keep coming back to. And you know the school formal?'

'Huh, the formal? Yes.'

'I was going to ask you to be my date.'

Hannah's brows furrowed. 'But you went with Tracy.'

'I know, but I only asked her because I saw you with Matthew. You were kissing behind the canteen, right when I was looking for you.'

Her hand went to her temple. 'You saw that? But... it was

only quick. You mustn't have seen me push him away. I didn't want him to kiss me.'

'You didn't?'

'No. I only went with him to the formal because…' her voice trailed off when Scarlett murmured again, 'because when I…' she walked towards the back door, 'when I went to ask…'

'Ask what? Hannah?'

She opened the door and immediately knew something was wrong. Scarlett lay on the verandah in her spot, her chest rising and falling quickly with shallow breaths, and then pausing periodically. 'Scar.' She knelt down and held a hand to her dog's head. It was warm and clammy.

'Hannah? Is everything okay?'

'I'm sorry, Luca, I have to go. Something's wrong with Scar.' She ended the call in a hurry and put the phone on the outdoor table.

'Scarlett, honey, what's wrong?' Hannah's chin quivered and she patted her dog's fur. She refilled the water bowl with fresh water from the tap and brought it over. 'Here, my girl, have some.' But Scarlett didn't seem to have the energy to drink. She went into the kitchen and grabbed a water bottle with a squeeze top and tried to drip some water into Scar's mouth. Her dog's mouth moved a little, trying to drink it, but her tongue seemed too dry to lap it up. She persisted, dripping more water in, then wetting her hands and dampening the dog's fur to cool it down. It wasn't like before when she had almost choked on a gumnut, it was different. It seemed like she was fighting a sudden infection, or that her body temperature regulation wasn't working properly. She stood to grab her phone to call the vet's after-hours number, but Scarlett murmured again, as though not wanting Hannah to leave her side. Something told Hannah to just stay put, to cuddle her, to talk to her to soothe her.

'It's okay, girl, I'll sit with you right here. Everything's okay.

Shh...' She stroked her fur. 'There's been a lot happening around here hasn't there? I've probably been a bit preoccupied. Sorry, Scar.' Her chin quivered again, and she didn't want to accept what may be happening.

The dog's breath was sporadic and part of Hannah wanted to rush around and do things, call for help, try to fix it somehow, but the other part made her want to just stay right there with her beloved animal and be fully present in the moment, holding her tight, keeping her calm, and letting her know she was loved and not alone.

Hannah watched warm oranges and reds float onto the sky's canvas... a scarlet sunset. Just like on the day she'd first been brought home. Tears welled in her eyes but she tensed her eyelids to hold them in, continuing to speak soothing words, as much for her as they were for Scarlett.

She straightened up a little at the sound of car tyres on the pebbles. Then a car door. Then footsteps, around the side, becoming louder until Luca came into view at the corner of the verandah.

'Hannah, is everything okay?' He rushed to her side, kneeling down next to her. 'You hung up suddenly and I wanted to make sure.'

'She's... I think she's...' Hannah's tears overflowed and spilled down her cheeks.

Luca touched the dog's head gently. 'Do you want me to call someone?'

Hannah shook her head. 'It's okay, I don't think there's anything we can do,' she sniffed. 'I just want to... to be with her right now, not leave her side.'

'Then I'm not leaving yours.' Luca nestled in behind Hannah and supported her weight as she hugged her dog.

Scarlett breathed tiny shallow breaths here and there. Her eyes glossed over, and then her chest stopped moving.

'Scarlett, I'm here. I'm here.' She stroked her fur continuously, hoping for one more breath, but it didn't come.

All was silent and still, waiting in case, but when Hannah looked up at the sky—its scarlet colour had darkened to black. She let out a sob, and then another, and cried the hardest she'd cried in a long time. Hannah's body went limp with her overwrought emotions and Luca held her and rocked her, saying nothing, simply being there.

CHAPTER TWENTY-NINE

After dawn the next morning, Luca returned to Iona, carrying a bunch of flowers. Hannah's parents were there, helping to prepare Scarlett for burial.

'That's a lovely gesture, thank you, Luca.' Kathleen accepted the flowers.

Doug was making a ditch in the dirt, near the willow tree, where Willow also lay buried.

'Here, let me give you a hand.'

'Thanks, mate.' He handed the shovel to Luca who continued digging.

Hannah picked up the large stone she had been engraving with a knife; it simply said 'scarlett', with a heart shape around it. She carried it to the head of the grave, and steadied it in the ground so that it stood upright.

'That should do it I think.' Doug said to Luca, who rested the shovel against the tree.

He gave a nod and looked in the direction of the house. 'Can I help carry her?'

Hannah nodded, grateful he was here. She could probably lift her, with some help from her parents, but her dad's back wasn't great and neither was his heart, and all the emotions had weakened her body.

When they reached the verandah, Hannah's heart sank again. Her beloved Scarlett was there, but at the same time, still and rigid and lifeless, she wasn't.

Luca bent down and gathered her in his arms, and Hannah helped, adjusting the knitted blanket around her.

They carried her to the grave.

'Do you want to take this off?' Luca asked, eyeing the blanket.

Hannah shook her head. 'It can stay with her.'

'You sure, darling?' asked her mother.

'The vanilla. It smells like me. I want it to stay with her.'

Her mother nodded.

Luca lowered Scar into the grave, and Hannah's chest heaved. She got out her phone and played a song; a peaceful, restful piece of music that she hoped would somehow send her soul on its way peacefully.

As the music played, Hannah dropped one flower at a time into the grave, on top of the blanket-covered Scarlett.

'Goodbye, my girl,' she whispered.

'You'll be missed,' said her dad.

'We'll never forget the joy you brought us.' Her mum placed a comforting arm around her daughter's shoulder.

Hannah sobbed softly, her mother sniffling and her father wiping the corner of his eye.

She was sad, but she was lucky. She'd lost Scar, but she had her parents. Though it wouldn't be forever, nothing was, but she was lucky for now.

Hannah peered into the grave and took one last look at her dog. She kissed the underside of her fingers and blew her a kiss, then turned away. 'Okay, it's time.'

Her dad nodded and he and Luca moved to the grave. She

could hear the scooping sound of soil being shovelled again, dropping it back into the grave and blanketing Scarlett, and when it was done, she turned around and clamped her lips together at the sight of the dirt mound.

Scarlett's new home, forever part of Iona.

'We'll come back with a nice morning tea for us all,' Kathleen said, before getting in the car. 'See you again soon, darling. Luca, you're welcome to stay and join us.'

'Thanks. I have to get to work in another hour though.'

She nodded, taking her seat, Doug getting in the driver's side. They drove off, a haze of dust from the ground following them as the tyres rolled down the driveway.

'Is there anything else I can do for you?' Luca asked, placing a hand on her arm. 'Help with packing, sorting out Scarlett's things?'

Hannah's chin quivered. 'Yes. Better sooner rather than later. I'll need to throw out her food and water bowls, and her dog bed, and any leftover medicines I'll put in the car to take to the vet.'

'Okay.' He walked with her inside to the laundry, and gathered up some of her things. 'So there's nothing you want to keep?'

'No. I have my photos. And the memories.'

He nodded. 'I'll take these away for you.' He left the room and returned, but by then the absence of all her things sent her legs buckling from underneath and she sat by the washing machine on the floor, hugging her knees to her chest, tears flowing again.

He knelt beside her. 'It's okay. Cry if you need to. It hurts but it'll help.' The feeling of his hand rubbing her back gave some comfort and warmth in the cold, stark laundry room.

'I don't know what to do without her,' she sobbed. 'She was my best friend. Like a sister, a friend, and a child all in one.'

She sobbed further on realising that maybe Scar had filled part of that gap that only becoming a mother could fill. Now the gap was gaping wide open, aching and raw.

'I don't know what to do... How can I move forward... how can I *leave*, without her to come with me?'

Luca's rubbing stopped. He sat in front of her. 'Hannah, what you do is completely up to you. If you want to go, go, but if you want to stay, stay.'

She dabbed her eyes with her sleeve. 'But I can't, you've bought the place, it's all settled, I've confirmed my new job and had the orientation. And besides, staying might just be as hard, without her here.'

'I'll be here. In town, if you want to take some extra time at least before moving out, I understand. Stay as long as you need.'

Confusion swirled within. What did she *really* want? Was her new beginning still as exciting as it had seemed on the first of June?

She thought of the past year, and how she had worked hard and done her best, moved on from Samuel only to be rejected by Nathan, and now Luca. Here, after all this time, but with no guarantee if he had really changed or could really stick with something and see it through. The uncertainty made her uncomfortable and she was done with waiting for things to be right. If she left and moved on, it would be in her own terms and she would feel in control. If she stayed and it didn't work out, once again she would be heartbroken and have her chance at a fresh start delayed even more.

No. She couldn't risk it.

She wiped her tears and held onto the washing machine to help her stand. Luca held onto her elbow. 'I'm okay.'

'You sure?'

'Yes. Scarlett dying is a sign. It's time to go. It's the end of an era and it's time for me to start a new one that's right for me.'

She wiped her eyes again and walked out of the laundry room, Luca following.

'Right. Okay, well, maybe it's best if I leave you to get some time on your own and rest a bit before your parents get back,' he spoke softly. He wandered to the front door. 'Let me know if there's anything I can do. I'm always here for you, Hannah, I mean it.'

He stepped through the door and off the porch, and the sight of him with his head lowered and hands in pockets made her heart lurch.

He had been so good to her, with everything. And being here last night and today meant a lot.

'Luca?'

He turned.

'I'm sorry. Thank you. For everything.'

He nodded. 'It's nothing.'

'It's everything.'

'Well, as I said, I'm here. You know where I am.' He turned again, but Hannah followed him to his car.

She held out her arms.

His eyebrows rose, and for a moment looked at his car, then back at Hannah, and moved towards her with a slow exhalation as his arms embraced her.

She pulled back after a while, and eyed him curiously. 'Were you *really* going to ask me to the school formal?'

A small smile grew on his lips. 'Of course. As I said, I saw you with Matthew and assumed you were into him, so the next day I asked Tracy,' he explained. 'We didn't get to finish discussing this on the phone last night when you went to help Scar... but what were you about to say?'

'The next day after Matthew kissed me, I was going to ask *you* to the formal. Before Matthew could ask me. I wanted to go with you. But when I finally worked up the courage, I saw Tracy with her arm around you, and I figured you'd be going with her.'

'Oh man, really?' Luca ran a hand through his hair.

She nodded. 'Luca, you have no idea...'

'No idea what?'

She bit her lip, then scratched her cheek. 'How much I liked you. How much I wanted you. We were great friends, but I always felt something more for you.' She lowered her head a moment then looked up and into his eyes. 'I assumed you considered me only a friend, as one of the guys. So after my one attempt to ask you out failed, I gave up. I thought if you liked me in that way, you would have asked *me*.' She pointed her hand to her chest.

'And yet I was going to.'

'Which I didn't know.'

'And I didn't know you were going to ask *me*.' Luca shook his head. 'And then the formal happened and Dad died, and we left. And we didn't get to say goodbye.'

'I know. I was so upset, mostly for you and your family. But I always felt a sense of loss at having missed out on something with you.' She crossed her arms and rubbed her elbows.

'Hannah, I would have loved to have something with you. I think part of me was scared because I didn't want to affect our friendship. I knew our bond was deeper than others. I may have had my fair share of girlfriends but they were never you.'

He brushed his hand against her cheek, but she turned her face away slightly as the touch threatened to unravel her emotions again. 'Well, at least it's now all out in the open. Thanks for being honest. I feel like I can move on now.'

'You don't have to,' he said. 'We can still work something out, see what's possible.'

She took a deep breath and said, 'I think I just need to stick with my plans.'

Luca sighed. 'Okay. I only want you to be happy.' He glanced up at the sky and twisted his lips to one side. 'But can I ask you something?'

'Sure.'

He held her hand up. 'Hannah Delaney, will you come to the formal with me?'

She laughed, a stark contrast to the emotions of before. 'What?'

'Will you come to the formal with me?'

'But, Luca, we're not in high school anymore.'

'I know. So I'm going to do what I should have done back then, and give you a night to remember.'

Her cheeks warmed. 'Luca, we kinda already had one of those, if you recall.'

'Yes, we did indeed. But I'm not asking for the same thing. I'm simply asking you to our formal. Tonight. A nice dinner at home, we can get all dressed up, I'll bring you a corsage, we'll play daggy music from twenty years ago and slow dance in the living room. What do you say?'

Her mouth gaped open. 'But you do so much cooking, surely you don't want to prepare another special meal tonight on your night off?'

'I'll bring takeaway pizza then.' He shrugged.

She tried to hold back a smile. 'Tonight, huh? Pizza? Daggy music? Okay then, you're on.'

'Yes! Finally, after all these years, I get to take my perfect date to the formal. Be all dressed up and ready at six thirty, I'll do the rest.'

'And, Luca, you know it's just to make up for lost time,

right? That's all?'

'I know. We'll keep it simple. I have no expectations, I just want you to have a beautiful night. We can even light a candle in honour of Scarlett.'

'Thanks. It'll be a good chance to properly say...'

'Goodbye,' they said in unison.

Luca arrived at six thirty sharp, and while waiting at the door he smoothed down his gelled hair to take a few stray strands off his forehead.

The door opened. She stood there in the same black dress she'd worn to the launch, her hair pinned back into an elegant bun at the nape of her neck, and wearing simple circular earrings. 'It's all I had that wasn't packed away,' she said, her voice soft and worn-out from crying but beautiful as ever.

'You look even more beautiful than the night of the launch.'

'I hope my face isn't too red.'

'So what if it is? Red's my favourite colour.' He winked, then looked at her dress. 'Oh, and black.'

'I'm sure it is,' she said, welcoming him in. 'Smells yummy, now I'm hungry.'

'Two delicious pizzas await.' He plonked them on the island bench.

'Two? I'm not sure I can eat a whole one.'

'Then I'll eat one and a half.' He grinned. 'Now, I have something for you.' He took the corsage from a bag and held it up. 'It's jasmine and some other flowery dangly thing.'

She chuckled. 'Flowery dangly things are my favourite.'

'Oh good.' He pinned it to her dress. 'There you go. Now for a photo?'

He held up his phone and she stood near the dining table, one hand leaning on it, a smile on her face. *Click!* 'Lovely.'

'Now you.' She took his phone.

'Don't need one of me.'

'Of course we do. One of each of us, and then together. It's what we would have done at the real formal.'

'True. Okay then.' He stood by the table with one leg crossed over his ankle, and flashed a goofy grin.

'So natural in front of the camera.' She laughed as she took a couple of photos. 'And now, a selfie I guess. Since there are no doting parents to embarrass us and... Oh, Luca, I'm sorry. It just slipped out.'

'It's okay.' He had barely had time to process what she'd said before she'd apologised, and he was surprised to find it didn't make him sad. Somehow, opening the restaurant had laid a lot of things to rest, cleared a lot of built-up emotion, and given him a way to channel his emotions into something positive. 'My mum would have probably insisted on making your dress,' he added. 'And if not, she would have studied every inch of whichever one you wore and analysed it... how it was made, where the fabrics may have come from, the types of stitching used.'

'I would have been perfectly fine with either option.' She smiled.

His mum would have liked her. They had met, but she would have liked her even more now as a grown woman. Her persistence, her independence, her determination and her values.

She's a lot like her, in a way.

'And nice suit, by the way.' She did a quick scan of his outfit and nodded her approval. 'Very snazzy.'

'Snazzy?'

'What my mum would have called it back then.'

'Oh,' he laughed.

'She'd be proud of you, your mum. And your dad,' Hannah said. 'Even if you hadn't set up the restaurant, they'd still be proud of you, for the person that you are.'

She always managed to speak right to his heart. 'Thank you, means a lot. And I know your parents are proud of you. Staying on the farm or not staying on the farm, they're just as proud either way. They only want you to be happy and do what's right for you.'

'Thanks. I know that now. I don't feel as guilty anymore.'

'You shouldn't.' He opened his bag. 'Oh, I have to put these up, hang on.' He untangled the fairy lights and attached them to the curtain rods.'

'Ohh, how nice,' she said.

Then he opened the pizza boxes and steam rose up. 'Oh man, this smells jump-on-the-couch worthy,' he said, remembering doing that as a teenager.

'Like when you discovered that new flavour of potato chips?'

'Yes! You remember?'

'I remember absolutely everything,' she said with a knowing smile, then glanced at the couch. 'Shall we?'

His eyes bulged. 'Jump on the couch? Now? I'm a bit heavier than I was back then!'

'Me too. It's okay, I'm not keeping the couch, it's a bit old and I won't need it at Karen's.'

'In that case...' He kicked off his shoes and held her elbow steady as she got out of her heels.

They got up on the squishy seat cushions and her delightful giggle made his day. This was how he wanted her to be, to feel. Whatever she wanted to do to feel that feeling and laugh that giggle, he wanted that for her.

'Ready?' he said, holding her arms and her holding his.

She nodded.

'And... jump!'

They bounced and bounced, laughed and laughed, she almost toppled over and he caught her, he almost toppled over and she caught him. Her hair came undone from her bun and she didn't seem to care, she flicked it around her face like a woman at a heavy metal concert. His hair loosened from the hold of the gel and he flicked his around too.

'Oh, my belly!' Hannah laughed and cried out. 'My abs!'

'Mine too! And I didn't know I had any!'

They belly-laughed for ages, jumping until they could no more, then toppled onto the couch together, entangled in each other's arms and legs.

Hannah scrambled up, smoothing down her dress. 'Now I'm really hungry, let's eat.'

He put the pizza on the dining table and lit a candle in the centre, then dimmed the room lights. 'Oh,' he remembered, 'music.' He switched on his nineties playlist and Hannah's eyes widened with recognition.

'I remember this!'

They ate and reminisced, laughed and chatted, ate and drank some more.

When they were finished, he flicked through a few different songs to a love ballad, then stood and held out his hand. 'May I have this dance?'

'You may.' She smiled, her face dewy and rosy.

He carefully kicked a few boxes out of the way, making an impromptu dance floor. 'I wanted to find a mirror ball, but it was too short notice, sorry,' he confessed.

'The candlelight is just fine.'

He slid his hands around her waist, and hers found his shoulders, then she hung them gently around his neck. Together they swayed, back and forth, to the music, and Luca sang along to the lyrics. 'You're the most beautiful girl in the room,' he said.

'Oh shucks. You're just saying that.'

'No, I really mean it. I really, really do.'

'Well, thank you kindly. And you're the handsomest man, I mean boy, in the room.'

'You think? Aw geez.'

He drank in her smile with his eyes, memorising it so he'd have something to hold onto when he needed it.

The dance and music continued, and he knew it was coming to an end, so he simply kept his focus on her eyes, wanting to memorise them too. His entire being wanted to gather her up in his arms and never let her go, but he had to remain strong. What was best for Hannah was what was important, not what his desires were.

She never took her eyes off him either. Perhaps she was doing the same.

Their breath merged as one and swirled about their faces, and intoxicating him with its sweetness, its life. As soon as the song ended, before he could change his mind, he let go of her waist and stepped back. 'Hannah, my dear,' he forced himself to say, 'it has been a delightful evening, but I must go and let you get home at a decent hour. Or get home at a decent hour myself, more like it.'

'Like a gentleman.'

'Of course.' He gave a bow, then smiled, and took the rubbish to the bin and cleaned up the table. Then he made his way to the door. He had to leave quickly before he couldn't. Before he did something to ruin everything and make this day more upsetting for her. 'Thank you for going to the formal with me.'

'No, thank *you* for asking. Even if it was twenty years later.' She winked. 'And it helped, doing this tonight, after what happened with Scar. Thank you.'

'My pleasure. Goodnight, Hannah, and...' he inhaled

deeply, scared the words would hurt his throat as they passed through into the air between them, 'goodbye.'

'Goodbye,' she said, her chest rising quickly with a breath and then falling with a sigh.

He gave her a smile, breathed in, then turned and exhaled, stepping out the door. He got in his car as she waited on the porch.

This was it. The time had come. He turned the key and the engine growled to life.

She gave a wave, but then her smile turned downward.

Oh no.

He wanted to leave her with a smile on her face. He didn't want to remember her like this. Didn't want her to feel like this.

He furrowed his brows, eyeing her to check if she was okay.

But then she dashed off the porch and came running towards his car.

What?'

He opened the door and got out. 'Hannah, what is it?'

She leapt towards him and flung her arms around him. 'I don't want to say goodbye! I thought I did, but I don't. I can't!' She held him tight and he couldn't help but mirror her embrace.

'Oh, Hannah. What are you saying?'

She pulled back to look in his eyes, her hands on his cheeks. 'I want a fresh start, of course I do, but the thing is, I've realised, despite the risk and the uncertainty... I want it with *you.'*

His heart leapt from his rib cage and he tried to find the right words. 'Oh my God, Hannah, what...'

'I don't know how to do this, I don't know exactly what to do, but I can't have you leave here tonight and I can't leave here next weekend. Oh, Luca. I think I've made a big mistake.' She covered her face with her hands.

'Hey, hey. It's okay. Let's talk about it. Are you saying you want to stay here at Iona or you want to stay in town and be with me?'

'I'm not sure. Both. I don't think I want to leave my home. And I don't want to leave without giving things a chance with you. But I don't want to get in the way of your dreams, of your new home.'

'Hannah, don't you see? *You* are my dream too.' He caressed her cheek. 'I made a silly little wish, not too long ago, that if there was a way for me to have my dream of my own successful restaurant, but also have you stay here somehow and be with me, then please make it come true.'

'You wished... for me?'

He nodded.

She smiled. 'I thought only girls did silly things like that.'

'Nope. Us boys do them too.' He smiled back.

'But what do we do about the house? About my job? And Karen's got everything ready at her house. And I've told everyone I'm going... It's all set, all done.'

'Then let's *undo* it.' He grasped her arms. 'It'll be messy and weird and crazy, but we'll work it out somehow, and hey, we launched Home in six weeks from scratch, we can do anything. I'll speak to Lily about the house, and I'm sure Karen will understand and help you talk to your boss and they can probably give your job to one of the other applicants, and I'll give you work with me running all my special events and theme nights!'

'Luca, it seems so crazy. I feel so stupid.'

'Hey. Not at all. Sure, I love this place, but I am perfectly happy to stay on with Nathan while we see how things go. And you call the shots. I'll be fine. It's still your home and I'm not going to get in the way of family history.'

'Luca, you're absolutely amazing, you know that?'

'Yup.' He grinned.

'Can we really do this? I mean, *undo* this?'

'Consider it... undone.' He held out his hand.

She shook it, then did the handshake, then he lifted her up and carried her up on the porch, through the front door, and straight to her bedroom.

CHAPTER THIRTY

THE FOLLOWING JUNE

'Ahh, why is it so hard to get out of the shower?' Hannah said, as warm water ran down her body, the firm pressure both relaxing and invigorating her.

'It has nothing to do with it being winter and everything to do with me.' Luca kissed her cheek and hopped out. 'But alas, I must get ready. And you too. We don't want to be late for Stefan's birthday party. Ooh, he's going to love his birthday cake, really outdid last year's!'

'You did, honey. A chicken cake with egg-shaped cupcakes. He'll love it as much as a five-year-old,' she said. 'I'll just be a few more minutes in here.'

'Okay, I'll go get dressed, then feed Mocha. That puppy eats more than I do.'

She smiled. Luca had moved into Iona with her three months ago, and two weeks ago they'd decided to get a new addition. It was nice to have a dog around the house again, even if she did scratch and chew everything in sight.

She could hear him getting dressed in the room, his zipper zipping up, his belt buckle buckling. She would never tire of those sounds.

When a few minutes were up, she reluctantly turned off the shower and stepped out, grabbing her towel and wrapping it around her. She wiped a section of the mirror so she could see her reflection, then applied some moisturiser.

'Hannah?'

'Yep?'

He didn't respond.

'What is it?'

'You coming?'

'Soon, I just need to put on a touch of make-up. One minute.' She squeezed a smidgen of liquid mineral foundation onto her fingertips, then rubbed it over her face.

'Okay then. I'll ah, just leave this here then while I go feed Mocha,' he said, with the sound of putting something down on the bedside table.

'Leave what?' she asked, her gaze still on the mirror as she applied her make-up.

No response.

She turned around and looked through the entrance to the ensuite, but he'd left the room.

'Leave what, honey?'

She walked out and peered around, then her sight rested on the bedside table. Between her lamp and her photo of Scarlett, was... a pebble.

She gasped, picked it up. It wasn't a stone, or a rock, but a definite, smooth, small pebble.

Hannah glanced to the side through the bedroom doorway, to see Luca standing there, leaning against the wall with one foot crossed over the other leg, a huge smile on his face.

He didn't have to speak for her to know the question, and she didn't have to reply for him to know her answer. She simply held the pebble to her heart with tears streaming down her face, and nodded her acceptance as she walked forward and met him at the doorway, her arms embracing him and his embracing her.

EPILOGUE
SIX WEEKS LATER...

'Phew,' Luca said, lowering Hannah back down after carrying her through the doorway and into the bedroom. She stood and he looked at her with eyes that radiated pure love. 'You really are beautiful, Mrs Antonescu.'

'You're not too bad yourself, Mr Antonescu.' She smiled widely.

'I'm so glad,' he said, coming in closer, 'that one of my mother's favourite creations got to be worn by one of my favourite creations.'

Hannah glanced down at the beautiful V-shaped beaded bodice of her wedding gown, and the sparkly hem near her feet. 'I'm honoured to wear it. And what do you mean, *your* creation? Are you likening me to one of your meals?'

He chuckled. 'Well, looking at you does make me want to gobble you all up.' He slid his arms around her and nuzzled her neck.

'Can't believe we'll be on a plane tomorrow,' Hannah said.

'I know, right? And then a boat, or was it a ferry...'

'Something on water anyway. As long as we get safely to the Isle of Iona, I don't mind if it's on a flying carpet.'

She kissed his neck too.

'I can't wait,' Luca said. 'And...' he fiddled with the back of the dress. 'I can't wait to get this beautiful creation off you.' He carefully slid the zipper down, although it stuck a little at her lower back. 'Hang on...' He gave it a nudge. 'There we go.'

She stepped out of the dress. 'Lucky I got to wear it... a few weeks later and it probably wouldn't fit anymore.'

'Yes, lucky. We did well to plan a wedding in six weeks,' he said, undoing his tie and unbuttoning his shirt.

'It worked for the restaurant, no reason it wouldn't work for our wedding.'

He nodded. 'It was such an amazing day. Even the chickens enjoyed it, I think.'

She smiled. 'They did.' They'd had the ceremony in one of the paddocks, chairs set up, a temporary gazebo erected with fairy lights, and a few of their closest loved ones. It was everything Hannah had hoped for and more. A simple but special occasion that suited her and Luca to a T. No huge fancy expensive wedding, just the basics, and in the surroundings of home. Perfect.

He undid his belt and trousers and let them fall to the floor.

'Mmm,' she said. 'Looking good, hubby.'

'You too, wifey.'

She giggled. 'We could jump on the bed I guess, but...'

'Hmm, tempting. But I don't know if that's appropriate.' He held his hand to her lower belly.

'You know, if it's a girl, I think we should call her...'

'Winifred.'

'No,' she gave his arm a whack.

'Pollyanna?'

'No.'

'Hmm...' He tapped his temple. 'Milifiscentannaliserisa.'

'What on earth?' She chuckled.

'Hey, just throwing out options.' He raised his arms.

'Jasmine,' Hannah said softly. And with that, she lit the jasmine candle he had given her, which she had only used sparingly for special occasions, to make it last.

He rubbed her belly in tender circles. 'Jasmine,' he said. 'I love it.'

'I love you.'

'I love you too.' He kissed her lips, and she pretended to feel nauseous, heaving her chest.

'Oh no, you okay?'

'Ha, gotcha.' She winked.

'Oh, Hannah, don't go tricking me like that.'

'Couldn't resist.' She grinned. 'I just wanted to see how you'd react if I really did have morning, or night-time sickness. And what if I get it on the plane, or boat, or on the island?'

'Then I'll look after you, don't you worry.' He brushed his thumb across her bottom lip. 'I'll always look after you, my amazing, beautiful Hannah.'

'Promise?' she asked, looking up into his dark, deep, eyes that she would have the pleasure of looking into forevermore.

He leaned in for a slow, firm, loving kiss, his lips promising even before he spoke.

'I promise.'

THE END

ALSO BY JULIET MADISON

Also in The Tarrin's Bay Series

The January Wish

February or Forever

Miracle in March

April's Glow

Memories of May

Fast Forward

ACKNOWLEDGEMENTS

Thanks once again to Bloodhound Books for supporting the Tarrin's Bay series, and my editor, Belinda Holmes, for working on it with me.

Big thanks to my loyal readers who have supported this series – I hope you enjoy it!

To my partner, Zeynel, thanks for your presence and support, especially during my surgery and recovery in 2018, and for inspiring me with your real-life cooking and teaching me a few things about working in a kitchen, not to mention the ins and outs of raising chickens! I hope I did it justice in this story.

Thanks to my lovely Facebook friend from the other side of the world, Hillary Peatfield, for coming up with the name of the dog in this story, Scarlett (Scar), and Willow for my character's childhood dog.

And to my son and fellow writer, Jay, who can write faster than me, thanks for being my daily inspiration. To my parents, thanks for your never-ending support with everything, and to my family and friends for supporting me.

ABOUT THE AUTHOR

Juliet Madison is a bestselling and award-nominated author of books with humour, heart, and serendipity. Writing both fiction and self-help, she is also an artist and colouring book illustrator, and an intuitive life coach who loves creating online courses for writers and those wanting to live an empowered life.

With her background as a naturopath and a dancer, Juliet is passionate about living a healthy and positive life. She likes to combine her love of words, art, and self-empowerment to create books that entertain and inspire readers to find the magic in everyday life.

Juliet lives on the picturesque south coast of NSW, Australia, where she spends as much time as possible dreaming up new stories, following her passions, being with her family, and as little time as possible doing housework.

You can find out more about Juliet, her books, and her courses at http://www.julietmadison.com and connect with her on social media at Facebook http://www.facebook.com/julietmadisonauthor and Instagram http://www.instagram.com/julietmadisonauthorartist

A NOTE FROM THE PUBLISHER

Thank you for reading this book. If you enjoyed it please do consider leaving a review on Amazon to help others find it too.

We hate typos. All of our books have been rigorously edited and proofread, but sometimes mistakes do slip through. If you have spotted a typo, please do let us know and we can get it amended within hours.

info@bloodhoundbooks.com